PRIMORDIA III

THE LOST WORLD—RE-EVOLUTION

D1731487

SEVERED PRESS
HOBART TASMANIA

PRIMORDIA III

Copyright © 2018 by Greig Beck

WWW.SEVEREDPRESS.COM

ISBN: 978-1-925840-43-8

"Time is like a road with infinite intersections and our travels along it are influenced by events, choice and luck. Some of these roads run parallel and others diverge greatly, and if we were to go back and choose another, then our lives, and perhaps millions of others, would be changed forever."

Greig Beck, Primordia III

PROLOGUE
RE-EVOLUTION: 001

The changes were so small at first that most people didn't even notice.

The brilliant red northern cardinal was quite common and could be found from southern Canada, through the eastern United States from Maine to Texas, and all the way down south through Mexico. With the male's brilliant red plumage, head crest, and black mask, plus its distinctive song, it was no wonder it once made such a prized pet.

And then one morning there was a blackout, only for the blink of an eye, like something had briefly moved across the sun. Then afterward, the cardinals were gone. All of them.

It wasn't like the ground was littered with dead birds, or they'd all migrated to somewhere more interesting. It was more like they never existed.

Books made no mention of them. No pictures existed. And they didn't just fade from memories; they were erased. All that remained was a nagging sense of...*wrongness*.

That was the first occurrence. And there was more, and worse, to come.

PART 1—Laramidia and Appalachia—the lands before time

"It has long been an axiom of mine that the little things are infinitely the most important." — Arthur Conan Doyle

CHAPTER 01

SOUTHEASTERN TIP OF NORTH AMERICA, 100 MILLION YEARS AGO

Andy carefully lowered the sail, an inch at a time. He had to be careful and quiet—several times his boat was investigated by creatures that glided beneath him in the warm, soupy water, rolling to look up from the depths with one large eye and regard him with interest or disdain, but thankfully, not hunger.

It had taken him months to hop up along the coastline, trying to stay far enough out to avoid the big crocs, but also not so far that he went over the edge of the shelf into the deep blue-black water, and ended up in mosasaur territory.

Luckiest man in the world, he had thought. *Only* man in the world, he corrected.

At a long spit extending out into the sea, Andy allowed the small boat to drift in toward the marshy shoreline, and felt the bow slide in on the bank's mud and stick fast. He lowered himself down below the gunwale, just letting his eyes rise to the top edge and moving them over the landscape.

The heat beat down on his neck and shoulders and he sniffed, smelling the warming silt, bringing with it the odors of brine, sulfur, rotting vegetation, and also something sweet that might have been animal decomposition.

"*Gluck.*"

"*Shush.*" Andy grabbed the small pterosaur's beak with a hand missing the two small fingers and held it for a moment. He gave it a stern look for a few seconds, and then released it.

The tiny creature cocked its head, and briefly turned one ruby eye on him, before hopping closer.

Andy shook his hand and flexed the remaining fingers; it still hurt even though it had been over a year since he lost the digits. He opened the hand to look at it. *That's what happens when you doze in a boat while leaving one hand dangling over the side*, he thought. He was lucky that whatever creature had traveled up from the depths and grabbed his hand was small, and its teeth razor sharp—otherwise, he might have lost more than his pride and a few fingers.

He sighed and turned back to the bank. The ground looked muddy but not bog-like, and he had pulled up in the mouth of an estuary. There was a river further in, and huge tree limbs grew over its top, making it look like a giant, mysterious green cave. Either side of the jungle was thick, and though it didn't look impenetrable, it would be harder going than trying to navigate the waterway.

But, he'd have to keep the sail drawn in. It didn't matter much as there didn't look to be a breath of wind in there, and for sure he'd get snagged on the lower branches.

"Anyone home?" he whispered, and then chuckled. He was impatient to jump out and stretch his legs. But if the years had taught him one thing, it was that the creatures that lived in this time were masters of camouflage and ambush. Caution and patience had kept him alive so far, and that's how he wanted to keep it.

The scream that pierced the air made him cringe down low for a moment. Even the small reptile flattened itself to the bottom of the boat. Andy looked up, and then higher. There was a solitary tree close to the waterline that stood about 70 feet tall and had all the branches on one side wind-blasted off. In its few remaining spiny-looking branches, medium-sized pterosaurs jostled and argued amongst themselves for a moment before settling down again. And then they turned to watch Andy with gimlet eyes and pointed, toothed beaks.

"Friends of yours?" he asked, but his little buddy said nothing, probably spooked by the bad language used by his bigger cousins.

Andy also desperately wanted to see his country, long, long before it actually *became* a country. He wanted to stand on hills, or in valleys, or on raw coastlines, seeing them in their infancy, and then picture what they would be like in the future.

He wanted to visit fossil bone beds, and other places where he had found prehistoric remains, with the hope of perhaps seeing those very beasts when they were alive. How cool would that be? *Impossibly cool*, he thought.

His determination was proving a challenge to logic and reality, but he was still alive, and had only had to pay with a few fingers so far—a small price.

"*Are we there yet?*"

"Huh?" Andy turned to look down at the small creature that just cocked its head staring up at him. He shook it away. He knew it was his imagination wanting to fill the void of loneliness with an imaginary friend. *I'm not insane yet,* he thought, and then he grinned. *Not fully anyway*.

The small bird-like reptile climbed on his leg, and he gently stroked its leathery skin. "Yeah, we're here."

Andy smiled down at his tiny friend. He had found the baby creature when it had been abandoned after its hatching. One wing was permanently stunted, and at first, he thought he'd simply eat it.

But then he wondered about the studies that queried dinosaur intelligence—were they smart? Could they ever be trained? He wanted to find out, so he kept it, and it had quickly bonded to him. And, ridiculously, he to it.

What started as a scientific experiment had yielded his only friend in the world. And a few years back, he began talking to it, and then one day, it talked back.

No, it didn't, he reminded himself. He was a scientist and knew enough about people being alone to recognize a psychosis. Deep down, he knew that the words were really coming from somewhere in his own mind. The problem was, he didn't really care that much.

And though he might not have admitted it, talking to someone, or some *thing*, was important to maintain his motivation, and remaining sanity. He thought he wouldn't mind being alone. But he did. So it was kinda nice to be able to share his thoughts about this place with another being.

Gluck rested its long, beaked head on his thigh as it nestled on his sun-warmed leg. He guessed the tiny pterosaur wanted to be off the boat as much as he did.

Many times, Andy had pulled in at the coast on his voyage, but for the most part, he'd slept in the boat and dropped a homemade anchor of a rock tied to a length of vine to keep him in place. He'd just covered himself over in the sail and prayed he got to see the next morning.

He knew that the ocean was fraught with danger, but sleeping in the jungle meant finding shelter, like a cave, and then barricading himself in, or up a tall tree, or burying himself in mud, as he had heard Ben Cartwright had done. None of the options were as easy, or any lower risk, than just lying down in a gently rocking boat, and hoping for the best.

Andy was a paleontologist, and one thing he knew from his fossil bed excavations was that at river mouths and broad estuaries like this one, where fresh and salt water mixed and where the environment was warm, calm, and teeming with life, big things lived.

The beasts came here to lay eggs, rear young, and to hunt. If he stayed in the center of the river, he'd probably be safe, or at least safer, from attack from the shore. But in the river center was where it was deepest, and here there were also aquatic creatures that hunted. Big creatures.

Andy continued to wait and watch. Impatience got you dead, real quick. His food had run out, and his drinking water was down to about a single tepid inch in a gourd. He desperately needed more supplies.

Andy's tools comprised of a spear, a slingshot, and something that looked like a deformed tennis racket that he used as a net. It was amazing how many small sea creatures came all the way up to the boat to investigate—close enough for him to simply scoop them out.

"Hello there." Andy saw a small herd, or maybe flock, of a dozen or so bipedal creatures tentatively come down to the water. They were bird-like in their movements and slate grey with black-banded tails held out stiffly behind them. He bet they were lightning fast, and he marveled at the way they took turns darting down, drinking quickly, and then darting back, while a few stayed with heads high in the air, looking one way then the other.

But speed and lookouts didn't help when you can't see below the water. And he was right—the attack came fast. The torpedo launched itself from the river with blinding speed and brutal power.

"Yep." Andy watched, transfixed. "Someone *is* home."

The creature was about 10 feet in length, and looked like a cross between an alligator and a seal. He rattled off some suspects. "*Uberasuchus*, definitely a *mosasauroid*, and maybe even a form of *Pannoniasaurus*—bloody beautiful."

The tiny pterosaur climbed higher on his leg and looked over the gunwale.

"*Gluck.*"

"Yeah, sure, but are you thinking what I'm thinking?" Andy grinned. "I think for us, that was a good thing."

Andy knew that the upside of seeing the attack was though the predator might have been big enough to attack Andy if it had the chance, it wasn't big enough to take on his boat. Added to that, it had just fed.

"We can do this."

He lifted the paddle and gently stroked in toward the mouth of the estuary. The water depth shallowed quickly as they passed over a sandbar, and looking over the side, he saw silver bony fish darting back and forth in the lukewarm water.

On the bottom, a five-foot, leathery-looking disc glided over the sand. The primitive stingray was mottled like a parlor rug, and had more of a shark-like tail, not the whip-like ones of modern times. Andy knew they were another ancient species of cartilaginous fish that'd been around for 200 million years, or rather, 100 million more than now.

Once over the sandbar, the water deepened again, and Andy moved away from the river mouth center where the water was becoming a dark green. The estuary was over 100 feet across and quickly narrowed to about 50 further in where the river began.

He gently paddled to within 10 feet of the bank where he could see the bottom—far enough away from the shore to hopefully dissuade larger land-based predators from lumbering after him, and close enough that if he did get attacked by an aquatic carnivore, he had a chance of making it off the water.

Looking over the side, he saw that the silt was striped with mollusk tracks, some of them quite wide. If he got the opportunity, he'd grab some as they'd be a couple of mouthfuls of great protein.

There were also a few nautiloids hovering mid-water for a moment or two, before they all turned in the same direction to zoom away when he approached. He'd tried eating them before but found they exuded something cloyingly sweet that tainted their flesh.

Ripples ahead made him stroke a little harder, and just below the surface, several foot-long fish were heading toward the bank. Andy gave the boat one more powerful stroke, letting them glide, and then grabbed his net. He lunged, scooping back toward him.

"Yes." He netted one, bringing it into the boat where its muscular body flipped and shivered, making a sound like drumming against the wood. Andy put his foot on it to quiet it, and Gluck immediately set upon it.

"Hey, wait up there, little buddy." He pushed the pterosaur away, and it glared and opened its bony-looking wings in annoyance but then stayed close so it could keep its beady eyes on the fish.

Andy took his foot off it and tipped it out of the vine net where it flopped to the boat bottom.

"*Whoa*, weird. What are you?"

The thing was grey, but without scales, sort of like a catfish, and had what could have been bristles all along its streamlined body. No obvious gills, and a flattened head. But the weirdest thing was that its flippers appeared strong, and they ended in tiny-clawed toes.

"Rudimentary limbs? *Synapsid*? *Therapsid*?" It was the name given to the earliest of creatures that began to transition to mammals. "Don't remember you from the fossil record." He knew though that thousands upon thousands of species just never became fossilized due to being in the wrong place, were the wrong composition, or were just too damn rare to begin with.

It flipped one last time, and he put a foot back on it to keep it still. "I wonder what you'll become in another 100 million years?" He chuckled. "I mean, what *would* you have become?"

Gluck waddled forward and pecked at it again.

"I know, right, it's amazing, but formally out of the evolutionary gene pool. Because today, it's dinner."

"*Hungry.*" Gluck pecked harder.

"I know you didn't just say that." Andy pushed the small pterosaur back a step, but it bustled forward. "Okay, okay." Andy set to cutting up the strange creature, some for his companion, some for himself, and some left to dry in the sun.

CHAPTER 02

SAM HOUSTON NATIONAL FOREST, MONTGOMERY, TEXAS—PRESENT TIME

RE-EVOLUTION: 002

Montgomery wasn't a big town by anyone's standards; in fact, only 621 people at last count. It was sparse, friendly, and close to the National Park and beautiful Lake Conroe. Summers were hot and humid, the winters mild. Many say it's more subtropical than true Texan weather.

No one could really remember when the first cats and dogs went missing. But it might have been around the time of the blackout. It only occurred for a few seconds, and not everyone even saw it, but straight after, everyone learned that any pet left outside at night never came home in the morning. Bears and mountain lions were suspected, action demanded, and hunters were dispatched.

Then, they caught something.

The three hunters stood around their kill. It was laid out in front of them, and though a few people held phone cameras loosely in their hands, no one took pictures as they all simply stared in silence, brows drawn together in confusion.

It was a bird, sort of, stretching 10 feet from beak to claw. It was a little like an ostrich, except the head was two feet in length, ferocious-looking, and with a huge trap-like serrated beak. The claws on the end of its powerful legs would have been more at home on some prehistoric creature as they were fearsome-looking scaly talons.

The plumage was red and brown, and flightless wings were tucked tight in against a barrel body.

Mitch Connors, the local MD, and the closest thing they had to a science type, leaned in closer, and then grunted.

"Terror Turkey."

The crowd turned to him.

He nodded. "Yep, now I remember, called a *Phorusrhacid*. Rare, but they come out of the forest this time of year." He looked up at the crowd. "Dontcha remember?"

Billy Douglas began to slowly nod. "Oh, yeah, I do. *Now* I remember."

Then they all did.

CHAPTER 03

WASTE KNOT CLIFF FACE, SOUTH DAKOTA—1,200 FEET UP.

RE-EVOLUTION: 003

Ben Cartwright hung on the cliff face, resting and sucking in deep breaths. He turned and looked out over the landscape. The cliff face he and Emma were on was of medium difficulty, but it was high, and afforded a view for miles over the forested landscape.

Elm, spruce, ash, and other tree varieties all competed for sunlight and created a multi-hued mosaic as they crowded together over the breathtaking landscape. Ben grinned; it looked inviting, safe, and felt like home.

He couldn't help his mind going back to a similar vista where he looked out over another forest from upon high—that one, the Cretaceous jungle of 100 million years ago. Back then, there were more dangers in a single square mile than this place where there was the occasional bear, mountain lion, or skinny wolf. In that time and place, there were things that were monstrously huge, cunning, and hunted with senses well beyond those of the soft, pink, hairless apes called mankind.

When he was trapped there, he'd had to hide buried in mud, in caves, and on treetops. He'd eaten carrion, insects, grass, and anything he could find to stay alive. His body became crisscrossed with more scars in a few months than his entire time with Special Forces operations.

He was about to turn away, when an odd tingling feeling washed through his body. And then everything blacked out.

"What the…?"

It was over as quickly as it started and Ben looked up to see if something had passed over the sun, but the sky was as cloudless and azure as ever. Looking down again, his eyes narrowed as he gazed out over the trees—something about them now. *Different.* He hung on the rope and tried to tease it out, but it wouldn't come.

It's nothing, he thought, and pulled himself back to the moment. He was here now, home, and he had survived his ordeal. He was safe.

Ben grinned, then laughed out loud, and then threw his head back. "*I'm alive.*"

"*You won't be for long if you don't hurry up, buster.*"

Ben grinned wider and looked up. Emma was already at the top, standing on the very cliff edge, unafraid, with her hands on perfect hips.

Her tanned, muscled shoulders gleamed with perspiration in the sunlight.

He chuckled and started to climb again. Though she was the expert climber, she had taken him on more climbs now than he could remember. It had made him stay fit, in top shape, and though there were silver streaks in his hair, he was still as tough as iron—at least in his book.

He began to climb faster, and his arms and shoulders screamed. He bet he'd need a good soak in a warm tub, plus a few cold beers after this one.

He reached the top and shook his arms and hands out, letting the muscles unwind. He grinned at her.

"Funny, it looked a lot easier from all the way down there."

Emma smiled back, her green eyes crinkling at the corners. To him, she was still as beautiful as ever, and though the years had lined the corners of her eyes and mouth, and the sun had given her a million more freckles across the nose and cheeks, she still made his heart leap.

She held her arms wide. "But didn't I just hear you say you feel alive up here, Captain Cartwright?"

"I sure did. After all, you have to be alive to feel pain, right." He grimaced theatrically.

"Oh, you big baby." She walked right up to the cliff edge again and peered over, absolutely fearless. "Climb down, or via the path?"

He held up both hands. "Two votes for the path."

She laughed. "Deal, but we jog, okay?"

He groaned. "Can we enjoy the view for a few more moments?"

He sat down on a rock, she beside him. Nine years had passed since Emma had ventured to the dark heart of the Amazon Jungle to find him and bring him home. The psychological scars for both of them ran deep, and would take a lot longer to heal, but would never ever fade from their memories.

Ben looked up at the sky. Soon, the comet, Primordia, would arrive back again. Frankly, he didn't want to give a shit, but every year at this time, it managed to creep back into his consciousness. It was an evil anniversary that had burned itself deep into his brain.

He felt Emma's thigh rub up against his and he felt he was the luckiest man alive. He sighed and looked back out over the view. The trees drew his attention again.

"Hey, Em, the forest, what's different about it?"

She stood and walked to the precipice edge and put a hand above her eyes. Her head turned slowly as she scanned along the treetops. She began to shake her head and looked over her shoulder.

"Sorry, I love the view, but I'm usually more focused on the rock faces." She turned and walked back to him, and came and tapped his broad chest. "You're the ex-special forces guy supposed to be observing things."

She was right, he was, and he did. He smiled crookedly up at her for a moment and looked back to the trees. He was sure those pine trees weren't there before. And they were huge, *abnormally* huge, and for some reason, familiar.

He wracked his mind, but it just wouldn't come. He gave up, smiling up at Emma who was still half-turned to him and looking out at the trees again. He smacked her tight butt.

"Okay, last one down buys the beers." He began to sprint.

CHAPTER 04

THE HELIOS STAR SYSTEM, ALSO KNOWN AS EARTH'S SOLAR SYSTEM

Comet P/2018-YG874, designate name, Primordia, had finished its elliptical curve around the sun and was on its way back toward Earth. In a few more months, it would be at its apparition point—the closest point to Earth where it becomes visible to the naked eye.

At that time, its astral effects would be felt, but only in one place on the globe—a tabletop mountain, or tepui, deep in the Venezuelan jungles of the Amazon. Primordia had done this for 100 million years, and maybe would for 100 million more.

Unless.

At the other end of space in a circumstellar disc in the outer Solar System, approximately 31 million miles from the sun in a place called the Kuiper belt, an astral body rushed to join the countless other fragments of space debris that already existed there.

Most of the astral bodies were small, made up of little more than frozen gases such as methane, ammonia, and water, and were remnants from when the Solar System was formed. But other suspended bodies were of titanic proportions, and were composed of dense rock and metals.

The newcomer was traveling at bullet speed as it entered the Kuiper belt, and just like in a game of pool, its velocity and mass on collision caused some of the other asteroids to be exploded away from it, and thus, out of the belt.

They were scattered throughout the solar system and beyond. But one of them was sent on a voyage into the heart of the Solar System—toward Earth.

CHAPTER 05

RE-EVOLUTION: 004

The flight home to Greenberry, Ohio took under two hours. Several times, Ben had felt the tingling waves rush through him, making his stomach flip. He also saw the light flick on and off briefly, like a temporary power outage makes the light bulb in a room blink. Once he turned to see Emma's brows knitted as well, so guessed he wasn't the only one.

The taxicab dropped them back at the huge family home by early evening. His mother, Cynthia, had passed away a few years back, and now Ben was the new owner. The family estate, assets, as well as the history of the house now all belonged to him, and his wife, Emma.

Ben dropped the bags on the front porch and checked his watch. Zach, their 6-year-old son had been staying with a friend, so this might be the last getaway he and Emma did by themselves. She was determined to take him with them next time, already having him practice on the climbing wall at the local gym.

Zach was being dropped back after dinner, and Ben looked north toward the tree line of their estate, gauging how much time he had to do his last chore. Belle, their aging Labrador, was also having a sleepover with their closest neighbors, Frank and Allie—who overfed her, let her sleep on their couch, and never even bothered to sound off at her when she tracked muddy paws in on the rug. It was a wonder she ever wanted to come home afterward, and probably wouldn't except Zach was her unofficial fur-brother.

The house was big and would feel empty now. Emma had opened the front door, and he tossed their bags inside.

"Are you gonna get Belle? You can forget about us, because she'll be the first one that Zach looks for when he gets back." He heard her rummaging inside.

"Yeah." He knew she was right. "Kids and their dogs, with Mom and Dad a distant second."

"Good man; I'll make you something for when you get back with our four-legged fur-bag." He heard her chuckle inside.

"Great." Ben reached inside and grabbed his car keys. "Make mine something that rhymes with: *cold deer*."

"Cold ear?" She leaned out and grinned. "You got it."

Ben laughed as he jogged down the steps and headed to the garage.

He took the SUV, revving some life into the cold engine, and then headed down their long driveway to the road.

The properties were big here, so it'd take him a good 20 minutes to reach Frank and Allie's place across a few miles and some gently sloping hills. They were a nice couple, a little older than Ben and Emma—he a retired engineer, and she still doing something in IT consultancy. Their own kids had grown up and moved away, and their big house just had them rolling around in it now, so any chance they had to look after Belle or Zach, they grabbed it.

Ben pulled into their laneway and headed up the small hill toward their bungalow. Oddly, Belle didn't come bounding toward him when she heard the car, or even as he stepped out.

He paused to look one way then the other—*probably being fed again,* he thought. Never get between *Belle the belly* and a snack, he guessed.

The porch light came on, the front door squeaked open, and Frank stepped out, holding a cup of coffee. He waved.

"Hi, stranger."

Ben smiled and walked up toward him. "Howdy, Frank. Nice evening."

"Sure is," Frank said. "Coffee? Beer?"

"Nah, I'm good," Ben replied. He turned about, hiking his shoulders. "Where's the old girl?"

Frank frowned. "Allie?"

Ben grinned. "Yeah, right." He came up to the porch and held out a hand for him to shake it.

Frank grabbed it. "Okay, welcome back, neighbor. So what can I *really* do for you?" He released Ben's hand and waited.

"*Uh,* the fur-kid?" Ben still waited for the joke to play out. "You must have really spoiled her this time for her to be keeping her head down."

Frank's frown deepened. "Not getting it, buddy?"

Ben liked Frank, but after being away for a few days, he just wanted to get his dog and then get home. "Belle, my dog; can I get her, please? I'm a little tired."

"Your what?" Frank stepped back a pace, as Allie came to the door.

"Hi, Ben, welcome back. Emma with you?" She looked from Ben to Frank and then back again. "Everything okay?"

Ben nodded, smiling again. "Yeah, sure Allie. Just came to get Belle. Can't find her."

"Belle?" Allie's mouth quirked up in a confused smile. "Who's Belle?"

Ben had had enough. "Guys, joke's over. I want to get home. Thank you for looking after her, but I need to get her home before Zach gets back."

Frank's face became serious. "Not sure what's going on here Ben, but you're making *no* sense."

"*Belle*." Ben's confusion was morphing into anger. "My dog."

"Ben, there is no one here named Belle." Frank's voice now had taken on an edge.

Ben felt the emotional climate shift. He was angry, but he could tell the man wasn't joking. "My dog?"

"What the hell is a *dog*?" Frank turned to Allie. "Best go inside now, dear. I'll deal with this."

Allie's forehead was creased with concern as she gave Ben a fleeting watery smile and then disappeared back inside, closing the door behind her.

Ben felt like he was on an episode of the Twilight Zone. "My dog, Belle. She's a Labrador. I gave her to you for minding."

Frank reached out and put his hand on one of Ben's broad shoulders, and gently eased him around. "Best you go home now. Get some rest, or something." He guided Ben to the steps. "We haven't looked after Zach for months, and certainly haven't looked after anyone named Belle."

"No." Ben shrugged him off and turned. "*Belle!*" he yelled at the house.

He walked fast ahead of Frank, who stopped at the bottom of his steps and watched him with a careful eye.

"*Belle!*" Ben yelled again to the grounds. He cupped his hands around his mouth. "Be-*eeelle*." But no dog came bounding back.

He whistled loudly. Nothing. It didn't make sense. The dog was well trained, and if she heard Ben's voice, she'd come sprinting to him no matter what.

Ben spun. "Joke's over, Frank. *Where's my fucking dog?*"

Frank was 15 years older and probably 50 pounds lighter, but he lowered his head and squared his bony shoulders. "Son, I have no idea what the hell you're talking about. You're frightening my wife, and pissing me off. Go home and cool down. *Right now.*"

Ben walked away a few paces, hands on hips, and threw his arms in the air. "Fuck it." He was more concerned about what Zach would think than anything else.

He stormed back to the SUV, climbed in, started the engine, and jammed his foot down on the accelerator, spraying dirt and gravel as he spun the car around and headed to the front gate.

On the way home, his mind whirled in confusion. He knew he'd dropped Belle off. He'd seen Frank ruffle the fur on her head, and Allie pop a treat into the silly dog's grinning mouth. He didn't know what game they were playing but he was damn sure he'd find out.

He grumbled in the cabin of his car; he'd come back tonight with a flashlight if he had to. He was an expert tracker, and as tenacious as a wolverine.

Back on his own property, he skidded to a stop out front, shouldered open the car door, and then jogged up the steps, still muttering.

He had a thought, and stopped—maybe she ran away and they were too embarrassed to admit it. Maybe she came home and found the house empty. Ben turned and cupped his mouth.

"Belle!" He waited a second or two. "*Be-eeelle!*"

Emma came out holding his beer. "What's going on?"

Ben spun to her. "The hell if I know." He rubbed both hands up through his hair, feeling that odd tingle in his stomach again. "Something…weird." He sighed. "Belle…you know Belle?"

"*Uh*, yeah." She held out his beer. "Has something happened to her?" Her brow was furrowed as she looked up into his face.

"Yes, no, *ah* God, I don't know." He grimaced. "I took her to Frank and Allie's, didn't I?"

"Of course you did." She half-folded her arms, still holding his beer. "Where is she?"

"They said I didn't." He scoffed. "In fact, they said they never heard of Belle." His voice rose and he couldn't help it. "They said they didn't even know what a goddamn dog was!"

"That's crazy; you must have misheard him," she said.

"No, I asked him several times—no Belle, no dog." He looked heavenward for a moment.

"Rubbish; we'll go together, talk to them." She paused. "Wait, let me grab a picture." She vanished back inside, still holding his beer.

Ben waited, feeling a growing sense of unease in his gut. He suddenly felt like he was being set up for some weird practical joke that everyone was in on except him. All that was needed was the creepy twist at the end.

He heard Emma rummaging, and then the tone of her voice worried him even more.

"Ben?"

He raced into the house and found her in the living room by the fireplace, her hands resting on the mantle. She shook her head slowly.

"It's gone."

Ben looked along the items there. Everything was as he remembered—small vases, a colored stone Zach had found, and multiple pictures in silver frames. There was his mom, dad, Emma's folks, a few of the property in different seasons, several of Zach, and then that was it.

There were eight pictures, like there always was. Ben craned forward to the frames—one of the pictures was different now.

He walked toward it on stiff legs, feeling like he was in a trance. It was Zach, after football practice, grinning like a loon as he had scored the winning touchdown. His helmet was lying beside him on one side, and on the other…nothing.

"Where's Belle?" He lifted it. "He had his hand on her head, and she was sitting, right, *here*." He pointed to the empty space.

Emma's mouth opened and closed and her eyes were blank with confusion. And he knew why—there was no golden dog, looking up at Zach with her typical, sappy, tongue-lolling grin.

Ben brought the picture close to his face, examining Zach, the grass, shadows, anything and everything, as he tried to find some sort of photo-shopping trick. He slowly shook his head.

"What the hell is going on here?" He looked at Emma whose face had drained of color.

His wife's eyes momentarily widened and she then raced to the kitchen. He heard drawers, cupboard doors, then the pantry opening and slamming closed, and things rattling. Ben followed her in.

"It's all gone." She looked at him and just raised her hands, palms up. "All gone; her bowls, her food, toys, everything." She just shook her head. "It's like she never existed."

"What's a dog?" he mumbled. "Just like Frank asked."

"This is a mistake." Emma took the picture from him, bringing it close to her face and squinting at it.

Ben suddenly felt a deep sense of loss as if the animal had suddenly died. "She was real." He lifted his gaze up at her. "What's happening to us?" He smiled but without humor. "Thank God you see it too."

"Or don't see it, you mean." Emma's frown deepened.

"Mom, Dad?"

Emma's eyes flicked up to him. "*Zach*…what'll we tell him?"

Zach came belting into the kitchen but paused to spin and yell back to the door. "See you, Tim! Thank you, Mrs. Abernathy, *bye!*"

"Thanks, Angie," Ben called, and heard Zach's friend's mom yell a farewell through the still-open door, and then close it for them.

Zach grinned widely, mop of black hair hanging over his green eyes, and rushed to kiss Emma and then hug Ben. He didn't even notice their strained looks and instead headed for the pantry for a cookie. He came back and smiled at them through crumbs, but then stopped chewing.

"Wassup?"

Ben looked to Emma and she back to him, both waiting for the other to speak. Ben guessed it was only a matter of time, maybe minutes, before

Zach asked where his buddy was, so…
"Zach, we think that Belle has gone missing."
Zach's brows pinched together. "Who?"

CHAPTER 06

PACIFIC OCEAN, JUST OFF PACIFIC BEACH, SAN DIEGO

RE-EVOLUTION: 005

Drake Masterson pulled on the rope tightening the sail in close to the hull, making the boat tilt toward the water in the breeze. Where he sat, he was acting as a counterbalance on the opposite gunwale, and the boat lifted the more it accelerated, requiring him to lean even further out.

He grinned as salt spray whipped his face, and his brawny forearms clung tight to the elasticized rope in one hand and the tiller with the other. The bay was warm this time of year, and a good breeze wasn't to be wasted.

Drake's security company was doing really well now. In fact, so well, he didn't need to be there to oversee it anymore. So he got to spend his time doing something he always wanted to do—go sailing.

Starting from scratch, he took lessons and learned how, bought a boat, and then let himself loose on the water. Out here, it was just him, the waves, the wind, and the blue sky. In a good breeze, it made him feel like he was flying in his 25-foot Catalina Capri 22, with its flared hull, fiberglass and wood-trim design, all finished with a full racing kit.

The beautiful little boat he had named the Nellie, after his mother, also had a small cabin, and many a warm night he had pulled into a cove and slept there, with just the lapping of the water and gentle lifting of the current to rock him to sleep. Sailing was his calm after so many of life's storms.

It allowed him one other thing as well—time to think. It had been nine years since he, Helen Martin, Emma Wilson, and Ben Cartwright had walked out of the Amazon Jungle. They'd been torn up pretty bad, but they were alive. Many who went in with them hadn't been so lucky.

The more time passed, the more Drake felt like it never really happened. It was just all so…unreal. Down in the deep, dark heart of the Amazon, there was a tabletop mountain, a tepui, where once every 10 years it became some sort of portal back to a time of 100 million years ago.

You had to get in and out in just over 24 hours. If not, the portal closed, and you stayed. He scoffed; they'd lost five good people in the few hours they were there. Six if you counted the kid who decided to stay behind. But Ben Cartwright had survived 10 damned long years there.

And they would have been 10 of the most hellish years any human being could imagine.

Drake found that anything and everything he had faced in this life, and that was a life lived fighting in Special Forces with Ben Cartwright against ruthless and bloodthirsty foes, was shaded by the creatures they encountered from that primordial time.

He laughed out loud. One thing was for sure: he gave thanks every day he was home, alive, safe, and in one piece.

Drake whooped loudly and pulled on the rope, forcing the main sail in tighter and lifting Nellie's hull a fraction more to squeeze a few extra knots from the sleek boat.

His gut tingled from the thrill, but then the boat slowed so suddenly he lurched forward, nearly slipping to the deck.

"What the hell?"

The boat gradually continued on and there hadn't been any loud or ominous sounds from below as if he'd hit some sort of submerged object like a log or crate or even sandbar. But he did feel like he had hit something. The only thing was, it felt more like he had hit a pillow.

Maybe it was weed, he thought, and looked over the side, and then saw half of a massive jellyfish go past.

"*Je-zus*," he whispered. The thing must have been 10 feet across. He continued looking out the back and saw another half appear—his boat had cleaved the gigantic thing in two.

"A monster."

Drake had heard there were large jellyfish in the freezing waters to the north that could grow to three feet across and weigh 100 pounds. But this thing would have been five times that.

"Weird." He sailed on, spending another hour tacking back and forth before heading back into the sailing club.

He kept the Nellie in the small club boatshed most days, but today with the weather good, he'd leave it tied up on the water so he could get back out first thing tomorrow morning.

He quickly grabbed his gear, tidied up, flushed down the sails, ropes, and deck with fresh water, and then climbed out to stand on the sun-warmed wooden pier to tilt his face into the sunshine and just absorb its warmth.

Life was good right now, and he wondered how his best friend, Ben, was getting on. He hoped he and Emma had found their little piece of paradise as he had found his.

He had everything he wanted. *Nah*, almost everything; he lost Helen, and now and then he missed her terribly. He wished she were here now so he could tell her about the jellyfish. He sighed, feeling the sun warm his cheeks. *Time moves on*, he thought, *and sometimes* things*, get left behind.*

Drake finally opened his eyes and turned to the clubhouse that had a bar and restaurant, and then faced the long stretch of beach to the south. The sun was just starting to sink, making the tide line glow orange. A few sand pipers on long legs waited for waves to draw back so they could race down to peck at small crustaceans that became momentarily exposed, and then striding back up as another waved lapped in at them.

While he watched, a large wave came in and the few pipers went to turn to outrun it when a section of the wave lifted and threw itself forward, like a watery hand.

It completely covered one of the birds, slapping down on it, and Drake then saw that the watery hand was actually one edge of a huge jellyfish like he had seen out on the water. The thing had trapped one of the birds and was slowly pulling it back into the surf-line. Revoltingly, he could still see the bird through the jelly body as it vainly struggled.

Drake turned about, hoping to see someone else to point the weird occurrence out to, but no one was there.

"That is fucked up." He quickly pulled out his phone to try and get a picture, but in the next few seconds, the massive jellyfish and the trapped bird were gone.

Weirdest thing, he thought. He'd ask someone about it at the club tonight.

CHAPTER 07

SOUTHEASTERN TIP OF NORTH AMERICA—100 MILLION YEARS AGO

Andy stopped paddling and let the rustic boat glide forward as their estuary stream opened out to a larger body of water. At the narrow mouth, the water surged a little as if the pond was a tad higher, and to enter, Andy would have had to either paddle hard or get out and drag his boat up into the bigger body of water.

If he did have to get out, he'd do it on the bank rather than wade in the water. Mainly because a while back the water had lost its clarity, and where he was now it was tepid, brown, and like weak coffee. It wasn't stagnant and the discoloration was more likely from the amount of rotting vegetation and tannins in the pond, and also the fact that it probably only got fully flushed out after a heavy rain.

None of this concerned him. But what did was he had seen the water lump at the far end when the body of something large came to the surface. It could have been a freshwater mosasaur, one of the many primitive crocodile species, or even a turtle the size of a small car.

If he tried to drag the boat from the water, the turtle he might be able to out run. But anything else and he'd be fish food.

Shit, he whispered.

"*Gluck.*"

Andy looked down at the small flying reptile.

"*Somebody home?*" Gluck had its head tilted to have one ruby red eye fixed on him.

He sighed and nodded. "Yeah, there is somebody home, and somebody that's big." Andy lent his forearms on the gunwale. "We can't go in there. They're home, and believe me, I'm betting they would *love* to meet us."

He continued to watch for many more minutes before coming to a decision. He cursed again, knowing it was going to cost him time and ramp up the risk. He began to paddle in to the closest bank.

Andy nosed into the reeds, making something slither away and vanish into the murky depths, and then the boat grounded and held.

He set about dragging it up higher to beach it, and then climbed back in to gather his things together into a satchel he'd made from woven fibers like the primitive tribes in Papua New Guinea. He'd drawn on his knowledge of ancient tribal craft, and had also managed to self-learn how to make a form of animal hide rustic boots, trousers, and vest. He had gourds for fresh water, now empty, and lastly, into the bag went Gluck who immediately settled down.

He knelt in the boat and took one last look toward where he had seen the large shape. His eyes narrowed as he scanned along the water's now-still surface. There was no breeze, and just the *zumm* of insects from the reed beds. The sun warmed the water and the bank, and he smelled the fresh silt, plants, and a dozen other odors. If he hadn't seen the thing come to the surface briefly, he would never know it was there.

He knew that big crocs like the *Deinosuchus* or *Mourasuchus* lived around this area at this time and could potentially follow him out of the water. But they were big, up to 40 feet, weighed many tons, and would be slow. And as the jungle looked dense here, they'd give up quickly.

He grimaced. There was one thing that could follow and catch him, probably before he even went a dozen feet, and didn't mind hunting in water.

"Please don't be a *Titanoboa*."

He continued to watch for a few more minutes, wishing his sister, Helen, was here to ask. She was the real expert on the giant snake's behavior.

There was something else he wanted to ask her: why did the snakes only seem to inhabit the plateau top? In all the time he'd been here, he'd never seen one away from the tabletop mountain. What was it about that site that they preferred? *A mystery for another day*, he thought.

Andy turned back to the jungle. There were trees that might have been mighty banyan with massive roots interspaced with ferns, bracken, palms, and all manner of weird tongue-like plants. Fungi grew from the bark in shelf-like plates of orange, brown, or brick red. And everything glistened like it was damp.

The deep jungle always worried him, and he much preferred the water where he could see what was coming—at least above the surface. Just looking at the tangle of green madness made him feel claustrophobic and nervous as hell.

One upside is at least I'll be able to forage on the way, he thought. He knew he wasn't eating enough plant material, and it didn't take long on a meat diet to develop things like scurvy and rickets, with the associated bleeding gums and then tooth drop.

Down beside the boat, some sort of mollusk was gliding along the bottom, and he reached over to grab it. It was the size of his fist, and immediately the foot extended from the shell like a long blue tongue. He leaned out again to rip up some leaves and rolled the large aquatic snail inside to keep it fresh, and then added it to his bag for a later meal.

He peeked in. "No fighting, you two."

"*Gluck.*" Gluck glared.

"I know it smells funny; and you don't?" He grinned and closed the bag.

Andy often wondered about whether anything he was doing now would make a difference in the future. Before he came, he had done some homework on the subject, and he'd read many theoreticians who said, *yes it would,* and many more who disagreed and stated that the future was immutable, and anything he did was destined to have happened anyway.

Perhaps without him, the future wouldn't have been as he remembered it. The bottom line was, the time paradox was unknowable.

Andy took one last look back toward the body of water, and then stepped out of his boat. He stood for a moment, turning slowly until a broad smile split his face.

"I christen thee, America."

He entered the jungle.

CHAPTER 08

ELMO, UTAH—THE BONE BEDS

RE-EVOLUTION: 006

Helen Martin carefully dusted the nub of long mineralized bones. Though there was only an outline of the skull showing, her experienced paleontological eye had already guessed it was going to be significant, and her excitement grew with every wipe of her brush.

It was from the *Triceratops* species and it was different—it had front-facing horns, unlike anything else they'd discovered here. And the head was big—six feet long and abnormally crested.

She paused to look at her surroundings: sand, clay, dunes, shelves of hard rock, and a few hardy plants.

The Elmo site was a veritable gold mine for dinosaur fossils, and especially *Allosaurus* skeletons. They were big theropods, with massive, boxy heads filled with tusk-like teeth. Finding a new *Allosaurus* skeleton was cool, but finding something even more rare was 100 times cooler.

She turned her head to sneeze, the dryness and dust tickling her nose, but in a good way. Though the area she and her team worked was dry now, in the late Cretaceous period, it was a lush swamp bordering an inland sea, filled with a variety of huge plant-eaters, and hunting them, the carnivores.

At that time period, there was an elevated sea level that split North America in two. The western landmass was called *Laramidia* and included what is now the west coast of Canada and the United States. To the east was the equally large *Appalachia*, the mountainous island landmass.

Helen wiped her brow and rested on her haunches. Her specialty had been prehistoric snakes, especially the *Titanoboa*, but for some reason, she couldn't bring herself to even look at that species anymore.

Maybe it was the fact that she had nearly been killed by one herself, and also had seen people crushed and eaten alive by the creatures. It had taken her years to get over the physical and psychological trauma she had suffered. Adding to her pain was the knowledge that her little brother, Andy, was still back there.

Her eyes glistened as she stared down at the nubs of bone showing. *Maybe one day I'll dig him up*, she thought, and then laughed. But there was little humor in it. Her nose tickled again, but this time it was from melancholy memories.

She hated that she was alone now. After they survived their ordeal, she and Drake had dated for a few years, but then drifted apart. She guessed they both reminded each other of a horrible experience, and distance from anything that reminded them of those terrible events was the only way to truly heal the psychological wounds.

"*Ooh.*" Helen felt the tingle ripple through her belly and placed a hand on her stomach, just as the sunshine flicked off and then a few seconds later, back on. She blinked, wondering whether she had only imagined it.

She looked around, finding her two students helping on the dig and earning bonus credits for their final. Edward Ramirez and Elizabeth Shelley were both competent, fun, and she could count on them to be meticulous in everything they did. Neither of them looked up or seemed confused about what just happened, so it must have been her imagination, or maybe even dehydration.

Helen uncapped her water bottle and sipped, letting her eyes travel over the dig site. There seemed more greenery now, or maybe she just hadn't noticed it before.

To her far left, Edward worked on a wall of shale-like material with an overhang of some sort of bush dangling over him. It was a great spot he'd found, as he had access to the fossil layers and a natural canopy against the harsh sunshine.

She watched him for a moment more and saw that the bush over him had what looked like large cherries in amongst its foliage—strange, as out here, most things struggled to survive in the dryness and nutrient-poor soil, so fruit was a luxury most plants couldn't afford to produce.

She was about to turn away, but then noticed one of the cherries, a particularly large and red one, seemed to be lowered down closer to the young man. In a few seconds, it was mere inches above him, and then to her amazement, it exploded in a puff of what looked like powder or gas.

Edward eased to the ground as though resting.

What the hell? She straightened, a frown creasing her forehead.

"Edward," she said loudly enough for the young man to hear. One side of her mouth quirked up in bewilderment, but in the next second, her confused smile fell away when she saw the tendrils drop from the bush above him.

"Hey!" Helen got to her feet.

Her other student, Elizabeth, turned.

"*Hey!*" Helen shouted again and quickly looked down at her tools, snatching up a small and sharp metal shovel. She saw the tendrils begin to gently wrap around the young man, and then once coiled, horrifyingly, his body began to be lifted from the ground.

Shit. She ran at him.

Edward was out cold, and Helen raised the shovel above her head, and then swung it forward like a machete, severing some of the thinner vines. But the thicker ones were elastic enough to resist her blows.

She went to snatch at the vine-tendrils but saw that they were covered in small, serrated thorns and these had already hooked themselves into Edward's clothing and exposed flesh.

Elizabeth joined her with a small pick, and together they bashed, hacked, and chopped at the vines and bush until the combined attack proved too much for the plant and the young man rolled free. Elizabeth dropped her pick, grabbed the young man by the shoulders, and dragged him away.

Helen stood, staring in disbelief as her chest heaved. She saw that where the spots of Edward's blood had dropped to the ground, tips of vines gently tapped on it as though like a cat lapping at a plate of cream.

She took a few cautious steps closer and then could just make out in amongst the plant roots there nestled bones—lizards, some birds, and even what might have been a coyote skull.

"What the hell is going on?" She turned about.

Elizabeth was gently wiping Edward's wounds with a damp handkerchief. "Vampire Dodder," she said. "We should have known they'd grow in this area."

"What?" Helen's mouth hung open, and she turned to stare for a moment. "*What* is that thing?"

Elizabeth tilted her head, confusion crossing her youthful features. "I only just remembered—the Vampire Dodder. It's a parasitic vine that can be a real problem. Pretty common in these parts; you know that."

Helen shook her head and felt slightly nauseous as another tickling ripple ran through her body. "I've never seen, or even heard of that thing before in my life." She turned back to the plant that had now reset its thorny tendrils, waiting patiently for something to blunder too close again.

Somehow something had changed, and the more she thought about it, the more she got a sinking sensation in her stomach. She rubbed her forehead, wondering why she seemed to be out of sync with everyone else. Why did the plant seem so alien to her, but normal to everyone else?

But then she did sort of remember. Not this type of plant, and not here and now. But when they were hacking through the jungle of the Late Cretaceous, there had been something similar. So what was it doing here, in this place, and in this time?

A worm of worry coiled inside her. She needed to talk to someone, urgently, and there was one someone she could trust who had experienced everything she had.

CHAPTER 09

PACIFIC OCEAN, OFF PACIFIC BEACH, SAN DIEGO

RE-EVOLUTION: 007

Drake was back out on the bay, heading out, and already about 2,000 feet from the shoreline where the water darkened as the sea bottom sloped away to about 200 feet of deep blue. There was a slight chop on the surface, but his streamlined Nellie cut through it like a hot knife through butter.

Several times last night and once this morning, the weird blackouts had occurred, accompanied by the tingling that started in his belly and then washed right through him. No one he talked to seemed to have noticed, and when he brought it up with a guy on the dock, he just stared back as though Drake probably needed to see a doctor, rather than it being an external phenomenon.

One thing that the Amazon had taught him was that life was short and should never be taken for granted. Enjoy it while you got it...so, he simply pushed it from his thoughts.

He flicked his head, whipping water from his eyes, and stared dead ahead. It was a good day for sailing, and he thought it odd that no one else was out here with him. In the distance, he saw there was a lump in the water, and he craned his neck trying to get a better look, but it seemed to vanish before his eyes.

One of those weird-ass giant jellyfish, he bet. This time, he decided to get a picture and kept heading toward it. But he gave the tiller a touch so he wouldn't sail right over the spot just in case it was something half submerged, like a log or lost shipping container. His Nellie was a Catalina Capri, built for speed and beauty, and definitely not for breaking ice packs.

The wind gusted a tad harder and the boat lifted a little and began to skip and dance across the surface. Drake was forced to lean back to stop it flipping. He was closing in on the spot he'd seen the dark shape, and as he leaned out even further, he caught sight of the thing almost right below him. His heart jumped in his chest.

There was a huge head only about 10 feet down, nearly as long as his boat, and it was attached to a long whale-like body—and worst of all, it was now trying to keep pace with him.

Drake couldn't tear his eyes away and saw it was turned slightly on its side so as he looked down at it, it was looking back up at him. Then to his horror, he could tell it was coming up.

"*Jesus Henry Christ!*"

He tacked away, his hands moving furiously to drag in ropes, keep the tiller tight, and also reposition himself to rapidly build up more speed. He twisted on the gunwale to look back and saw the lump in the water breach, coming after him.

There was a plume of water mist like that from a whale, but unlike a whale, there were two instead of one, as if there were two spouts close together, like from a freaking big nose.

Drake felt his heart galloping now, and he turned ahead to see just how far he was from the shoreline—still 1,600 to 1,800 feet at least.

He angled even steeper into the wind and headed directly in. Drake was skimming now, cutting it fine between top-speed and tipping over. And that was the last thing he wanted, because he had a pretty good idea that if he went in the drink, he wouldn't be climbing back out.

He snapped his head around for a quick look back and saw the lump still there, not gaining, but not falling away either. The huge bulk of the thing was making V-shaped waves as it chased after him. Whatever the thing was, it was damn big and fast as hell. But he had a good lead and with the wind up, he intended to keep it.

Then the Nellie hit something, soft and pillow-like, and he immediately knew he'd just run over another of those goddamn giant jellyfish. The boat's speed was cut by three-quarters.

Drake furiously re-angled the boat, tugged in the sail, and the Nellie gathered again as the breeze lifted the boat as if a giant hand gave her a gentle push along. He was soon back up to speed, but looking back, his lead had been cut in half.

Damn, damn, damn… This can't be happening, he thought. He left all this shit behind on that damned plateau nearly 10 years ago.

Drake whipped his head back again toward the thing following him, and then forward. His swift little boat was eating up the yards toward the beach. He didn't have time to get back to the club wharf, so anywhere dry would do.

He looked back again and gritted his teeth. Then he hit another jellyfish and grunted as he was thrown forward.

"Fuck the fuck off!" he screamed. He madly went through the motions once again to regain his speed. He looked back and felt a cold hand on his neck—the damned thing was gaining on him. It was 500 feet back before, but now only about 200. He turned back to the beach.

Come on, baby, you can do it.

Once more his boat skipped along, and then he hit every racing boat captain's number one enemy—the calm spot. Drake had to leap forward to stop from falling back into the water as the boat settled into the dead zone of no wind.

Oh, shit, no.

Then it was over and the wind started up again. But now he had to go from a standing start this time—slow, so slow. But up he climbed—5 knots per hour, 10, 15, 20… Drake looked back and could see the lump of the beast's back clearly now. It was a shining gray like a whale but with darker banding. It was so close he could see a few barnacles on its back, and horrifyingly, the two large predatorial eyes were fixed right on him.

His boat skimmed fast once more, and he counted down to the shore—400 feet to go, with the thing only 100 back now. He watched it for a moment more and saw it accelerate, trying to catch him before he got away.

He turned back toward the bow and leaned forward as if this was somehow going to make him and the boat a little more aerodynamic. How far must he go before the creature decided the water was too shallow? Or could it come up on the land—remember the damn jellyfish and the bird? *Impossible*, he thought, begging it not to be true.

Faster, faster, faster, he urged Nellie.

Below him, he started to see clumps of weed. It must have only been about 20 feet deep here. He hurriedly turned back and saw that the thing was gone. Or had dived.

No way, it was too shallow. The boat skipped toward the shoreline—80 feet, 50, 30, 10, and then he hit the sand and leapt out.

Drake didn't stop running until he was 50 feet up the first sand dune. He spun back.

The sea was calm. Except for the whitecaps, there was no monstrous lump or wedge-shaped head rearing up. But he knew what he saw. He grimaced as the tingling rushed over him again—and then the sunlight blinked off then seconds later, back on.

Drake looked up at the sky. *And what the hell is with that?* he demanded of the big yellow orb.

"You tryin' to commit suicide, son?"

"*Huh?*" Drake spun.

There was an old guy standing up on one of the dunes, holding his sandals with a pair of binoculars around his neck.

Drake pointed. "Did you see that?" His voice was higher than he wanted.

The old guy's face twisted in disdain. "Course I saw it." He stepped aside and thumbed over his shoulder to a sign jammed in on the dune.

Drake's mouth fell open in disbelief as he read the huge yellow sign's black lettering.

Kronosaur season—no swimming, no boating, and no fishing until further notice.

There was a stenciled image of the sea reptile he just saw.

"*What?*" Drake felt his eyes actually bulge. "Is this a joke?"

"Idiot." The old guy began to turn away. "There's a reason we stay out of the water this time of year. It's mating season for the big kronos. They make a kill, and they'll hang around all year."

"This is madness." Drake ran up the dune to grab the guy's arm. "When did this happen?"

The old guy suddenly looked a little worried by Drake then, who was still tough and brawny-looking even though he was now in his 50s.

"When?" The old guy shook his head, looking confused. "It's always been like this. Every season on the warm current they migrate up the coast." He backed up. "Just…just stay out until about October, *orright?*"

"Yeah." Drake nodded slowly. "Yeah sure."

The guy turned and vanished up and over the dunes. Drake looked back out over the water. It now looked ominous, threatening, and mysterious. He then stared down along the waterline where his boat was beached. He really wanted to believe it was some sort of prank on him. But he knew what he saw, and knew something bad had just happened that defied belief.

He felt the tingle in his belly again, and he knew whatever was happening was still happening. His phone rang and he pulled it out, looking at the caller id—it was Helen.

CHAPTER 10

WEIRD IS THE NEW NORMAL.

Ben Cartwright put the phone down slowly and turned to Emma.

"That was Drake. He and Helen are coming over; I mean, they're on their way right now. They want to discuss something important with us." His eyes were on hers. "He sounded a little agitated."

"They're back together?" Emma's brows went up. And then: "Did they say about what?"

"No." Ben slid his hands in his pockets and ambled toward her. "But I can kinda guess, can't you?"

"You think it's happening to them too?" Emma turned to stare at the empty fireplace for a few moments. "But why us? I mean, why is it just us seeing the weird things going on, but everyone else is acting like all the weird is normal?"

"The weird is normal." He paused, staring down at her. "The new normal."

She looked up quickly. "Do you think it's because we went, *um*, back?"

Ben shrugged. "I don't know. How? Maybe there are others, but then, why doesn't Zach see how strange it all is? To him and everyone else, it seems to them that it's always been like this, and we're the ones out of sync."

"Only we see the change," Emma said softly.

Ben walked to the window. "And it all worries the hell out of me." He spoke over his shoulder. "When will it stop? I mean, what comes next?"

The doorbell rang, and he and Emma got to their feet. "Time for some answers," Ben said.

Emma pulled the door inward as Ben stood at her shoulder. When Drake entered, she hugged him, and then allowed him to pass by her so he could shake Ben's hand. She went to also hug Helen and chat softly to her.

It'd been a while since they last saw each other or even spoke, and to Ben, they looked the same except their hair contained a few streaks of silver, and the sun had pressed a few more fine lines onto their brows and at the corners of their mouths. However, he bet that the haunted look around their eyes was something new.

"Come through, come through."

Ben led them into the living room where there was a coffee pot on the table, plus freshly sliced orange cake that Emma had baked that morning. Behind them, the fire popped, and the place looked and smelled inviting, hopefully a sanctuary from all the confusion.

"Where's boy wonder?" Drake asked.

Ben chuckled and thumbed toward the steps. "I'm betting either slaying dragons or chopping up zombies online."

"If only he knew what his father had done—slain some real ones; dragons, I mean." Drake sat down on the couch and looked at its clean surface. "Hey, no dog blanket covered in hair for a change."

"Yeah, about that." Ben looked grim and clasped his fingers together. "What's a dog?"

"*Huh?*" Drake frowned and held a slice of cake suspended from his mouth. "What does that mean?"

Helen also sat down and Emma spoke as she poured her a coffee. "You see, there's no such thing…anymore."

Drake and Helen sat and stared as Ben continued. "We had a dog, we know we did. But he's gone." He frowned. "No, he's not just gone; he never even existed. In fact, no dogs exist anymore." He looked at each of his friend's faces. "Except in our minds."

Emma's mouth was a flat line. "Something has changed. Somehow, our world has changed."

Drake lowered his hand holding the cake. "I knew it." He turned to Helen. "See?"

Ben sat on the edge of his chair, big hands grasping his knees in front of him. "I've seen things, weird things, that I don't understand. I think you have too, right?"

Helen nodded. "Yes, yes. Plants, carnivorous, that attacked my students. They never existed in our time before. *I would know if they did.*" She shook her head. "And my students acted like *I* was the crazy one for not recognizing them."

Drake nodded. "Yeah, that was the kicker for me; everyone else acting like I was the odd one out. I was out boating and got chased by something the size of a freaking whale. But it wasn't. Looked like a giant lizard that swam under the water…" He turned to Helen. "What did you say it could have been…?"

"*Kronosaurus, Tylosaurus*… maybe one of those, but both long extinct," she said softly.

"That was it—a *Kronosaurus*—yeah, a freaking monster. Just made it back to shore with my skin." He sat back and scoffed. "But what was even weirder was on the beach an old-timer chewed my ass off because I shouldn't have been out on the water." He scoffed. "You know why?

Because it was goddamn sea reptile season—*Krono season!*" His eyebrows were up. "What the hell? When did that happen? I mean, there were even signs stuck on the beach as warnings. They weren't there before, I know it."

Ben nodded. "The world is changing. We now live in a world where dogs don't exist, and sea monsters do."

"That's a shitty tradeoff," Drake said.

Helen's vision seemed to have turned inward. "Dogs never evolved. And other species never went extinct. Evolution is on a whole new pathway." She looked up. "Something happened to change everything...in the past."

"And is still happening," Emma said. "Hey, has anyone felt strange lately? Like, *um*, a tingle running through them?"

"Yeah, yeah, like a mild electrical current that runs from your head to your toes, and ends up in your belly," Drake said. "And the light flicks on and off—the sunlight."

"Yeah, me too," Ben agreed. "I felt it just before I saw the tree species change down in Utah. The weird feeling rushes through you as the lights black out, and then there's a change."

"And they're getting bigger," Helen said. "We did it, we changed something in the past, we broke the rules." She looked at each of them. "And now we're going to pay for it."

CHAPTER 11

TORONTO, CANADA—BAY STREET BUSINESS DISTRICT

Chess Monroe briefly glanced over his shoulder at Mohammed Ibn Aziz as he came down the main street flanked by three enormous men in dark suits that barely contained their hulking muscles. One walked in front, and the other two just behind each of his shoulders.

Aziz used to be the chief accountant for the Maghadam crime family, and since he had been picked up by the CSIS—the Canadian Security Intelligence Service—and threatened with life in prison, he was rumored to have flipped. Word was that he agreed to give evidence against the family for a new name, new home, and complete amnesty on all charges. He'd agreed, and all he had to do was survive until his single court appearance in a week's time.

No one was even supposed to know he had been picked up, and this one last venture outside was to his strong box at the bank to retrieve some documents he'd need to put the Maghadam elder's heads on the block. The State Prosecutor's Office would then do the rest.

The thing about organized crime, and the families who ran it, was they had enormous resources at their disposal—money, property, businesses, and contacts in everything from the highest office of politics all the way down to the most cunning street urchin. Therefore, for every snitch like Aziz, there was a counter-snitch prepared to give up their mother for a golden goose egg.

The Maghadams already knew about Aziz being picked up, they knew about him getting ready to testify, and they even knew about the visit to the bank, probably minutes after it was floated in at the CSIS.

Toronto's Bay Street was fairly busy at 2pm in the afternoon, and even though it was downtown in the financial district, its coffee shops were overflowing with outdoor business meetings, groups taking the opportunity to take a break and talk a little office treason, and also several weary shoppers walking from one set of retail hubs to the next.

The two men and a single blonde woman at one of the tables laughed and sipped coffee, and the woman leaned forward to cut some cake with a fork. If a trained operative were looking for potential risks, or something that stood out as incongruous, they would have seen that even though she wore expensive clothing, she held the fork roughly in her hand and her fist had knuckles that were raised and calloused.

Chess was one of the two men at the table with her. Both of them were also dressed well, in linen sports jackets, one blue, one brown, and pressed shirts, but they too had the facial features of men used to brutality rather than corporate finance.

Two blocks further down Bay Street, a van moved slowly and then double-parked. The single driver, a dark-haired, dark-eyed woman, had a small communication pill in her ear, and waited. In the back of the van, another man also waited by the sliding door.

As the Aziz party approached, from the café table one of the men facing the group counted the steps of the coming men and lowered the cup a fraction from his lips.

"Now."

The man in the blue linen sports jacket left the table to wander down the street in front of the approaching Aziz group. The two remaining coffee drinkers continued to sip their coffee, laughed, relaxed, and made small talk as they faced each other. However, behind their dark sunglasses, their eyes were fixed on the party of four now coming abreast of them.

Just down the street, the man in the blue linen jacket slowed so he was only a half dozen paces in front of the lead bodyguard. He spoke softly.

"Show time."

From his sleeve slid an 8-inch steel spike and he stopped, spun, and then lunged. Before the lead bodyguard could react, he had jammed the spike into the side of his neck.

Aziz's mouth dropped open and he held his hands up in front of himself like a small animal holding up its paws.

The two guards behind him went for the guns at their belts, but from behind, the man and woman who had been seated were already on their feet and up close. They shot them point blank in the back of the skull with silenced shots so soft it sounded more like a small child coughing.

The three guards were carefully laid against the brick wall, and as the van roared to a stop beside them, its door slid back. Aziz was grabbed under one arm and lifted toward the open door like he was a child.

"You got a date," Chess said.

The small accountant was pushed inside and the trio followed. On the street, few people were even aware something had happened.

In the back of the van, Aziz's eyes began to water. "Are you going to kill me?"

Chess shook his head. "*Nah*, we're just going to deliver you to the Maghadams. They'll kill you…eventually."

CHAPTER 12

"THAT'S WHY THEY CALL IT A TIME PARADOX."

Emma leaned forward. "Helen, you said that something was changed in the past, we broke the rules, what does that mean?"

"The butterfly effect is one name for it," Helen said.

"You mean the theory that if a butterfly flaps its wings in one place, it can affect another, like cause a hurricane?" Emma asked. "That bizarre theory?"

"Something like that, but it's an actual mathematical design theorem," Helen said. "Grew out of chaos theory and was put forward by theorists in relation to weather modeling and the path tornadoes took. It can also be adapted to anything that can be affected by minute changes. And time is certainly one of them."

Helen reached forward and grabbed her coffee cup, sipped, replaced it, but continued to stare into its dark depths. "I did some research when I first thought that something had been changed that might affect us." She put her cup down but held onto it.

"There are so many theories, such as the *grandfather effect*, *predestination*, *looping*, and something called *the Fermi effect*. Basically, some of them contradict each other, and some state that no matter what someone did in the past, it was meant to happen anyway and therefore of no consequence to the future. Others say it is impossible to make changes, such as that proposed by the grandfather effect theory."

"Going back in time to kill your grandfather," Drake said. "Like, how you can't really kill your grandfather, because then you would never have existed to have been able to kill him in the first place, right?"

"Exactly. Another theory that exposes the absurd complexity of it all is the impossibility loop." She laid a hand on Drake's forearm. "Say, an old lady gives a young man a watch. He then travels back in time and gives the watch to the old woman who is now a young girl. The young girl grows old and then gives it to the man. So, where did the watch originally come from?"

"Makes my damn head hurt," Drake said.

"That's why they call it a time paradox." Helen smiled. "But one thing's for sure, is that something we did, or maybe Andy did, has altered our version of time. And now it's catching up to us."

"Like toppling dominoes," Emma said.

"Yes. And the further you go back in time, that first tiny domino to get a push, can topple a slightly bigger domino. And then that one can topple an even bigger domino, and the bigger the dominoes that can fall, and the more time they have, the bigger changes that can occur."

Drake's brow was furrowed deeply. "But so what if you take out a few animals to eat a hundred million years ago? Or chop down some trees, or eat some berries and nuts? It's not like they're the last ones."

"But don't you see?" Ben sighed. "They might just be the ones that made all the difference."

Helen clasped her hands together. "That's how the domino effect works. Just imagine you went back in time 100,000 years. You find a berry and eat it. But that berry was going to feed a bug. That was going to feed, say, a bird that was going to feed an eagle that now doesn't lay eggs that season. And those eggs were going to feed a hunter-gatherer family."

Helen rubbed her temples and went on. "The family goes hungry, and now don't have children that year. One of those children was going to be a great leader and found a great nation that will now never exist. The human world will be changed forever."

Ben ran a hand up through his hair. "And now multiply that by a thousand times, by going back 100 million years."

"Yes, yes," Helen said softly. "Through one tiny change, one species may die out, and instead another may take its place. An alternate future is created."

"Jesus Christ," Drake whispered and stood up. He paused. "But...why is it happening now? None of this occurred when Ben was stuck there."

They sat in silence for a moment, all lost in their own thoughts.

"Maybe, *uh*..." Ben hiked his shoulders. "Maybe it was like keystones. Everything I interacted with wasn't important...wasn't key to our timeline."

"That's all I can think of," Helen agreed. "Some species, or even some particular animals, are pivotal to our timeline. You might be lucky a thousand, thousand times, and then the one berry you eat, or bird you kill, or fish you net, turns out to be the one that was important." She looked up at Ben. "That turns out to be the keystone to change."

"Lucky us." Drake exhaled through pressed lips. "Okay, I got another question. Why is it affecting us, here, when we were down in South America?"

"It'll be a global effect," Helen said. "As well as continental drift, the sea level was much lower many times over the past 100 million years. There were land bridges between Africa, Asian, European continents, and us, right here. Things, creatures, plants, moved back and forth."

"We just have to adapt," Emma said. "Maybe things will change for the better. Maybe we humans will be less warlike, maybe there'll be less disease, better food...we might have to just wait and see."

Helen's eyes were glassy. "Or maybe we won't exist at all." She gave Emma a watery smile. "Or a new disease might evolve, a new predatorial creature." She chuckled. "Or we might have decided to never come down from the trees."

"We could vanish altogether," Drake said. "Our...human line, our thread, might begin to be unpicked right before our eyes. One person at a time."

"And we might be the only people in the world to notice," Ben said morosely.

Ben felt the tingle run through him again and he grimaced. He saw Drake and Helen look to each other, and Emma reached out to place a hand on his shoulder just before everything went black for a second.

"Oh God, another one." Emma gripped Ben's shoulder even harder.

"Yeah, I felt it too." Drake straightened in his chair. "What else just happened this time? What else has turned up, or disappeared?"

Emma looked to Ben and he back at her—the same question hung between them. She jumped to her feet and ran to the steps.

"Zach?" She sprinted halfway up the stairs. "*Zach?*"

Ben rose, staring toward their staircase and feeling sick in his gut. He said a silent prayer.

"*What?*" It was the muffled sound of Zach's voice.

Ben exhaled, only then realizing he had been holding his breath. He slowly sat back down and sighed heavily.

"The human race is a frog in a pot with the water beginning to boil," Helen said softly. "And just like the frog, it doesn't even notice the changes."

"So what's worse?" Drake asked. "Not noticing and carrying on as the world gets more dangerous or people just start winking out? Or being like us, somehow immune to this collective obliviousness and actually witnessing the changes?"

"Worse for us," Helen said. "Because we won't know what to look out for. Remember your kronosaur?"

Drake nodded. "Oh yeah. And I didn't even get to tell you about the bird-eating jellyfish."

Emma came back down the steps, and her expression was relieved but strained. She came and sat up close to Ben and grabbed his hand in both of hers.

"What do we do?"

"Nothing we can do," Ben said.

"Isn't there?" Drake asked. "Sure, we can't do anything today, but it's now been nine years and eight months since we were on that damn plateau."

"So," Ben picked up. "In four months, Primordia returns. And with it, comes a doorway."

"A doorway back to stop anything else happening." Drake sat back.

"No," Emma said. "No way. We only escaped with our lives by the skin of our teeth last time. No way we're going back. Why the hell would we?"

"Andy," said Helen. "Whatever he's doing, we can't let it continue."

"*No.*" Emma was even more emphatic this time. "I'm not doing it."

"I agree," Ben said. "You stay." He drew in a deep breath. "But the thought of not going, and leaving our son in a world that is hostile to him, scares the hell out of me. You need to look after him. But I need to make sure this ends. Whatever *this* is." He smiled, but couldn't make it extend to his eyes. "Besides, it's basically a second home to me, right?"

Drake groaned. "It was my idea, so if you need a wingman…" He screwed his eyes shut. *Say no, say no, say no.*

"Thanks, bro," Ben said and leaned across to slap his shoulder.

Drake opened his eyes, held out a fist, and Ben bumped it with his own. "Done."

Ben looked at Drake with a level gaze. "We make Andy come back with us. Or we stop him doing what he's doing."

"Hey." Helen's eyes flashed. "What does that mean? Stop him doing what he's doing? How do you plan on doing that?"

Ben looked at Drake, and the two men knew exactly what that might mean. He cleared his throat. "We convince him to come back with us. Even if we have to tie him up and drag him home."

"Really?" Helen's eyes narrowed. "I don't trust you."

"Well, come with me, *us*, I mean." Drake lifted his chin.

"Seriously?" Helen frowned. "You're going to use this as a way to try and rekindle our relationship? Try and get me to come back to a prehistoric world where everything there is designed to tear you limb from limb? Oh, and you also insinuate you might harm my brother as well."

Drake grinned. "So I'm a bit rusty, huh?"

Helen looked furious for a moment and then burst out laughing. Ben and Emma did the same.

"You asshole." Helen wiped her eyes. "Okay. Because I know if he sees me, he's more likely to come with us."

"*Okay?*" Drake's brows went up. "Seriously? I was only joking about you coming."

Helen shrugged. "You'd be dead in a minute without me. And besides, I figure if we don't do something, then this world, or rather this time, might end up just as deadly as the one of the Late Cretaceous."

Emma sat back and folded her arms. She shook her head, and her eyes watered. "I'm sorry; I can't."

Ben reached across and put an arm around her shoulders. "I know, and you shouldn't. Your priority is Zach. As is mine. You need to stay to look after him. I need to go to ensure he is safe in the future. That we all are."

Emma nodded, but then paused. "Maybe he'll come home by himself. When the portal opens, he might just decide to come home."

"Maybe. And maybe the changes we've seen so far are all that is going to occur," Drake said.

"No, he won't come home," Helen said. "But, I'm betting his scientific curiosity will draw him back to the plateau to observe the doorway opening again. He won't be able to resist that."

Ben nodded. "He'll be there, and so will we. Snatch and grab, and then we bug out."

"I'll organize some hardware." Drake grinned. "And I'll make damn sure it's appropriate this time."

"Jesus, you guys." Emma shook her head. "Aren't you forgetting something?"

They waited.

Emma scoffed. "Ben, you first went when we were 30. That was 20 years ago. Now you're in your 50s. I know you guys have trained hard and maintained your fitness. But seriously, the one thing you both know is that surviving on that plateau is the most arduous thing anyone could do at any time anywhere."

Ben sat back. "We don't intend to be there long. We can't afford to be."

"So we'll need help." Drake rubbed his stubbled chin, making a rasping sound. He began to nod. "I know some people. They'll bulk us up on muscle and firepower. But they'll cost us."

"It's not right," Helen said. "Remember last time? There's no way you can make someone believe or be ready for what that place is really like." She turned to Drake. "All those years ago when Emma first spoke to you about it, did you believe her?"

"Nope," Drake said. "And even now, I still find it hard to believe it was even real. That was, until a few days ago."

Ben used a thumb and forefinger to rub his eyes for a moment. "I don't think we have any choice. The world is at stake, and it doesn't even know it." He opened his hands, palms up. "Sorry, Helen, but what we're doing is bigger than just our little lives, or even anyone else's lives who comes with us of their own free will."

Ben then gave Emma a crooked smile. "I know you get it. Bottom line, even if we don't go back, it seems the past is coming after us anyway. Maybe coming after Zach and all the other Zachs."

Emma seemed to melt and grabbed his hand. "No, I'm sorry. Bring Andy back, save our world and its future." She lifted her chin. "Just leave me a damn big gun."

CHAPTER 13

EAGLE EYE OBSERVATORY, BURNET, TEXAS—60 DAYS TO COMET APPARITION

"Hey…" Jim Henson adjusted the lens on his massive telescope and amplified his view aperture. He leaned across to bring the computer online, and then jammed his eye back over the eyepiece.

"What have you got?" His colleague, Andy Gallagher, sounding vaguely interested, continued to type data into his own computer.

"Got some traffic," Henson scoffed. "Little fella coming out of the void." He quickly leaned an arm out to type furiously with one hand. He then looked across to check he had the details right and began to record the astral fragment.

"Asteroid?" Gallagher asked.

"Yeah, nice size, and going to come close enough for us to get a real good look." Henson went from his eyepiece to the computer screen, satisfied that what he was seeing was now on the screen.

To the novice, the screen looked black on black with a smattering of pinpricks of light. But to a trained eye, it was an astral snapshot of a segment of space, well out into our solar system.

"Thought you were going to tell me that Primordia was on its way back." Gallagher leaned back in his chair and folded his arms. "Our lucky number year again —'8'—and our clockwork traveler, P/2018-YG874, is coming back for a visit."

"Yeah, sure, but this is something else." Henson froze, and slowly turned. "He-*eeey*, you don't think…?"

Gallagher frowned. "Don't think what?" His brows went up. "No way…*collision*?" He snorted. "Are you on drugs…? I mean, even *more* drugs?"

Henson guffawed. "Hey, what do I look like here?"

Gallagher grinned. "You look like Santa Claus, if he didn't comb his hair or beard, and wore sweatpants."

"You flatter me, sir." Henson straightened in his chair. "And Santa Claus with an astrophysics degree from Caltech, remember?"

"Yeah, and mine's from Princeton, honors, and we both know our orbital mechanics—space is basically empty, and the chance of two tiny astral bodies colliding is millions upon millions to one."

"And yet it happens." Henson folded his arms and watched the moving speck on the computer screen. "P/2018-YG874, *Primordia*, has been traveling perhaps for millions upon millions of years." He turned.

"Eventually everyone and everything's luck runs out."

"Impossible," Gallagher said emphatically. And then, "But it'd be pretty cool if it did." He looked up. "Hey, you spotted it, you name it."

Henson stroked his beard for a moment. And then raised a finger. "I name thee... *Lord Vader*."

Gallagher groaned as he grinned. "Lord Vader it is. And may the dark side be with you." He turned back to his screen. "So let's keep an eye on him, just in case."

CHAPTER 14

SOUTHEASTERN TIP OF NORTH AMERICA, 100 MILLION YEARS AGO

The huge theropod eased forward and gently placed a foot the size of a small car down on the soft ground. It did the same for the next step, and then became motionless for several minutes. It finally angled its head slightly, a little like a monstrous dog, as it listened for a moment, before taking another careful step.

It inhaled deeply, drawing in all the odors and scents of the surrounding jungle. It was tracking something, something it couldn't yet see, and for now could only smell. But its predator senses told it that the thing was close.

The alpha theropods were huge beasts and happy to feed on carrion, but also liked the thrill of the hunt and kill as well. Their eight-inch, tusk-like teeth were all backward curving, designed for gripping, tearing, and sawing through the flesh and bones of the massive animals of its time.

It remained frozen, and even with its towering size and bulk, it was near invisible in the dappled light of the jungle. Its mottled hide was a patchwork of brown and green with some banding on a thick tail held out stiffly behind it as a counterbalance for its huge head. At around 40 feet from nose to tail tip and weighing in at 15 tons, it was one of the largest carnivores in North America during the Cretaceous Period.

It turned its head again, slowly, scanning the jungle floor, but also searching for the scent trail. Minutes passed, and then it took another step, and then another, and paused to search again.

Whatever it was looking for was not being revealed. Whatever it was, it was better at concealment than the massive hunter was at hunting. Finally, it seemed to give up and it moved on, caring less about its noise and pushing aside trees as if they were long grass.

Andy stayed where he was, not moving a muscle. The mud he had coated himself with was layered on thick and was like axle grease; also, it was as uncomfortable as hell. But it kept the insects away and hid most of his weird and attractive mammal odors from the beasts. Most of them anyway.

He identified the creature as a member of the *Carcharodontosaurus* genus—probably a *Siats meekerorum*—that lived in this area just 100 million years before Andy's home time. Though there were theropods that were larger and heavier, this monster was one of the most powerful, and certainly most ferocious.

Andy continued to watch the path it had taken, or rather just bulldozed through the jungle, while still not moving out of his concealment. He remembered being involved in debates about whether these massive carnivores were hunters or scavengers—but now he knew. He'd seen with his own eyes the massive thunder beasts running down huge prey, using their bulk to knock them off balance, and then their car-sized head craning forward and massive jaws gaping wide to rip out throats or crush neck vertebrae. They were hunters all right. And damned good at it.

Finally, a tiny speck in the gargantuan jungle moved—Andy—coming out from amongst a tangle of mangrove-like tree roots. He opened his pouch and looked in at the tiny bird-like reptile. For once, Gluck kept his beak tightly shut, perhaps catching the scent of the apex predator and knowing that discretion wasn't just the better part of valor, but the only thing keeping them alive.

Andy took a few cautious steps, stopped, and just let his eyes move across his path. He was a speck in a land of giants, and he turned slowly, looking over his shoulder. He'd learned a lot in his years in this time period, and one of those things was that the massive many-ton predators had an ability to be wraiths when they were hunting. They could be as silent as ghosts; one minute you thought you were alone, and the next there was a 10-ton shadow only a few hundred feet behind you.

Andy couldn't count the number of near misses he'd had. *All my lives are used up*, he thought and grinned, his teeth and eyes glowing white through the caked mud.

It took him another 20 minutes before he felt safe enough to resume his normal pace. He stopped to lift his head and sniff deeply. He still wasn't close—there was no hint of salt in the air. And not the murky salts of mineral pools or sulfurous magma vents, but the clean smell of brine.

When he was growing up, the one eye-opening thing that grabbed his attention and thrust him on the path toward studying, and eventually becoming a paleontologist, was the fossil sites referred to as bone beds. These were places where the remains of many species of dinosaur were found, and in some cases all jumbled together.

The center of America had once been submerged when sea levels were hundreds of feet higher. In the hot and humid times of the Cretaceous, the ice caps melted and the ocean had intruded deep into the continent's heart. It had split the mighty landmass down the middle, creating two.

Andy had arrived on the eastern landmass called *Appalachia*. And across a vast inland sea was the western landmass called *Laramidia*. As the millions of years passed, the sea level dropped, and eventually, the inland sea became a massive lake. It had landlocked thousands of species of prehistoric creatures—some sprat-sized, and some the biggest sea monsters of their time. They became monstrous goldfish in a sea-sized bowl.

Finally, when the inland sea dried completely, the stranded animals became piles of corpses, and then fossilized. It became a kill box for the creatures, but a bonanza for future fossil hunters.

Since arriving in this time, it had always been one of his goals to see arguably the most famous of all the bone beds. But of course, today, in this time period, it wasn't a bone bed at all.

Andy sniffed again. *Damnit, I still have far to go, and it has already taken me…* He paused, having a thought, and reached into his bag, eliciting a *gluck* of annoyance from his little friend.

"Move aside, buddy." He pulled out a length of slate, roughly 12 inches long by 3 wide and 2 deep. On it was hundreds upon hundreds of scratch marks—his calendar stone. And at the top, his name in all capitals: "Andy." He'd carved it when he still had a knife, now long rusted away.

"Wow, guess who's coming back soon?" He looked up, but had no chance of seeing the sky through the thick tree canopy. Perhaps up there in the sky was the familiar eyebrow streak of the comet and its tail as it began its approach to our world.

"So what." He replaced the calendar stone. But then looked up again. *Imagine what the plateau looks like when the displacement actually starts to occur?* he wondered, and then cursed. *Damn my curiosity*, he thought.

Gotta see my interior seaway first, he whispered. There was one problem—what would be the United States in 100 million years' time was currently two massive continents. The western one, *Laramidia*, was a land of low plains. But unfortunately, he had arrived on *Appalachia*, and the mighty backbone of the Appalachian Mountains was already a line of towering peaks.

They were first formed around 480 million years ago during the Ordovician Period, where the mighty fold in the Earth's surface thrust up to be of equal height to the Alps. Since then, natural erosion had worn them down a little, but during the Cretaceous—now—they'd still be a formidable climb. All he needed to do was cross them.

Andy sucked in a deep breath and then exhaled long and slow, feeling the fatigue and years drag on his skinny frame. He peeked into his bag, and the small pterosaur lifted its head.

"*We can do it, Andy. And we still got time,*" it said.

He grinned and nodded. "Damn right we do."

CHAPTER 15

MAMA'S DAUGHTER'S DINER, DALLAS, TEXAS

Drake pulled up out in front of the small, flat building that was like an island in the middle of a large concrete sea of a carpark. Hanging on the facade was a huge oval pink sign with swirling calligraphy announcing the place as *Mama's Daughter's Diner*.

He switched off the engine, held onto the steering wheel, and craned forward, looking out through the windscreen at the small building.

Ben scoffed. "In here?"

"Oh yeah. Best comfort food in Texas," Drake said without turning. "They'll be waiting."

"And these guys are available for hire, *huh*?" Ben didn't look that optimistic anymore.

Drake grinned. "Sure; a few days in and out, plus throw in an extra two weeks for training and acclimatization, and all up I guess we only need to buy these guys for a month, maybe an extra week here and there."

"What should I pay?" Ben asked. "You know them."

"Too little, and they'll tell you to hit the highway. Too much, and they'll smell a rat." He bobbed his head. "*Nah*, there's no such thing as too much for these guys."

"Yeah, well, we don't have a lot of time to hold too many rounds of interviews. I'd prefer to offer top of scale than to haggle over pennies. Besides, since I inherited the estate, I've got more money than I can spend." Ben sat back.

"That's why you're my best friend." Drake chuckled. "But you're right; they're greedy, so a pot of gold at the end of the rainbow will get their attention."

Drake rested his forearms on the wheel. "I've worked with them, and then fired them because they were mavericks and risk takers. Don't want that in a legitimate security business." He turned and grinned. "But in a suicidal mission back to the dawn of time, well, they'd be perfect…and expendable."

Ben chuckled. "And so?"

"And so, a million bucks apiece. 10% on lift-off, the rest when we get home." Drake's face became serious when Ben's eyebrows went up. "You want them to say yes without even stopping and thinking about it, right?"

"Shit. Big payday." Ben blew air through his lips. "But at least I like the way you back-loaded the deal. After all, how many will actually be alive to collect?"

"All of them if everything goes to plan." Drake briefly looked around the near vacant carpark.

"What have they been doing since they left your fruitful employ?" Ben asked.

"Knowing them, bad shit. They're no angels." Drake elbowed his door open. "Let's go and meet them." He paused and then leaned back into the car. "Oh yeah, one more thing." He grinned. "Don't expect any of them to be shrinking violets."

"You don't say." Ben chuckled and stepped out himself.

Ben and Drake crossed the carpark and pushed in through one of the double doors, making a small bell tingle overhead. Both men stood just inside, surveying the interior; there were a few people scattered about, and on one wall was a sign that read: *No dessert till you eat everything on your plate.*

Ben smiled. "Mama sure sounds like one tough old bird."

Drake nudged him and nodded toward two huge guys at a booth. Only one was watching him, the other picked at a plate of food.

"Two there, two more at the counter, and one at the far booth."

Ben looked from person to person—two solid dudes at the booth, two women that looked like they chewed barbed wire for breakfast at the counter, and another guy the size of a small mountain in the far booth. They had spread themselves out to look random, but to the trained eye, it was more like they were expecting an ambush.

All except one seemed interested in the pair of new arrivals. But Ben bet his bottom dollar that when he and Drake had crossed the carpark they had all watched like hawks.

"And these guys are your buddies, right?" Ben asked.

"Sort of." Drake bobbed his head. "Like I said, they used to work for me…and I fired every one of them."

"Well then, this should go smoothly." Ben and Drake took a booth and the waitress came with a notepad.

"Coffee and a chicken club," Ben said. "Bacon extra crispy."

"Make it two," Drake added.

The waitress nodded and left and then Drake eased back against the vinyl and threw an arm out along the top of the booth seat. "Now we wait."

And they didn't have to wait long. One of the guys from the booth who had been watching them lifted his coffee cup and sidled over, sliding in next to Ben and bumping him along. Ben was a big guy, but this guy had to be 6"2', and had 20 pounds on him. Plus about a dozen years.

"Drake." The guy nodded.

"Chess." Drake smiled and continued to lounge back. He nodded toward Ben. "My buddy, Ben Cartwright. The guy I told you about."

Ben nodded, and Chess turned an eye on him to give him the once over and then looked back to Drake.

"You said you wanted to see us about a job?" His mouth turned down momentarily. "Pretty busy right now."

"Sure you are." Drake waited as the waitress slid their coffees in front of them and left. Drake lifted it and inhaled the aroma. "Playing pool, being hungover, and a bit of petty crime is a full-time job."

"Smartass," Chess snarled. "Is there a job or not?"

"Yep, and one that might be your last." Drake stared back with an unwavering gaze.

Chess frowned. "What's that mean?"

Drake chuckled, and Ben shook his head. "I mean, the payday is so good, you may never have to work again."

Chess waved it away. "Getting too old to be an outlaw, brother."

"Nothing illegal, as if that ever bothered you. But it is…unusual." Drake waited with a half-smile still on his lips.

"But I'm betting dangerous as all fuck," Chess shot back. "Right?"

"You bet." Drake laughed.

Chess stared for several seconds until the waitress appeared again. "Anything else for you boys?"

"Yeah." Chess looked up. "Five servings of pie for my posse, and put it on this guy here's tab. *Wait*, put all our bills on his tab." He grinned.

The waitress' eyes slid to Drake who nodded once.

"Okay." She hustled away.

Chess folded tattooed arms. "That just bought you both some listening time. Go on."

Drake looked to Ben who gave him the go ahead. He leaned forward. "A quick snatch…a rescue. A month's work between here and down in the Amazon. And when we're ready, in and out in two days. If everything goes to plan," Drake said.

"We've done snatches before, but the Amazon, man. Bad news." Chess whistled. "Have to think about it."

"A million bucks. Each," Ben said, evenly. "So think quick."

Chess didn't flinch, but the corners of his mouth twitched. He turned and waved for the other four members of his team to come and crowd into the next booths to listen.

Chess looked at each of them. "Guy here says the job pays a million bucks, *each*, for a simple snatch, *ah*, rescue." He turned back. "For that sort of cabbage, who is it, some drug lord, the president? Who?"

Drake shook his head. "Nobody you know, and nobody important. Who it is doesn't matter. But we need to bring them home from the Amazon, fast." Drake's eyes were level. "And yeah, you heard right, a million bucks each. $100,000 when you get on the plane, and then $900,000 more when you get off back home, *with* our guy." He lifted his chin. "And I never said the job was simple."

One of the women leaned toward their booth, and then right into Ben's ear. "Sounds like bullshit, man; what's the catch?"

Ben leaned away from her mouth. "Possibly, *probably*, going to be a suicide mission."

"*Ooh.*" She scoffed, turned to Drake, and thumbed toward Ben. "You gonna tell us who this guy is?"

"He's a buddy of mine; we used to work together. This here is Captain Benjamin Cartwright, formerly Special Forces. And he's also been where we're going. So if you sign up, you listen up when he speaks, because he's the boss." Drake grinned with zero humor. "And one more thing: he's also the guy that pays the bills."

"*Used* to be Spec Forces," the woman said. "And I've been to the Amazon more'n a dozen times. It's just another freaking jungle full of wet heat, bugs, and snakes. But for a million bucks, Mr. Fuckstick, I'd go to the moon."

Chess turned. "That's enough, Shawna." He thumbed to the four people in the booths surrounding them, starting with the two big men. "Buster and Francis. The mouth here is Shawna, and the nice one is Balls."

Ben tried not to laugh as he turned and nodded to each, finishing on Balls. She was a 30-something Latin American-looking woman with a slight dent in her lips, indicating an old split lip that hadn't knitted right. Her face was pleasant enough, but her eyes were dead. Ben had seen that look before, usually in Vets that had seen it all. He didn't think for a second she wasn't as tough as they come. Ben looked again at each of Chess' crew. In fact, they all looked fearless and formidable. *Good,* he thought.

"Got another name?" he asked Balls.

She smirked. "Bianca Alejandra Leticia Sofia."

"I see; *Balls*." Ben grinned. "I'm gonna go with Bianca; how's that?"

She shrugged. "For the money you're paying, you can call me what you like."

"Yeah, for a million bucks, we're all in," Chess said and looked over his shoulder at his pals. "Right?"

They all agreed. "Money for old rope." Shawna winked. "And we get

100Gs, just for saying yes?"

"No, you get 100Gs for getting on the plane, and *after* it takes off. *And* after your training. *And* when I'm happy that you're ready," Ben replied.

"Too many rules." Chess looked at Ben with disdain. "If you don't mind, we'll speak to Drake. We don't really know you."

"Too late; you said you were in, so basically you're on my payroll and work for me. Don't like it, the door's that way." Ben nosed toward the door and then shrugged. "We got plenty more down and out Mercs to interview, and the day is still young."

Chess' eye narrowed. "That right?"

"Now you're getting it." Ben just smiled.

Chess' jaw jutted. "Hey, Drake, I don't think I like your buddy." He lunged forward, grabbing for Ben's collar.

In the blink of an eye, Ben gripped his wrist, half turned it, and used his other hand to take the big man's hand and give it another twist, turning it upside down, and wrenching it all the way up to the man's shoulder. He then held it with ease, his eyes half-lidded with boredom.

Chess grimaced, his entire body leaning out, while Ben held him in check with just one hand. He looked like he was struggling hard not to show pain.

"You don't like me, but you'll take my money," Ben said. "That is, if you live to get it." He sat forward, still hanging on as Chess gritted his teeth. "And you know what? I don't want you to like me, because I don't want to like you. If you come on this mission, you may die. Maybe all of you will die, so I don't want to be your friend, or have to care about you. Got it?"

Chess' teeth were clamped.

"*Got it?*" Ben repeated, applying a little more pressure.

"Yes, *fuck*, yes," Chess seethed.

Ben let him go.

Chess sat back rubbing his shoulder and just glared. His friends looked like they didn't know whether to pile in on Ben or laugh out loud.

"Told you not to mess with him." Drake grinned as the five Mercs stared, but seemed more surprised than anything else. Drake raised his eyebrows. "What? You thought he was going to pay you a million bucks to have a holiday? We meant it when we said this mission is bordering on suicidal, and you've all said yes without even hearing the details."

"We've been to tougher places than the Amazon." Bianca lifted her chin. "And we're all listening now Mr. Special Forces... Mr. *Ex* Special Forces."

Ben turned to her. "Self-preservation finally winning over greed, *huh*? It's good to worry about your own skin."

She nodded. "Nothing I'm scared of. Not in this world."

"Nothing in this world." Drake chuckled. "In this world, at *this* time. And I used to be the same."

They paused as two massive chicken club sandwiches, overflowing with tomato, chicken breast, lettuce, tomato, peppers, and crispy bacon arrived at the table. Potato chips surrounded the plate.

Ben and Drake nodded their thanks to the waitress, and the aroma of bacon wafted over everyone.

Drake lifted his napkin. "Now, Captain Cartwright here is going to give you a brief overview, and I want you to listen closely. Then all of you take a few minutes to think about it and ask questions while we eat our lunch." He looked hard at each of them until they nodded.

Ben took a sip of his coffee. "Before I start, know that there is no dishonor in saying 'no' to us. And indeed, it might be the smartest thing to do. This job will be for insane people only. Drake and I will be leading a small team in. I hope we'll be leading that same team, plus one, out. If we make it, you'll all be rich. And if we don't, you won't need the money anyway."

Shawna sneered. "Is this where you tell us that what you're about to say is confidential?"

Ben shook his head. "I don't give a shit who you tell. No one will believe you anyway."

Chess rolled his shoulder and looked like he was about to take one of Ben's chips, but changed his mind. "Okay, Captain Cartwright, we're all ears."

Ben began.

CHAPTER 16

VENEZUELAN NATIONAL INSTITUTE OF METEOROLOGICAL SERVICES

"At last." Nicolás leapt up to pull the battered notebook from the shelf.

Mateo leaned back in his chair. "At last, what?"

Nicolás held up the book. "The big wet, the monsoon of madness, the wettest season, it's all due to return in just two months."

Mateo ran a hand through silver hair and sighed. "Oh, yes; your first love."

Nicolás flipped pages to his last entry, entered nine years and 10 months ago when he had only just joined the Meteorological Services. He left the book open and rested on his elbows, staring down and reading the notes again as he'd done too many times now to count.

The wettest season came every 10 years, almost to the day, and always over just one part of the Amazon. Down in the darkest center of the still mainly unexplored jungle, a localized hurricane developed, but coming out of nowhere and always centralized. Strangely, it *stayed* centralized and just over one of the towering tepuis or flat-topped mountains.

Then, in just 24 hours, it dissipated and vanished, as quickly as if a switch had been thrown and so completely it was like it was never there. The anomaly had intrigued him for 10 years since he had seen it right here with his own eyes.

Well, he thought, *as much as one could see*. Nothing could pierce its cloud cover—radar, satellite images, even X-rays were all deflected. But he had seen *something* in there.

Nicolás rolled his chair along to his computer and quickly searched his files. He found what he was looking for and pulled up the satellite video he had recorded from high above the plateau from all that time ago.

He had spent months cleaning it up and now he played it again, for probably the hundredth time. The silent film showed a balloon with people in it entering the cloudbank, and then what looked like it being attacked by something that came out of the cloud, something big. Using the passenger balloon for scale, the bat-like creature had to have been about 30 feet across.

Nicolás knew that the Amazon had her secrets, but none he thought as compelling and mysterious as this one. He looked over his shoulder at the sound of the senior meteorologist's voice.

"Hey, this year, we have all the new meteorological equipment you can use to measure the storm's intensity. Also, if you're really lucky, you may get permission to fly one of the drones in for a closer look."

Nicolás nodded with little enthusiasm and played the video again. "A closer look." He breathed slowly, watching the strange events, still trying to understand what he was seeing. He knew that the drones couldn't get too close or they'd lose power and fall to the jungle floor, as dead as a dodo.

He had researched the phenomena extensively, finding many references stretching back hundreds of years. With the Internet as his research base, he crosschecked other phenomena that occurred around this time and found a single peculiarity—a comet, called Primordia—that came close to the Earth once every 10 years, and always in years that ended in 8…just like the year when he had witnessed the balloon. And now, just like this one. A theory had formed that begged to be proven.

Nicolás drummed his fingers on his desktop. He'd waited 10 years for this event, and in a few months, it'd pass by for yet another 10. He sat for a few more moments and then leapt up, pulling the office stationary from a tray and scribbling furiously on one of the pages. He then handed it to Mateo.

The older man looked at it for a moment and his eyebrows rose. "You're taking leave?" He slowly turned in his seat, his mouth hiked in one corner. "And surprise, surprise, right when the wettest season is going to be occurring in the Amazon."

Nicolás nodded.

"You aren't planning on doing anything stupid, are you?" Mateo lowered the form. "Curiosity killed the cat, my young friend. And down in the Amazon, curiosity killed and ate the cat."

"I just want a closer look." Nicolás grinned and shrugged. "And after all, everyone knows that cats have nine lives."

CHAPTER 17

WESTERN MOUNTAIN SLOPES, APPALACHIA, 100 MILLION YEARS AGO

Andy paused to wipe his brow. He'd been climbing for many days and had many more to go.

Back in his own time, he'd been climbing in the Appalachian Mountains before when he was searching for fossil sites. Most paleontologists were curious about the ancient lifeforms up here, as there were large gaps in the primordial record due to the fact that most of Appalachia's fossil-bearing formations were destroyed by the Pleistocene Ice Age.

But back then, or forward then from now, though the mountains were large, they were nothing like the formidable peaks they were here and now. In the Cretaceous, the mountain range traveled all the way down through Alabama and into the northern edge of the ocean that was the submerged state of Florida.

Where he was right now, he estimated he was only at about 4,000 feet elevation. But further north, they would be three times that and impassable to someone like himself. Over the next 100 million years, they would be weathered down to leave their granite cores and their slopes mostly covered in a gentle forest.

Andy looked out toward the west where there was a world of green as far as the eye could see. There was a steamy mist hanging over the treetops, and it was unbroken, primitive, and teeming with life. It was a green world, all except for right at the very edge of the horizon where something glinted like polished silver.

He was past the worst of his climb now, and he expected it would get easier as he descended. The atmosphere was pleasant here, cooler, but still with humid breezes wafting up through the valley's conifer forests and fern-filled meadows that interspaced the mountains. Where he was, the trees were sparser and generally growing in stands like tall conifer oases, with strappy-leafed plants at their base and more exposed rock.

So far, he had encountered a variety of smaller dinosaurs and several carnivorous theropod species, but they were small enough to not be a bother to him. Most he recognized, but some were unidentifiable, sporting strange beaks, horned or crested heads, and one that was even covered in what looked to be long rudimentary hair. These were the species that were probably unique to this area and were scrubbed from the fossil record by erosion.

However, he had several encounters with nodosaurs, the large, herbivorous, armored dinosaurs resembling tank-sized armadillos. Interestingly, it was one of the few dinosaurs that he felt he'd already seen from his own time. That was because in 2011, a specimen was found deep in a mine so well preserved that its head and front half of its body were still intact, and even more amazing, not compressed, but in a 3D form.

The nodosaur fossil was so amazingly preserved that it was still showing some coloration—spots and coffee-brown patches surrounding the huge osteoderms, the huge spikes and plates, and the smaller coin-sized scales in between.

Andy had approached one of the great beasts, thinking they might be like armored cows. But he ended up having to run for his life when he was charged. Even though the nodosaur was a plant-eater, it was 18 feet long and easily a 3,000-pound behemoth that had two 20-inch-long spikes jutting out of its shoulders. *Instead of being like a cow, it's more like a bad-tempered mutant rhinoceros*, Andy thought as he had scrambled into a stand of trees.

Luckily for him, they shared another rhino-like trait in that they had terrible eyesight, so once Andy stopped moving and hid, he probably vanished to the brute. In addition, a tiny brain meant it lost interest quickly.

A big body, and sparse food, meant it was rightly being territorial, he surmised. From then on, he had learned to give them a wide berth whenever he encountered them.

In the mountains, the opening of the landscape presented him with another challenge. Andy was used to scurrying between tree trunks, under palm fronds, and slithering through bracken to get where he needed to go. But up here, he had to cross areas of open slopes.

He had been crossing a fern meadow on one such slope, thinking how quiet it was, wishing he had his sister here to enjoy it with. But that daydreaming meant he had let his guard down. He became inwardly focused and stopped using his spatial awareness, just for an instant or two, and then from overhead the sunshine had been blotted out for a moment.

Andy was immediately on guard, but still instinctively cringed down and froze, just for a second, as a breeze wafted down on his long hair.

Something heavy landed behind him, and he didn't even bother to turn; he didn't need to. He knew enough about this place to know that if something was creeping up on you, it wasn't because it wanted to make friends.

He began to sprint for the next stand of conifer trees and the terrifying scream from over his shoulder came from an enormous throat that told him he only had a short head start.

Andy was only 50 feet from the trees when he chanced a glance over his shoulder—and it was as bad as he expected. The monstrous pterosaur was around 70 feet tall from nose to tail and had a wingspan of over 50 feet.

He immediately knew what it was and cursed himself for not expecting it: a *Quetzalcoatlus*. It was a pterosaur species known from the Late Cretaceous of North America and probably the largest flying animal to have ever existed on the planet.

The worst thing for Andy was they had good locomotion on the ground using their folded wings as front legs, and with their giraffe-like long neck, they could lunge forward to spear their prey in a serrated beak that was itself around eight feet in length.

Andy pumped his arms and legs, and upon reaching the stand of trees, dived and crawled in among bushes and tangled roots. He scared a small creature from its hiding place that squealed and made a break for it—the four-legged, barrel-bodied thing could not have known that Andy wasn't the real threat, and its fast-moving shape distracted the monstrous flying reptile that caught the fleeing creature with ease.

"Sorry, pal," he whispered.

Andy flopped back, breathing hard. He stayed down, hoping the massive flying reptile wasn't smart enough to be able to tell the difference between a small four-legged dinosaur and a weird, hairy, two-legged human.

Andy sucked in air and watched as the *Quetzalcoatl* shook the creature in its beak to break its neck, and then lowered its giant frame to then spring upward, spreading bat-like wings larger than an airplane. It immediately caught a thermal on the slopes and rose higher into the pale blue sky.

He watched it with open mouth and marveled at its magnificence. He'd been here 10 years and every now and then he saw something that made him think it was all a dream. It vanished behind the peak, and he relaxed a little.

"You asshole, you should have known better," he groaned to himself. *I'm either getting old or dumb*, he thought. He knew that giant pterosaurs lived in this time *and* in this area. And just like the condors of home that also had large wingspans and preferred high altitudes for their nesting so they captured the updrafts to make take-off easy, of course the Cretaceous giants of the air would be nesting in the mountains.

Dumb. And dumb gets you dead, he cursed.

"*Gluck.*"

Andy eased up to sitting and opened his bag, seeing the miniscule version of the thing that nearly ate both of them staring up at him.

"*Nasty bird.*" Gluck seemed to frown, but only for a moment. "*Andy good?*"

Andy sucked in one last big breath and nodded. "Yeah, Andy good. This time." He looked around. "But Andy needs to pay attention or we both won't be good."

He looked out through the trees and into the distance. He could still make out the reflective glint on the horizon. He knew it had to be a large body of water.

"My sea," he said and looked down into the bag. "But I think we'll travel at night until we're out of the mountains; otherwise, we'll both end up as bird shit."

"*Gluck.*"

"Yeah, I'm hungry too." He closed the bag. "We'll make camp soon and have dinner, I promise."

CHAPTER 18

1958—THE WETTEST SEASON

PROJECT ARCHIMEDES CAPSULE, 87 NAUTICAL MILES ABOVE SOUTH AMERICA

Lieutenant Redmond "Red" Gordon was jammed in tight. There were so many dials, tubes, buttons, switches, and electronics surrounding him that he could feel the electromagnetic waves all the way to his back teeth. Added to that, they made the heat in the compact space capsule nearly unbearable and the bulky flame-retardant suit he wore was like a layer of canvas pillows.

But he was thankful for the padding now, as the blast-off and acceleration had been like riding a 1,500-pound rodeo bull, and after several hours of being strapped in place, every single fiber of his body ached and screamed to be able to stand up and move around.

Gordon was an engineer and test pilot with the U.S. Air Force, and he had been selected to pilot the new ballistic rocket system that was to make him the first man to fully orbit Earth, beating Russia by just a few years.

In his ear was the constant professional command center babble of NASA, the newly formed space agency, and his constant companion, ground control leader Mitch Brammel. He looked up to the countdown clock and saw he had mere hours until he'd commence re-entry and be on his way to splashdown in the Florida Bay where he bet helicopters were already hovering.

The Archimedes was coming up over South America, still at a height of 87 nautical miles, as Gordon began the re-entry checklist with ground control; all was going to plan. Until everything went dark. So dark, he thought for a few seconds that he'd gone blind.

"Command center, come back." Gordon licked suddenly dry lips. "Command center, come back. *Ah*, Mitch, are you there?"

There was nothing, no sound, not even any static. There was only his own rasping breath.

"Ames Command Center, this is Major Redmond Gordon requesting immediate response, come back."

Nothing. He was in a void of nothingness where there was no sound, no light, and no constant hum of the electronics. And the craft even felt different now. There was no sensation of the sliding acceleration as he skimmed above the atmosphere in a space orbit heading toward re-entry.

"Damnit, Mitch, where are you?" Gordon cursed and brought a fist down on his thigh. His stomach began to flip and he knew why—gravity was kicking in and he knew he was in free fall.

"*Ah* shit."

Gordon shook his head. "Come on, guys, don't do this to me." He tried the comms again, and again, and again, and by the fourth time, he knew he was alone.

The words: *total system failure*, screamed in his head.

"I've damn well trained for this," he told himself to regain some calm over the waves of panic wanting to wash over him.

There were manual procedures, processes, and instruments for him to use, and he reached forward to a small compartment and grabbed a glow stick, broke it, and held it up. Manual clock face dials told him his speed, orientation, and altitude. Thankfully, he was well inside the atmosphere now but had reached a terminal velocity, and he had no idea over what.

Now, there would be no automatic ejection of his capsule from the booster, and no capsule ejection meant no deployment of the parachutes. He had zero idea where he was, but he'd have to deploy himself or he'd be a smudge on some road, swamp, mountainside, or beach somewhere.

Gordon sucked in a deep breath and shook his head to try and flick away streams of greasy perspiration that ran down his face.

The altitude dial spun fast, and he counted down the seconds. He grabbed the manual disengagement lever and prayed he wasn't too high or too low—too high and the air was too thin for the chutes to grab and open. Too low and he'd never slow himself enough to walk away.

"Command center, I am manually disengaging and deploying. Mitch, I'm coming in hot." He swallowed. "Hope you're there when I arrive, buddy."

All or nothing, he thought, and gripped the red lever. "5-4-3-2-1...*disengage*."

There was a massive kick as small explosive charges blew the rocket's nose cone, and his tiny claustrophobic home spun away from its ballistic missile thrusters. Gordon felt himself tumble once, and then the air brakes kicked in as the chutes now automatically unfolded—thankfully, they filled—and began to slow him down.

Gordon stared hard at the altimeter as the feet counted down. He had jammed the glow stick in beside it, and it was a tiny pool of yellow light beside the dial that was now his whole world. He felt like some sort of tiny insect that had crawled into the back of a giant's crystal radio set as he watched and waited.

He blinked away more sweat; he had a ways to go, as he was still 2,000 feet up. But it would be eaten up fast. He gripped the armrests, preparing for whatever came next—he'd strike hard if he hit water or green. If it was rock, chutes or no chutes, he'd more than likely break apart.

In a few more seconds, he was at 1,500 feet, and then strangely he felt the first strike. He bounced, struck something else, and then felt the tin skin of the capsule being thrashed and pummeled as there came the sounds of branches snapping and leaves slapping at him.

In another few seconds, he landed softly and bounced—like in a hammock. He waited for a few seconds and then began to grin.

"*Ho-le-y crap*." He started to chuckle. "Thank you, mother nature."

He looked up at the instrument panels that were all still as dead as dodos. "You're no help."

He immediately began to unbuckle, unstrap, unhook, and unwind from the multitude of safety harnesses, monitors, and communication's equipment, and then he shifted forward to grab handholds so he could lever himself up to the door.

Gordon had to use the spanner to literally unscrew the metal door, and after 20 minutes was able to shoulder the lid off where it fell to the ground. He looked out.

Green.

Everything was green.

He flipped his faceplate up and was hit by a wave of cloyingly sweet scents, wet heat, and a cacophony of jungle sounds.

He leaned out further and looked around—he saw he was hanging about six feet up from the ground in some sort of massive banyan tree that must have been 300 feet tall if it was an inch.

The foliage above was too thick for him to get his bearings, and he even had no idea which country he was in. He didn't think he'd made it as far as the Florida Everglades, but who knew.

Gordon ducked back inside and pulled out the emergency bag tucked under the cockpit seat. It contained rations, water, and a couple of flares. He then twisted his helmet a half turn to remove it and let it drop down to the ground.

It bounced on a solid but plant-littered base, so he threw a leg over and jumped down.

Red Gordon stood with his hands on his hips for a moment, trying to decide if he should wait by the capsule or try and set off. Even if he was in the U.S., he could wander into a swamp and end up gator food. And if he were in the Amazon, well, then getting lost would mean he'd really be screwed.

He looked up again. The tree he had landed in was probably one of the tallest around…maybe he could climb up and see if he could get his bearings further up.

He tried to map a path to the upper branches. The limbs were huge lower down, and there were plenty of handholds—yeah, it was doable. He took a quick sip of water, left his bag with his helmet behind, and started up.

It was easy at first; the branches were broad, and now and then Gordon came across weird lizards that got up on their back legs and hissed at him.

He'd never been to the Amazon before and guessed he was just seeing their typical lifeforms. He'd make a mental note to ask the science geeks when he got back.

At about 120 feet up, he paused to listen as something large moved below him. He heard the sounds of trees being pushed aside and the snuffled grunts from a large throat and mouth. Suddenly, he caught a glimpse of an enormous grey-banded back as it broke for a few seconds before it re-entered the dense growth again.

Did they have elephants here? he wondered. While he continued to stare down, there was a thump of something landing behind him, and turning, he saw another goddamn reptile standing upright, this one about three feet tall. It was a mottled green and had a long, pointed face, like a beak.

"*Shoo*," he said as it fixed him with one ruby-red eye. Gordon had the weird feeling it was looking him up and down as though sizing him up…for dinner.

"Go on, get lost." He waved a hand at it, and the thing screeched and unfolded bat-like wings…*goddamn wings*!

"*Piss off*!" he yelled and it flapped away like a wet sheet. Gordon shook his head. "Goddamn weird place."

He started up again, now getting to about 200 feet up. He didn't suffer from vertigo and he was extremely fit, so even though the going was tough, he was managing just fine.

He was still within the canopy so as yet he couldn't see out, but he could just make out that where he was now put him at the forest ceiling, so when he got a little higher, he'd be above it.

In another 10 minutes, Gordon edged out on the thinnest branch he could, holding the one above it for balance. He got as far to its edge as he could manage before it started to bend precariously under his weight.

The test pilot then leaned forward to bend the branch down, opening a hole in the banyan's foliage.

Red Gordon looked out, and his mouth fell open.

Miles and miles of green.

He was higher than the far jungle, much higher, leading him to believe he was on some sort of flat-topped mountain, and that accounted for his crash landing before he actually made true landfall.

There were no roads, no settlements, and nothing resembling human habitation. In the distance, he saw a line of mountains and before it a lush green valley that was shrouded in mist.

"Where the hell am I?" he whispered.

Staring upward, he could see the sky was marred by a long eyebrow-like streak, and soaring above the heads of the distant trees were what looked like small airplanes.

No, not airplanes, they flapped wings and were some sort of bird—some sort of giant freaking birds.

His branch quivered, and Gordon held on tight. He sniffed, frowning, as he smelled something like piss or sour vinegar and checked his hands for plant sap.

"Phew."

He tried to change angles to see in another direction, but his branch quivered again, and then to his shock, began to bend, downward…far downward.

"Hey?"

He turned, and then froze. At the base of the limb where it met the tree trunk was a monster, a snake, big around as a Longhorn steer. It was so motionless he might have thought it was a statue, except a tongue thicker than his arm flickered out as it tasted the air, tasted him, and then drew back in.

Its brown, green, and black scales made it almost invisible in among the foliage and dappled light, but its two dead eyes were like giant glass beads, and he had no doubt they were fixed on him.

Its body curled around the trunk and trailed away beyond his vision, but the head slowly lifted and then began to come forward, its gaze never wavering from him.

Gordon couldn't look away. He'd once seen a big anaconda eat a possum and had a pretty good idea what this thing had in mind.

"Stay back," he said with a quaver in his voice as he edged another foot away. His branch bent further, and he quickly glanced down, looking for an escape route.

Could I leap to the next branch down? he wondered. The snake glided ever closer, and with the sound of creaking wood, the branch bent even more.

Gordon knew he had no choice. He released the branch above him to wobble on his thin perch for a moment as he tried as best he could to judge the easiest hand holds below him. Then he leapt.

Red Gordon never got five feet. The snake struck out, catching him in mid-air. Its mouth clamped down on his torso, and it rolled him back up in its coils. The snake was so large the light was blotted out around him, and he felt the massive pressure begin.

The mouth released him and he was thankful for the padding of his suit as he had felt the teeth in his flesh, but they hadn't penetrated too far into his body.

"Oh God." He lost all feeling below the waist. Then the coils tightened again and he both felt and heard his hip and ribs begin to pop and crunch like kindling.

"No," he gasped as his head felt like it was going to explode from the pressure on his circulatory system. The last thing test pilot Major Redmond Gordon saw was the coils parting slightly to offer him head first into a toothed maw the size of a doorway.

This time, he knew he would feel the teeth.

CHAPTER 19

AKRON OHIO, WAREHOUSE LOGISTICS, SHED-11

Ben, Drake, and Emma were all lost in their own thoughts as they arrived at the warehouse they'd been using as a staging area for the past few weeks. Every time they felt they were ready, they found another dozen things that needed to be done. The logistical things could be managed. But it was time that was their enemy, and unfortunately, not their only one.

The weeks went by and more incremental changes occurred around them. Some things once familiar now vanished, and new things appeared—a large yellow beetle called a 'cob,' for obvious reasons, was found to have a taste for rubber. You needed to check your car before driving, as its favorite meal was the wheel tread, and a single beetle could leave a whole tire completely bald. Several of them together, and you were looking at tattered shreds on steel rims.

There was now a domestic pet called a molecat that was taken into family homes—it was the size and shape of a cat, but was without eyes. It found its way around and also everything it needed by using its hearing and sense of smell.

There were gross changes as well, such as a species of lamprey, those ancient fish-like creatures with circular mouths filled and rasp-like teeth. When it rained, the new species left their waterways and slithered up onto the land, making a meal of livestock. And if they managed to get into your house and found you sleeping, they'd latch onto a limb or torso and leave a painful, weeping sore when they were done.

Nearly every day now, the tingling in their gut followed by the blacking out of all light was occurring. They all knew that whatever was happening was accelerating. No one doubted that there were big changes coming. And they just prayed nothing happened before they had a chance to change it all back.

*****

Drake and Ben walked along a row of their tactical hardware laid out on the warehouse floor. Emma was at the far end also checking off some of her own new equipment arrivals.

"Cheer up," Drake said.

"I feel like shit," Ben said.

"What, about bringing in those merc knuckleheads? Forget about it; they know how to deal with deadly risk. They're hard-asses, and bastards all of them, but damn good at what they do. Plus, they've got jungle experience and are totally fearless. They'll do their job."

"They didn't believe me," Ben said. "I'm, *we*, are walking them into a freaking prehistoric meat grinder."

"They've risked themselves before, and if they make it, they get a million bucks. Believe me, for that amount of money, they'd go even if I told them they'd have to duke it out with Satan himself." Drake half smiled.

"If we didn't need 'em, I wouldn't bring 'em," Ben replied.

Drake cocked his head. "Hey, you ever heard of the old diving axiom about always swimming with a buddy?"

Ben shook his head and Drake grinned wider. "It's so it improves your chance of not being the guy who gets eaten by a shark."

Ben scoffed. "So I should bring them, just so *they* might be the ones killed instead of me?"

"That's right," Emma said, wandering over. "That's *damn* right." She lugged a few big boxes with her.

Drake shrugged. "What can I say? Two against one."

"You, Ben Cartwright, are going to save your family, and maybe even the entire human race. Those mercenaries are going to make some fast money." Emma dropped the boxes she carried with a thump, and then folded her arms. "That's why they call them mercenaries."

"Brutal," Ben said.

"But accurate," Drake added.

"Damn straight." Emma squared her shoulders.

Ben could see she meant every word and was prepared to fight him on it. "Okay." He knew that either the mercs went with him, or maybe she'd decide to go as well. And that was something he couldn't bear. He changed the subject. "What have you got there?"

She crouched by one of the boxes. "We learned a lot last time we went in. Getting there, and I mean up there, proved to be the first and one of the biggest hurdles."

"You can say that again." Ben waited.

She laid a hand on one of the boxes. "Flying up to the plateau top is out, as the magnetic pulses knock out electronics, and even using gliders would be impossible due to the wind turbulence. And we found out the hard way that ballooning is subject to attack."

"And external cliff face climbing is dangerous for non-climbers— sheer walls at over 1,500 feet," Ben said.

"Deadly," Drake added.

"Yeah, I was there, I remember." She half smiled up at him. "Climbing is slow, arduous, and like you pointed out, high risk for novice climbers." She held up a finger. "But what if we could make climbing safer, and faster?" She pried open the lid on one of the crates and lifted out what looked like a black steel box, 6 x 12 inches, that had a round opening at each end.

She held it up. "Gentlemen, I give you the power winch. The lazy rock climber's speed lift." She turned it on its side, holding it flat on her hand. "Can lift 400 pounds of equipment or two people at once. Dual rope feed, and two speeds—3 miles per hour for slow ascent, or rapid lift at 10 miles per hour—you'll basically fly up." She pointed. "Rope feeds in one end, and the grip teeth suck it in and spit it out back." She looked up at the men. "Simple, won't jam, and so easy, even ex-Special Forces guys can operate it."

Drake whistled. "I like it. Especially that bit about it being good for lazy climbers and dumb Spec Forces guys."

"That'll work," Ben said. "But one question. The cliff faces of the tepui are between 1,500 and 3,000 feet. And the winch works on pulling us up a rope—so how exactly do we get the rope up the wall for it to feed in and out?"

"Good question." She flipped open the second box and pulled out what looked like a cross between a rifle and spear gun. "Cliff dart with titanium tip. Just aim and shoot. It'll penetrate even granite at 300 feet, and the expansion collar will immediately lock it in place." She stood, holding the gun. "I've used these before; once they penetrate the rock's surface, that's where they stay. They're good tech."

Emma held it up with one hand, sighting along the barrel. "You aim it at where you want it to go in, fire, and then it takes the rope up with it. Then all you need to do is feed it into your winch, and up and away you go."

She held up a hand when she saw Drake frowning. "Yeah, I know, the cliff face where you're going to be climbing is around 1,500 feet, so once you're at the top of your rope, you'll need to reload and fire again. Then you'll need to move from rope to rope—I've done it before, and you can too."

"Show us," Ben said.

Emma quickly mimed the aiming, firing, and then showed them the winch pulling in the rope, and when it came to the end, how to change from one rope to the next without any slippage. It looked simple, but Emma was an expert.

"We'll need to practice that," Ben said.

"We all will," Drake added.

"Okay, your turn." Emma pointed. "What toys did you bring?"

"Glad you asked." Drake grinned, and as he walked, he waved a hand over the edge of a sheet where all their weapons were laid out. He stopped. "Okay, for close contact, we got our standard knife kit—hunting and Ka-Bar with Tanto edge. Also, I managed to get a good deal on some new Glocks—short recoil-operated, locked-breech semi-automatics with a box magazine, and all in a non-reflective polymer-frame with a nitride finish."

"Light and low-jamming, nice ones," Ben said, crouching to pick one up and hold it in a two-handed grip as he sighted at the far wall.

"My thought was to pack a punch, but be mindful of our weight-to-defense ratio. Last time, we found some of our hardware came up a bit short against the bigger plateau residents. So with that in mind, and also not wanting to load us up with hundreds of pounds of steel, I stuck with the Mossberg 12 gauge, but kicked it up to tactical level with the Venom rotary kit for rapid cycle times, greater shell capacity, and lightning fast reloads."

Drake picked one up. The shotgun now had a circular magazine on its side. He ran his hand up and along the weapon. "Forend with action bars and grip, 10-round rotary magazine, and barrel clamp." He held it out front, aimed it from his waist and then from his shoulder, before lowering it and grunting his satisfaction before laying it back down.

"Now we move up to the real kick-ass tech." He picked up a powerful-looking rifle that was matte-black with a skeletal framework. He looked down at it almost lovingly for a moment before holding it out to Ben.

Ben took it and hefted it. "Barrett M82—the Light Fifty." He then held it under his arm, testing the balance. "Big punch."

"Yep, can't go past the .50-cal, Barrett M82, recoil-operated, semi-automatic, anti-materiel, anti-personnel rifle. Like you said, a big punch, but with a significantly lighter weight compared to previous models."

"You got us the shorter barrel—smart," Ben said.

"Sure did; in closed-in spaces, it's good to have that extra maneuverability. And that's not all I got." He ducked down to pick up a magazine box and flipped it open. In it were large shells with a green-on-white tip.

Ben scoffed. "Holy crap, are they Raufoss?"

"You bet your ass." Drake kept grinning.

"A what?" Emma asked, taking out one of the shells and holding it up.

Drake took it from her and held it up like he was examining a diamond. "Ladies and gentlemen, I give you the Raufoss Mk 211." He turned it in his fingers. "It's a .50-cal, multipurpose, anti-material, high-explosive incendiary plus armor-piercing projectile. The multipurpose bit

I mentioned is because these bad boys have a tungsten armor-piercing core, plus an explosive and incendiary component. Comes in handy for penetrating armored targets and causing internal damage after that penetration—basically, it'll punch its way in through the toughest armored hide, and *then* explode."

He turned. "So, to quantify that, your standard .50-cal will put a hole the size of your fist through steel. But a Raufoss round will penetrate even the toughest of armored bodies, and then blow bucket-sized chunks of flesh all over the field."

Emma nodded. "Okay, I feel a bit better now."

"Me too," Ben said. "Considering we only want to be there for a single day, if we were going anywhere else, I'd say you've gone well over the top. But we all know what we're going to be up against, so well done."

"I just hope your friends do as well. Chess and...who?" Emma half smiled.

"Chess, Francis, Shawna, Buster, and... *Balls*." Drake grinned. "And by the way, Balls is a woman."

"Of course she is," Emma said with a smile. "Tell me about them."

Drake rubbed his chin theatrically. "Well, Chess is sort of their leader. He's a big S.O.B., but Ben already established the chain of command with him." He winked at Ben.

"I can imagine." Emma rolled her eyes at Ben who just shrugged as Drake went on.

"Shawna is blonde, busted nose, and used to be a bail bond hunter. She's tough as nails and knows every curse word known to mankind, and a few she's made up. Francis is a big guy, real big, and ex-MMA. He doesn't say much but he's a coffee-colored mountain and good with a gun, knife, and his fists. Even Ben would have trouble with this guy. Next up is Buster; he used to do some freelance work in South America consulting to the drug agencies. Apparently got caught and tortured, so is still a bit twitchy."

"A problem?" Ben asked.

"Nah, bit of high blood pressure and plenty of scars inside and out, but he's all good now." Drake shrugged. "He'll keep his end up."

"And Balls?" Emma grinned.

"She's a tough little one, and a fighter. Smart as a whip, totally fearless, and a crack shot. She's also probably the brains of the group."

"And you fired her?" Emma asked.

"Yeah, like I said, she likes to fight, but a little too much." Drake's mouth turned down momentarily.

"Quite a team you've pulled together," Emma said.

Ben nodded at Drake. "They're friends of his." He chuckled. "Oh yeah, he didn't just fire *her*, he fired all of them. So I expect employee loyalty will be off the charts."

"And that's why you pay them the money *only* when they get home," Drake replied.

"Yeah." Emma's mouth set in a line. "Just make sure you *come* home; everything else is secondary. Drake, you tell them that if Ben doesn't return, as far as I'm concerned, they can all go to hell."

"That's the plan," Ben said. He grabbed his friend's shoulder and pulled him close so he could feign whispering into his ear. "I'm sure she means both of us."

"Yeah, right." Drake checked his watch. "Okay, we're done here. I'm gonna pack all this up and send it on ahead. It's five weeks until Primordia passes over and our doorway opens. We set off Monday morning." He held out his hand to Emma. "You two have a nice weekend and I'll see you when we get back."

She grabbed it and pulled him close into a hug. "Take care of yourself, and take care of Ben…for me."

He nodded. "Seems to be a full-time job these days." He turned to Ben. "Monday morning, big guy, we've got a date… 100 million years in the past. See you at the airport."

CHAPTER 20

"AT THE VERY EDGE OF THE WORLD, I BEHELD WHERE TIME BEGAN."

EDGE OF THE WESTERN INTERIOR SEA, 100 MILLION YEARS AGO

Andy woke and came to his senses almost immediately as he had trained himself to do. He had found a hiding space beneath a huge tree that might have been some creature's burrow that looked as if it hadn't come home for a while—one trip out too many, he surmised.

He and Gluck had moved in and set to barricading themselves in for the night. Morning sunlight just peeked through the cage bars of roots as it had peeked over the horizon.

The tiny flying reptile had wedged itself under his arm as though hiding and was delighted he had finally woken.

"Morning, Daffy."

"Gluck." It angled its head, turning one eye on him. Andy grinned down at it.

"Say: *thuffering thukotash.*"

"Gluck."

Andy grinned. *"Thuffering…"*

"Gluck."

"Thukotash."

"Gluck."

"Thuffering thukotash."

"Gluck, gluck."

"I think you've finally got it, little buddy." He rubbed its head, and Gluck climbed up on his thigh, flapping its leathery wings and pulling on the hairs on his leg.

"Hungry."

"You're always hungry." Andy found the last bits of his dried meat and shared it with the animal. Gluck gobbled it down and then went to climb higher on him, as if trying to get under his arm.

"That's all I got, but big day ahead. Got another sea to check out. We're here just in time, 'cause in another dozen million years, it'll be gone. Blink of an eye, really." He chuckled.

"Many legs." Gluck burrowed under his arm.

"Huh?" Andy tried to push Gluck off, but the tiny pterosaur stayed put, and when he went to lift him, he felt it shiver. Andy knew it wasn't from cold as it was already about 80 degrees and humid, so even hairless, featherless reptiles were in their comfort zone. Gluck started to make tiny noises almost like a mewling whine.

"What's the matter with you?" he whispered.

He looked around, but there seemed nothing inside to worry them, and he began to wonder whether there was a threat outside their root cave. He looked down at Gluck, who was staring back up, but not at him, at a place just over his head.

Andy slowly lifted his gaze.

"Oh, shit."

On the roof of their cave was a spider the size of a dinner plate. It was muscular, its body was shiny black like polished plastic, and finger-thick legs covered in hair were spread wide.

Multiple eyes were like drops of oil, and he knew it was watching them. Normally, Andy would just give it space, as small ones like this rarely contemplated attacking something the size of Andy, but a few pounds of skinny pterosaur would have been perfect for it.

No wonder the little guy was trying to get under Andy's arm, as the spider might have been stalking him for a while.

"Okay, okay, everyone just stay calm."

While keeping his eyes on the spider, he quickly set to packing up and once done, to unblocking their tree root cave. The spider rotated on the roof so it could continue to track them, and without even being asked, Gluck climbed inside Andy's bag.

"Good thinking—out of sight, out of stomach."

He kept one hand on the bag top to keep it closed and then carefully peeked out through the last logs he'd set up. He had to stay that way for many minutes, just letting his eyes run over the jungle floor, then in and around the fronds, stems, and branches. And finally, up above them.

He'd found that morning was a good time to move around—many of the larger daytime predators hadn't yet roused, and the night shift of carnivores had clocked off.

"All clear… I hope."

Andy pulled the last of the logs out of the way. He lifted them and placed them to the side, gently, quietly, trying to use all his senses to detect whether anything had taken an interest in his tiny corner of the jungle.

So far, he heard something small in the tree canopy overhead and the patter of morning dew as it dropped from the large pad like leaves to the detritus on the jungle floor.

He took one last look at the spider, which had now crept down from the ceiling to where he and Gluck had slept, perhaps hoping to find traces of the pterosaur.

"Thanks for letting us stay." Andy saluted it. "Just glad you guys never made it to our time."

Then he was out, with his life's belongings packed up, as well as the only friend he had in the world safe inside his bag.

He set off, away from the sun to the west where he knew the inland sea would be, and also following his nose. Andy was excited, curious as all hell, and working hard to slow his impatience. He smiled, thinking that when he was a paleontology student, if anyone had said to him that one day he'd actually see living, breathing Cretaceous Period dinosaurs, he'd have told them to kick the drugs.

Now, he wasn't just seeing them, he was living among them, and about to cross off one of his ultimate bucket list objectives. He sniffed again, inhaling the brine. His excitement started to peak.

Andy eased through the jungle, darted forward, and then hid. He watched for movement, and when he felt safe, he repeated the entire process over again, and then all over again, and again. It took him two full hours to move through only a thousand feet of jungle, but by then, he began to hear the sound of water against rocks.

Andy got down on his belly. He flipped his bag over onto his back and crawled. In another few minutes, he came to the very edge of the vegetation line and saw the sparkling blue before him. He stood, easing upright beside a tree trunk, and stared out over the vast expanse of water.

"Yes. Oh yes."

He slowly slid down the trunk to sit cross-legged and partially hidden under some strappy fronds. He felt a little discombobulated knowing that he was the first, and only, human being to ever see this place. And no one ever would again, because by the time man evolved, this vast sea would be long, long gone.

Andy sighed. "At the very edge of the world, I beheld where time began." He peeked down into his bag. "Do you know who said that?" He looked back out at the sea. "I did, Andy Wilson, just then."

It was hard to picture, but one day if there even was a cliff top here and he stood on its edge, he would be looking out over an Alabama or maybe Mississippi landscape.

Gazing out over the endless expanse of sparkling water, he noticed it seemed to be in lanes. *Perhaps depending on depth?* he wondered. In close to the shore, it was a lighter blue, and a little further out, it became a darker blue lane, and then a few hundred feet out further again, it looked to be the blue-black of significant deepness. He frowned, perplexed, as he looked along the different hues, knowing that this inland sea wasn't all that deep.

"Maybe it's some sort of tidal or continental current movement," he guessed.

Andy peered over the edge. The cliff was a few hundred feet high and where he was ended at deep water. The sound he heard was the surf crashing against its face. It was clear, clean, and he knew it would be warm. While he watched, a surge wave came about a thousand feet out from him. Something big had sped forward and attacked something else below the surface.

He waited for another moment and saw the huge back of the beast lump the water and then dive deeper. As it vanished, he saw there was no scythe or flipper tail, but instead a long, flattened oar with distinctive scutes along its top that were like teeth but were actually bony external plates overlaid with horn. It immediately told him it was one of the mighty sea reptiles, like the massive *Tylosaurus* that grew to 50 feet in length. But this one had looked even bigger, and around this area lived the *T-rex* of the ocean, the monstrous *Hainosaurus*.

Andy stared, willing it back to the surface, and it didn't disappoint him. It surged back up, shaking its head like a dog just below the surface. The creatures had a distinctive long snake-like body, and in fact, they were thought to be related to real snakes. And with their expanding jaws, they ate other animals whole, including other mosasaurs.

As it sank, the sea surface was stained red—whatever it had charged at, it had caught.

Andy exhaled; he'd seen a few of the giant sea reptiles on his sea voyage, but luckily, they didn't think he was interesting enough to investigate, or worse, eat.

He got down and crawled along the cliff edge for a few hundred feet to an area below that wasn't under water, and once again went all the way to the very edge of the cliff to lean over. First thing he noticed was the discoloration marks against the cliff's rocky surface at about 50 feet up from the current waterline.

"*Ha*, the sea level was once higher," he said softly. "So it's already in retreat."

Down below him now was a plain of exposed mud, and he could see what looked like some sort of crustaceans making foot-wide tracks in the silt as they came out of the water, fossicked in a random pattern, and then headed back into the sea. They looked like some sort of king crab with their rounded bodies, like flattened helmets and long stiff tails sticking out the back.

Andy looked back and forth, trying to find a way down; other than being curious to investigate a few caves at the cliff base, those crabs would make an easy-to-catch meal. He crawled along the lip a little more.

As he shuffled along, he thought he heard a cracking sound like an old board being bent back. He froze and listened for several moments, but it wasn't repeated so he continued to worm along, looking for a pathway down.

Puffs of dust blew up around him, and the creaking was back, louder than before.

"Oh crap." He froze again as the entire cliff edge began to crumble. Right in front of him, clods of earth and then rocks began to fall off and tumble in space for a while before smacking into the glistening mud hundreds of feet below.

Popping and more puffs of dust were now coming from behind him as well. Andy tried to edge back but it seemed just the additional pressure from using his hands on the cliff edge was enough to destabilize the lip.

There was a crack like a gunshot and then a table-sized chunk of rock and soil began to slide free—with Andy on it.

"*Shi-iit!*" he screamed and threw his arms out wide to try and hang on as the entire section he was laying on fell away. His bag was up-ended, and he threw a hand down to slap it shut, just catching it before Gluck fell out, but not in time to save his heavier calendar stone that fell away into space.

The slab of rock hung down at a 45-degree angle but didn't break off and Andy hung there, closing his eyes to pray for a few seconds. After another moment, he gently pushed the tiny flying reptile further back in the bag and opened his eyes.

I'm still here, he thought. Hundreds of feet below him, he heard the booming smack and ensuing echoes as large rocks hit the mud. *Gotta go*, he urged and began to use his fingertips and toes to carefully crawl inch after inch up to the firm ground.

After his long years in this place, his body was all stringy muscle and zero excess fat, so he managed to pull himself up without too much strain. He slid himself back up off the hanging rock and then rolled on his back right on the new cliff edge, breathing hard, and after a few moments, he built the courage to look back down.

Way down below, there was no sign of his calendar stone, but the silt beach was littered with debris and impact craters. He could imagine the super hard stone smacking down into the silt, and then something landing on top of it, burying it forever.

After another moment to give his heart rate a chance to return to normal, he crept back to the tree line and then with his back braced against a huge trunk, he was able to relax.

"What a day," he whispered, as the sunlight was only just now beginning to strengthen. "And it's only just begun."

CHAPTER 21

MONTGOMERY COUNTY, ALABAMA, THE FOSSIL BEDS—TODAY

Janine and her husband, Hank, were amateur fossil hunters, and twice yearly they saved enough to spend a week down at the Montgomery fossil beds. Though the entire area's geology was comprised of Cretaceous Period fossil-bearing stone, she and Hank knew a few places that the others didn't.

A hundred million years ago, this many-miles-wide dusty plain was under water, and when the seas finally pulled back, it left behind a wealth of bones.

"Got something," Hank said.

"Me too," she replied.

Both worked about 20 feet apart, and Hank lifted his head. "What have you got?"

"You first." She grinned.

Hank pointed with his soft brush. "Tylosaur tooth—big guy. Must have been a 50-footer at least."

"Wow," she replied, impressed. Carnivore teeth were highly prized as both personal specimens and also in demand at sales. "Not sure what I've got yet. Might not even be a fossil."

She was carefully excavating what looked like a foot-long rod of a different type of stone embedded in the matrix. It seemed to be ancient slate, which wasn't usual for this area, and she was beginning to wonder if it had been washed in from somewhere else when the matrix around the specimen crumbled away, half the rod popping free.

She carefully lifted the piece and turned it over—there were hundreds of marks on it that seemed all in rows and didn't look natural at all. *That's weird*, she thought, but none so much as the markings at the top of the stone.

"Well, what have you got?" Hank called.

"*Um*...hold on." She quickly dug out the other half of the stone and lifted it, dusted it off, and then turned it over. She carefully brought the second piece together with the first—they fit like a jigsaw. Janine looked at the markings.

"*Andy.*"

She stared hard, her brain not comprehending what she was seeing. She knew the rock here was Cretaceous to Late Cretaceous—100 million years old if it was a day.

She frowned down at the stone, but there was no mistaking it: the word "Andy" was scratched into the top.

"*Well?*" Hank stopped digging and while on his knees, he straightened, obviously interested in his wife's sudden silence and concentration.

Impossible, she thought. And then: *ludicrous*. Janine began to shake her head. "Nothing; must just be some site contamination." She let the two halves of the stone drop to the dirt.

CHAPTER 22

ROCKY RIVER, OHIO—LAST NIGHT

Sunday evening and their final night together, Ben and Emma, plus an animated Zach, headed into town for a meal at Bearden's at Rocky River. It had been Zach's favorite ever since he was old enough to sit up in one of the long booths.

Not only did they have a cool car stuck on the front of their cottage-style diner—with working headlights—but they also served his all-time, ever-lovin' favorite meal: the Peanutburger—a steak burger, with the works, and all topped with melted peanut butter.

Emma grinned as she drove; it sounded gross, but the tender, juicy steak with the salty, melted peanut butter tasted like heaven. Probably about a million, billion calories, she bet, but tonight, it'd be one each, plus fries, then pie for dessert, and all washed down with endless sodas—*what the hell*, they were celebrating.

No, they weren't, she thought as her smile flattened; she'd make a show of celebrating, laughing, and smiling, but they were saying goodbye to Ben before he and his team headed off. She knew exactly what he'd be walking into, and she knew he'd already been trapped there once, for 10 long, horrifying years.

Ben became trapped the first time because he saved her, and now he was doing it for Zach, her, and the entire world. He was the most selfless man she had ever known.

Emma blinked away watering eyes. He was also the most insane man she had ever known. The risk of being trapped there again or being torn to shreds was so high it was off the charts. She felt a lump in her throat, and her morbid train of thought was only broken by Zach's laughter from the back seat.

"Dad, I'm putting my fries *on* my burger this time."

Ben turned in the seat next to her, looking back at his son. "Oh yeah? Well, I'm putting my fries *on* my burger, and I'm asking for extra crispy bacon, two layers, to jam on that bad boy as well."

"I'm doing that too," Zach said enthusiastically. "What else?"

"Fried egg," Ben added.

"*Um*, okay." Zach's grin widened. "And…?"

Ben *umm'd*, and Emma nudged him. "That's enough. After that, your blood pressure will probably make your head explode."

"But what a way to go." Ben laughed as he winked at Zach who joined in, having no idea what blood pressure meant, but probably thinking it sounded pretty cool.

They were heading along Lake Road with the river on one side and the urban area on the other, when Emma felt the familiar tingle in her stomach.

"Oh no."

The lights went out, and just for a few seconds, it was like being in the vacuum of space. Then everything came back on.

She turned to Ben. "What just…?

"Watch out!" he yelled.

Emma's head whipped back to the front as a man stood in the center of the street. She nearly stood the car on its nose as she stopped so suddenly, and the guy raised both hands, fists clenched as though he was going to bring them down on the hood.

"What. The. Hell?" Ben stared open-mouthed.

The guy had on gray overalls and only stood about five feet tall. But his shoulders and arms looked so powerful they nearly burst through his clothing. His fists were still raised and his hands were large, gnarled, and covered in hair.

"Oh, Ben," Emma began and pushed herself back in her seat as they stared at the man, and he stared back at them. "His face."

Emma couldn't look away from that visage—his tiny, dark eyes stared out from under a jutting, shelf-like brow-ridge, and his jaw was weak and receding. Hair grew all the way down to his bushy eyebrows, on his cheeks, and sides of his face, as well as hanging long and wiry hair to his shoulders.

"Don't stare," Zach said. "It's rude and they don't like it."

Zach leaned between them and made some shapes with his hands. The small eyes of the deformed-looking guy followed his fingers for a moment and then looked like he snorted from wide nostrils before moving on.

"The Neans are okay." Zach sat back. "But they really hate being stared at just 'cause they're a bit ugly."

Emma and Ben watched as the hunched man crossed the road in a bow-legged gait to join with more people exactly like him—men and women.

"Neans," Emma said softly.

"As in, *Neanderthals*." Ben half turned. "How long have you known about them?"

"*Huh*?" Zach frowned. "About the Neans?" His frown deepened and his mouth curled up a little in the corners as though waiting for the punch line. When it didn't come, he went on. "Like forever."

"What do they do?" Emma asked.

"The tough stuff usually. They're really strong." He pointed. "See the guy in the blue cap? That's Gorin; he's the Ohio state arm-wrestling champion."

Ben and Emma continued to stare, and Zach sighed theatrically.

"Can we go now?"

Ben and Emma looked at each other, and she could tell exactly what Ben was thinking: the Neanderthals never died out in this version of reality. The next version they might be gone again, but one thing was for sure: the changes were now working their way up the evolutionary chain and were about to reach them. They might be next.

"Yeah, sure, buddy. The peanut, bacon, and egg burgers are on me." Ben glanced again out the window at the group of powerfully built hominids. And Emma noticed that he slumped a little in his seat.

PART 2—JUST A SINGLE TICK ON THE EVOLUTIONARY CLOCK

"Time was a film run backward. Suns fled and ten million moons fled after them." — Ray Bradbury, A Sound of Thunder

CHAPTER 23

EAGLE EYE OBSERVATORY, BURNET, TEXAS—5 DAYS TO COMET APPARITION

"Impossible." Jim Henson stared into the viewing piece of the 12.5-inch Newtonian reflector. The massive steel tube was now pitted with rust spots on the outside but was too expensive to replace and even cleaning the entire telescopic infrastructure was a bitch.

However, inside the highly polished glass lenses and mirrors, plus large view aperture, still gave the man crisp images of the solar system. Henson typed rapidly into his computer and then stared.

"Predictive position plotting now gives us a 91% chance of a strike." He sat back. "This is big."

Andy Gallagher leaned away from his computer screen. "P/2018-YG874, Primordia, has had close calls before. Besides, it's basically a massive chunk of iron. It'll survive."

Henson typed and shook his head. "Primordia is huge, but this little guy is no lightweight. Its composition is…" He read from his screen, "…around 20% being a mixture of nickel, iridium, palladium, platinum, gold, magnesium, plus some osmium, ruthenium, and rhodium thrown in for good measure. But its base, and 80% of its composition, is also solid damn iron." He looked up. "It's an astral ball bearing."

Gallagher bobbed his head. "A ball bearing meets a wrecking ball—no contest. My money is still on a no-strike—they'll miss by a thousand miles."

"You're forgetting something." Henson folded his arms on top of his prodigious belly. "Primordia is magnetic."

CHAPTER 24

Emma and Zach dropped Ben at the airport and she pulled in at a far runway, slowed, and then stopped. He sucked in a huge breath and stepped out.

Ben immediately saw at the end of one of the longest runways a massive airplane sitting there.

"Wow, Dad, is that one yours?" Zach grabbed his arm and hung on, his mouth hanging in an open-mouthed grin.

"Yep, that'd be it—the LRS-B." Ben could just make out Drake as well as his mercenaries standing around outside. But the airplane exceeded his expectations. It was a retired Long-Range Strike bomber, or LRS-B—matte-black in its radar-reflective paint, looking like some sort of hulking metallic bat.

"Looks fast," Zach said.

"Subsonic maximum speed. And it can fly for 5,000 miles before we need to refuel." He looked down and smiled. "In mid-air."

"Oh wow." Zach nodded. "I so want to go on it."

"Looks fast, *and* expensive," Emma said, standing beside him and folding her arms. "Does the military know you are stealing one of their stealth planes?"

"*Hiring*, not stealing, and at great cost. And the LRS-B is an obsolete model now, even though it still has state-of-the-art propulsion, computer systems, radar technology, and can even withstand heavy weapons attack." He winked at her. "And you don't want to know what it's costing to hire it, including a pilot, fuel, a drop-crate, plus extras."

"The GDP of a small country, I bet." She lifted her chin. "But worth it I guess to get there fast and without anyone asking too many questions."

"Yeah, the radar deflection alone will allow us to sneak into South America without them even knowing about it." Ben got Zach in a headlock. "Hey, I'll give you a tour when I get back, promise."

Zach nodded and laughed, and then pointed to the men and women watching them from in front of the bomber. "Are they your friends?"

Ben turned, first to the group and then back to Emma. She rolled her eyes. "Friends, yeah."

Ben just smiled. "Well, they're definitely going to be my travel buddies. But my real friends Drake and Helen are there."

Zach stared for a while and then turned his large eyes up to him. "Dad?"

"Yeah?" Ben crouched and Zach dropped his gaze to his shoes. He wiped his nose. "What's up, buddy?"

Zach continued to keep his head down and when he spoke, his voice was tiny. "I don't want you to go. I have a funny feeling in my tummy."

"A pain?" Ben grabbed his shoulders.

He shook his head. "Just…can you not go this time, and maybe just your friends go?"

Ben hugged him, and for a second, he wanted to jump back in the car and go home and lock the doors. He wanted to spend whatever time they had left with the people he loved most in the world.

Zach sniffed, wiped his nose again, and then reached out to grab Ben's sleeve with his fingertips. Ben felt the agony of indecision; if he went home, they might have months, weeks, or only days together before things changed to become insane. But if he went and was successful, they may have the rest of their lives together.

There was no choice. "I've got to, Zachy. But wherever I am, know that I'm thinking of you. And I'll feel good knowing that you're thinking about me." He raised the boy's chin to look into his eyes and leaned forward to whisper, "I'll also feel good that you're here to protect your mom. She gets a little scared by herself." He leaned back. "Can you do that?"

Zach gave him a tiny smile and nodded.

"That's my boy." Ben hugged him again.

Zach held his arm for a moment. "Can you bring me something back?"

"Sure, like what?" Ben asked.

He hiked bony shoulders. "I dunno; just something cool."

"You got it." He ruffled the boy's hair. "See you when I get back, big guy. Don't forget; look after your mom for me while I'm away."

Zach nodded solemnly. "I will, I promise."

He stood and Emma put an arm around his neck. "You're mad, and I love and hate you for it." Her eyes were glistening as she spoke, but she tried to hold a watery smile. "Bring me something back as well." She brought her face close to his. "You…just you."

Ben turned to kiss her. And then stared into her eyes. "Just promise me you and Zach will be here when I get back."

CHAPTER 25

AMAZON JUNGLE—61 HOURS UNTIL PRIMORDIA APPARITION

Ben sat next to Drake and Helen in the cavernous rear of the strike bomber. The plane was an enormous piece of modern flying technology, but for all its size, the jets were whisper quiet and allowed all three of them to become lost in their own thoughts.

Ben's mind took him back to the airport, and he now thought of a hundred things he should have said to his family. He also tried hard to dampen down the niggling thought that it might have been the last time he'd ever see them. He felt a lump in his throat and swallowed hard to make it go away.

He exhaled and looked across at Drake's mercenaries. Most dozed with sprawled legs and mouths hung open. Chess' snoring sounded like someone tearing up canvas sheets. But it didn't seem to bother the brawny Shawna beside him who was also lights-out.

The huge Francis had his hands clasped together and eyes closed, and Ben wondered whether this was how he relaxed or perhaps he was saying some silent prayers.

Ben then glanced across to catch Balls, or Bianca, smiling at him. She winked and then continued to hold his gaze. For the last few days, she'd been extremely helpful, friendly, and way too flirty. Ben nodded back and knew that Emma would have vetoed her coming along if she had seen any of that.

He let his eyes slide to the last of the group, Buster. Ever since they had departed, the guy had worried him. He'd seen good soldiers become strung out on adrenaline before. Most handled it well when they were young or trained to deal with the stress. But some entered a state of permanent agitation and became hyper-alert, hair triggered, and/or short-tempered. Buster's eyes were open and constantly darting. Drake said the guy would do his job; he hoped so, as they'd have enough problems to deal with once they walked into their own private hell.

A red light came on overhead, the lights dimmed, and blackout globes lit up. It meant it was time to move into their drop crate, a little bit of new technology they were using for landing that removed the necessity of a formal arrival or letting anyone know they were coming. And it didn't even need a runway.

Other than them, the drop crate was the only thing in the rear of the bomber, and they filed in and took their seats along either side. It was armored and looked like a cargo container except it was packed with modern technology. The drop crate would slide from the rear of the plane and then a rotating wing on each corner would deploy to lower them to the ground.

There was minimal guidance, and it could only be moved by increasing or reducing power to one or more of the mini-chopper wings. Drop crates were primarily used for cargo drops when the materials needed to be kept intact. It had been used for personnel before but wasn't recommended, and it also wasn't really meant to fly, just supposed to find a suitable place to land without breaking the equipment, or bodies, inside.

The other reason they now needed to use it was that Ben and Drake had discovered that for some reason the airport at Caracas didn't exist anymore, and the capital city of Venezuela that they knew had a population of over 2 million was now little more than a ramshackle town. It seemed a recent re-evolution change had wiped most of it away.

Also, the major river they once traversed, the Rio Caroni, a once mighty coffee-brown water laneway snaking through the Amazon jungle, was down to a trickle in this area. Whatever was happening to their world wasn't just affecting the population and cities, but now also the geography.

The other obstacles Ben found they needed to surmount were that there were now few modern settlements, no guides, and the Amazon jungle was deemed a largely unexplored no-go place. This last bit filled Ben, Drake, and Helen with trepidation—they always knew it was a place where dangers lurked everywhere, but it was eminently survivable if you had the right experience. But now, something else had obviously changed in there.

Ready for drop, the pilot intoned from the overhead speaker.

Ben sucked in a deep breath. *I guess we'll all find out soon enough,* he thought as he tightened the straps across his upper body.

From outside the fortified container came the faint whine of hydraulics and Ben expected it was the bomber's rear cargo door yawning open. He suspected there would now be howling winds inside the rear cabin, but they were sheltered, locked inside their steel cocoon.

Around them all crated up and tied down were their weapons, climbing gear, and supplies. Ben closed his eyes for a moment as he felt nervousness creep into his belly.

On my mark, 3, 2, 1…mark. So long and good luck, people.

"Here we go," Drake said. He pulled an extendable arm around in front of him that was a little like an airline tray table and opened the small screen.

There was a clunk, a drop of about an inch, and then the sound of rollers for a few seconds. Finally, there came a sensation of weightlessness. Their tiny steel world dipped, the overhead rotors whirred to life, and then the drop crate automatically righted itself in space.

On Drake's control console were four small toggles, which he worked, shifting power to one or the other as he checked for a suitable landing space that was devoid of water, rocks, or trees.

They'd hoped to set down about a day's march from the plateau, as it was the most level ground for hundreds of miles, and then have 48 hours to be there when Primordia was directly overhead.

"There," Drake said.

Ben leaned across and saw where his friend was pointing—there was a small clearing, just 50 square feet, that would fit them in with little room to spare. There were tall trees surrounding it, but as there were no huge canopies to contend with, the rotors only extended a few feet out from all four corners.

"Get ready, people, coming in on, 10, 9, 8..." Drake's hands were a blur as he shifted power around the rotors to guide the crate in. "3, 2, 1..."

Then the lights went out.

"Oh no," Helen whispered in the darkness as Ben felt that weird butterfly fluttering sensation that started in his stomach and then tingled all the way from his scalp to his toes.

The light came back on and Ben noticed they had only been around a dozen feet up when the lights were out, and when they came back on, they were still a dozen feet up, even after the lapsing of what he thought had been a few seconds. It was as if time stood still in those void-like moments.

The container gently settled and Ben looked one way then the other. "Everything okay?"

Drake and Helen's faces were pale and cautious, but the mercs just looked bored.

"Sure, why wouldn't it be?" Chess asked.

"Hey, where's Bianca, *uh*, Balls?" Ben asked, frowning. He quickly looked to the door, but he already knew it was still sealed tight.

"Who?" Chess asked.

"Damnit, Bianca Alejandra, and whatever the rest of her name was. You guys called her Balls?" Ben said and pointed to the vacant space beside Francis. "She was just there."

"Balls?" Francis looked down to the empty space next to him, and then slowly shook his head. His voice was basement deep. "Ain't no one there now, and ain't no one been there. Don't be losin' it now, brother."

Ben cursed and ran both hands up through his hair. Helen leaned across to him. "It's starting on us now: erasure."

Ben looked up at her. "Let's hope we're in time."

CHAPTER 26

WESTERN INTERIOR SEA SHORE, 100 MILLION YEARS AGO

Andy finally made it down onto the debris-strewn beach and he stood on the silty shoreline, flexing his aching fingers from the climb, and looked back up; the cliff top was far above him, and he had no doubt if he had fallen when the edge broke off, he'd have been killed. Or even if he had survived, and only ended up with one or more broken limbs, in this place, it would have been a death sentence anyway.

His first order of business was to grab up several of the flattened helmet crabs that meandered along the sand making wide tracks. They were slow and in no time, he had several large ones stacked like plates under his arm.

Andy quickly turned to the ocean, always mindful of being in an open space. It was shallow at first but darkened quickly to deeper water. The amazing thing about it was that it surged sideways along the rocks and sand as if it was a monstrous river.

The surge moved rapidly, far faster than walking pace, and he guessed it traveled for miles; hundreds even, on the turn of the tide. Given there was around six hours for a full change of tide, he bet if he was in his boat, he could travel for miles.

Right now, it was heading north, but sooner or later it would stop, then become calm for a while as the tide had reached its zenith or nadir depending if it had been on the run in or out, and then it would turn to begin its southern run. Maybe all the way down south where the inland sea reached the open ocean. It might even join up with one of the continental currents and travel all the way to where he pulled his little boat up at the estuary mouth all those months back.

"Need a boat." He looked up and saw the stand of trees at the cliff line. He thought about it for a brief moment but then gave up. "Too hard, too long." He sighed and turned back to watch the surge for a little longer.

A thought crossed his mind: he could actually use it to travel further up inside the continent, at least along the coast of Appalachia. There were places he was still desperate to see in the lands that would one day merge to become North America.

He turned southward: or should he try and head back down to South America again to watch the effects of Primordia? After all, Appalachia and Laramidia would be here tomorrow and every day for millions more years. But the comet Primordia only ever came once every decade.

What a sight it would be to watch as that plateau became shrouded in its curtain of rain and that tiny section of Amazon jungle was somehow thrown forward, or them backward, so the two time zones briefly overlapped.

Truth was, a small part of him was calling him home. He held up his hand that was missing the fingers. He smiled at it and flexed it—the damned thing still hurt. His body was all skin and bones, covered with a hundred different scars. Added to that, his back teeth were loose and he often suffered from chronic diarrhea from eating things that he obviously shouldn't.

Andy knew in his heart that this was no place to be an old man and alone. He exhaled and watched the water barreling north. *Maybe I can just head back down and when I see the portal open, I can decide then.*

He flexed his hand again—it ached, and there was even a tiny nub of bone showing. It wouldn't be a bad idea to get some supplies, medicine, knives, and whatever.

"If they even come," he whispered, but then: "*Nah*, Helen will."

He smiled at the mental images of his sister forming in his mind. First there came the ones of a little girl falling off a swing, and then her standing in the water with a beaming grin, her Sammy the Seal pool float around her waist. Next came her in a prom dress and being taken to the dance by the college meathead called Jack Harding, who probably had the IQ of a tree stump.

His vision blurred as his eyes watered as his mind took him home— then came university, and he and she had graduated together as the first brother and sister paleontologists in the state.

Andy suddenly realized he missed her terribly. In reality, he missed everybody and anybody. He peeked into his bag. "Sometimes your conversation skills just don't cut it, my little friend."

"*And yours do?*" The tiny thing tilted its head. "*Gluck.*"

"Exactly." He looked back at the surging sea and watched as a massive tree trunk, hundreds of feet long and probably twenty feet wide, passed him by on its way up the coast. Its branches and roots acted like stabilizers so it didn't roll or bob.

His mouth dropped open as it continued on by, fast, and traveling at about 10 knots in the surge—that was a good running speed.

"I need a boat," he repeated, and his mouth curled up at the corners as a plan began to take shape in his mind. Andy turned to look down the coastline and then back up. The tree was still in sight, but now already about 1,000 feet further up the coast.

From where he stood, there was nothing but cliffs, rubble and little else down the coast. But just further up from where he stood, there was a small spit of sand and stone. The tree must have passed so close to it; it would almost have been leaping distance.

"*Maybe,*" he whispered.

He started to walk up along the beach, picking up more crabs and other things that could be edible as he went. *Supplies,* he now thought.

He needed a boat, and Mother Nature provided one for him. If things went to plan, he'd be on that damned log for hours, and if things *really* went to plan, maybe even days.

As he watched, the surge began to slow. "Here we go." It was the change of tide, and soon the opposite surge would start and keep up for hours. He had to be at the spit waiting for the tree trunk or he'd miss his ride.

Andy started to run alongside the now glass-calm sea, his feet slapping in puddles that sprayed his legs with warm water. But then from the corner of his eye, he detected a flicker of movement.

"*Shit.*" He leapt to the side as the long shining body launched itself from the water.

He scrabbled backward as the jaws snapped shut and kept snapping as the thing moved seal-like up onto the beach after him.

It was a mosasaur, a small one at about 25 feet long. The calm water had created a window-like surface, and coupled with Andy jogging along the sand, he had attracted a predator whose eyes were adapted to focus on moving prey.

However, the water was its kingdom, and on land it was well out of its element. The mosasaur gave up and flipped itself back into the water, but Andy could still see it gliding along under the surface beside him.

"Dumb, dumb, and dumber," he berated himself. He walked even further from the water and sat down. "Now what?" he wondered.

He had to get to the tree stump, which meant even if it came real close to the spit, he would still need to cross some of the water by swimming. If he dragged this thing up the coast with him, he wouldn't make two feet of open water, let alone a few dozen.

He picked up a stone from the sand and threw it out into the water.

"Fuck you!" he yelled.

There was a surge toward where the rock landed, and he watched for a moment with narrowed eyes.

"Okay, you find that interesting, *huh*?" He picked up some more and threw them again and again. This time, the mosasaur came to the surface, and he managed to land one smack onto its back.

With a gout of water, it thrashed away. Andy watched for many more minutes, but there was no dark shape gliding back and forth.

"And goodbye to you too... I hope."

Andy looked up at the sun—it was still only at mid-morning. Everything he owned was with him or on him, and he had miles to travel. He decided. He began to walk up the beach to the cliff wall, and then turned to head north toward the small spit that was like a natural wharf that would take him out from the coast.

If he was going to hitch a ride, he knew he would have to cross some water—so the farther he could get out onto that spit, the better.

It took him 30 more minutes to reach the spit, and in the far distance, he could see the massive tree starting to make its way back down toward him. It was moving slowly, probably only a few miles per hour right now. But as soon as the tide really began to turn, it would pick up speed. He needed to be on it and settled by then.

The rock wharf extended out like a finger for about 50 feet, and by the way the water pushed up in a small wave at its end, there must have been a sand spit as well.

Andy turned to look up the coast again—the log was about 500 feet from him, and now picking up speed. There were plenty of leafless branches and gnarled roots for him to use as a ladder to climb up when he got there, and he mentally went through the motions he would use—swim, grab on, climb up, don't look down, don't look back.

He turned and faced the water again. Just beyond the spit, the shelf would drop away to at least 50 feet in close, maybe more, otherwise the tree trunk's branches would get snagged up on the bottom.

Andy opened his bag and reached in for the last remnants of a shirt that was just a length of rag now. He carefully picked up Gluck and began to wrap him up like he was swaddling a tiny infant. The small reptile had felt it before and didn't complain too much.

"Gonna get wet real soon. Wish me luck, and you hold your breath."

"*Good luck, Andy friend.*"

"Thank you. And I know you didn't really say that." He smiled. "But I don't care."

Gluck never made another noise as Andy pushed him down deep into the bag and tied it closed. He then secured it over his shoulder.

He rolled his shoulders like an Olympic swimmer getting ready for a heat and looked to one side of the rocky spit then to the other. The water was fairly shallow so the risk was minimal. But further out...

He carefully moved along the rocks, slowly, arms out. His gaze went from the tree stump, to the rocks, and then to the water—*I need eyes in the back of my head, plus a few more on the sides*, he thought.

When he reached the end of the rocks, he saw that there was a sand bar extending for another dozen feet, just about a foot below the waterline.

Beyond, the water was dark blue and he could see the rip lines as it was beginning to pick up speed as it headed down south on the outgoing tide.

Andy looked toward the massive log again that was bearing down on him and also picking up speed. He only had a few minutes more before he had to commit—he wanted, *needed*, more time, but any second now, it'd be at the go/no-go split.

His heart galloped like a racehorse in his chest.

"Shit, shit, shit," he whispered from a cotton-dry mouth.

Damnit, he thought. *Gotta catch my ride, see Helen again.* He stepped down onto the sandbar.

CHAPTER 27

"NEW THINGS ARE APPEARING, AND OLD THINGS ARE WINKING OUT."

Ben waited while Drake slid the door back on the drop crate, and as soon as it was open, the heat, damp, and smells of the jungle rushed in. He inhaled the wet smell of decay, the cloying sweetness of scented blooms intermixing with the sharp tang of acidic plant resins. There was also the smell of the rich soil and corruption—life and death in equal measures was all around them.

Walking further out into the small clearing, Ben could almost physically feel the waves of raucous sound from a million insects competing in song to attract a mate, give a warning, or just enjoying the warmth of the sun. Things flitted through the jungle canopy, some small and brightly colored and others larger shapes that caused the leaves to rain down like confetti.

"Welcome home," Drake said.

"God, I missed this place," Ben said.

"Really?" Drake's brows went up.

Ben turned and grinned. "*Nah*, not one bit."

Helen joined them. "And then we were seven."

"Yeah." Ben sighed. "And only we noticed her gone." He looked at Helen. "Like you said, it's reached us. But I don't understand how it just took her? What happened?"

Helen shook her head. "Who knows? Maybe somewhere back in her lineage something happened to change direction—an ancestor had a son instead of a daughter, or maybe never had children at all."

"We could be next," Drake added.

"Sobering." Ben looked over his shoulder at the mercs and then lowered his voice. "Do you think…it *will* affect us?"

"Who can say?" Her mouth turned down. "But my guess is that the bigger changes will start to happen soon and become evident." She looked up at him. "But evident only to us." She looked down at something moving through the grasses at their feet and crouched to scoop it up.

Helen opened her hands and let Ben and Drake crowd closer. "Like, what's this thing?"

In her hand was a tiny creature that just covered her palm. It was the size of a mouse, except instead of fur it had pebbly skin and a beak rather than a long whiskered snout.

"Some sort of…" Drake just snorted, "… ugly little bastard?"

The thing mewled like a cat as Helen turned it one way then the other. "Well, it looks like an *Aquilops*, a distant relative to the huge *Triceratops*. But it's different—new things are appearing, and old things are winking out." She put it down. "But one thing's for sure, it shouldn't be here."

"Neither should we," Ben said. He turned and whistled to Chess and waved the mercs on before turning back to Helen and Drake. "Seems we're in a race. We find Andy and bring him back before we get erased from history. We can't afford to lose."

CHAPTER 28

SWIMMING IN THE WESTERN INTERIOR SEA, 100 MILLION YEARS AGO

Andy sunk down into the sand a few inches and felt the strength of the current in bath-warm water as it came to just above his knees. The sand spit was only about 10 feet wide and was like a shoulder that sloped to rocks on either side.

He licked his lips and tore his gaze away from the water, saw the tree trunk approaching now just another 100 feet further north and, worryingly, was going to pass by a lot further out than he anticipated.

50 feet, he thought apprehensively. He tried to do the math—a single swim stroke would drag him forward about 3 to 4 feet, so maybe 15–16 strokes, 20 tops, and he'd be there. Once he got into the shadow of the log, anything in the water wouldn't be able to see him.

As the tree approached, he was able to get a better look at its characteristics: leafless branches, some massive, extended 20 feet in the air and all clustered around the front end. And at the other end, the roots were like a massive 10-foot-wide tangle. But there was plenty of room in among them for one skinny paleontologist to hide—he'd be caged in, but everything else would be caged out, so that's where he'd head for: the rear.

Andy stood just back from the very end of the spit and waited. He mentally calculated the timing he would need—dive in, stroke hard, try and intercept the log as it passed by. If he went too early, he might be carried away in the tidal surge. If he was too late, he might never catch up to it. He needed to time it so the trunk was right in front of him when he was out there. The absolute least time he spent in the water, the better chance he had of surviving.

He quickly crossed back to the rocky spit and picked up a piece of loose stone. He brought it back and flung it far out into the sea—nothing surged toward it, and other than the ripples from the moving water, there also seemed nothing else lurking. He counted down, flexing his hand and bending his knees that felt weak and trembling.

10, 9, 8, 7, 6—look left and right—3, 2, 1…

He dived. Even though the water was tropical warm, he felt a chill run right through his body. He swam hard, too hard, thrashing like a machine. *Slow down!* his mind screamed, but his primitive brain refused to listen, and he thrashed onward. He knew his flailing strokes would attract predators but he wanted to be out of the water more than anything else in his life.

Andy didn't want to, but he opened his eyes. Down below him was a flick of movement, and it caused a little bit of piss to shoot from his groin.

Oh fuck, he thought. *The mosasaur was down there.* He lifted his head—just 15 more feet.

The long and straight trunk towered above him and he thought its size meant it might have been some sort of early species of Sequoia that had been around since the Jurassic. For something so colossally huge, it was moving fast, way too fast.

The jig was up and he had nothing to lose but his life. His fear shot adrenaline into his system and with it came a burst of energy. He threw his arms over and kicked hard. He was no champion swimmer, but he bet he would have left Michael Phelps in his wake.

On his back, his satchel, even though mostly closed, was acting like a water parachute and slowing him down. There came a surge from beneath him, and his stomach fluttered as it was exposed to the depths. Andy swam with his head up now, counting down—10 feet, 8, then 5.

He didn't want to look down or back anymore, just willing himself to thrash toward the tangle of tree roots. In another few seconds, he was jammed in among them and kept going until he was in their very heart, just as something welled up, nudged the massive tree trunk, and covered him in spray.

"*Ha!*" he yelled and spun back. "*Fuck you.*" He turned around and hung onto some roots and puffed hard like a steam train. He felt ill and his stomach threatened to lose the precious little food it had in it. But he swallowed hard and willed it down, and also forced himself to breathe slower. He could do nothing about his heart rate that was still sprinting in his chest. He'd had close calls before, but there was something about dark water that scared the shit out of him.

In another few minutes, he had regained enough energy to clamber up onto the top of the log. It was wide, stable as he had hoped, and he flopped down to lean his back against a stout gnarly root. Andy lifted his face to the sun. It warmed him, and he thanked whatever gods were up there for looking after him.

"Oh no." He suddenly jerked forward and dragged his bag around in front of him, quickly untying it and searching for his little friend. It was a wet jumble inside, and he remembered the bag filling and slowing him down. Anything could have been flushed out.

A tiny sneeze and a head shake. "*Gluck.*"

Andy let out a relieved chuckle.

The little pterosaur blinked up at him. "*Thanks a lot.*"

"Don't ask, buddy; you don't want to know." He lifted the flying reptile from the bag and gently laid it on the trunk's surface in front of him. Gluck hopped in a circle and then stared out over the tree trunk's side at the water.

"Yep." Andy did the same. "We're on the bus." He watched as the shoreline hurried past. He must have been traveling at a good 10 miles per hour by now, and he could see the landscape of late morning, with all its marvelous creatures hunting, killing, fleeing, or dying in their primitive and brutal world.

As the cliffs gave way to more open landscape, he saw a *Triceratops* with a huge bony crest and three horns, two massive ones up top each easily six feet long, and astoundingly, the colors were magnificent, in brown, brick red, and some green. One pawed at the ground like a bull and snorted, and must have weighed as much as a school bus.

Andy lifted his hands in a box shape and brought them to his eye. "Click." He lowered his hands. "Just one photo, that's all I want." He sighed as he continued to watch the show.

There were also herds of hadrosaurs, with sail-crested heads. "*Corythosaurus*." He said, and then: "No, bigger, maybe even *Hypacrosaurus*."

He straightened when he spotted the box-like head peeking between some trees. "Look out," he whispered and pointed. The carnosaur burst free, and the herd of hadrosaurs panicked. But the massive predator's hugely muscled legs pounded down on the ground, going from 0 to 30 miles per hour in a blink, and then caught a medium-sized hadrosaur, holding it with a foot, and bringing its six-foot jaws down on a long neck. Even from where he sat, Andy could hear the vertebrae crack from the thousands of pounds per square inch bite pressure.

"Wow," he mouthed. "That's the photo I want."

It all suddenly made him remember why he was here—he could be killed, horribly, any second. But this world at this time was magnificent in its ability to terrify, but it was also so beautiful that it made his heart leap in his chest.

"Ouch." Something jabbed his leg. He lifted his bag and saw one of the sharp crab legs was protruding through his bag. His stomach rumbled, reminding him it had been many hours since he last ate.

He drew the bag between his legs and fished out the first of the crabs. They had a huge disc-like head, long spindly legs, and a whip-like tail that contained next to no meat.

"It's not your lucky day." He broke the legs off and the tail and placed the pieces on the log before him. It took him several more minutes to tease out the meat from the legs using the hard spiky tail like a spear, and he shared some with his ever-hungry small friend—the meat was raw, cold, salty from the ocean, and damned magnificent.

Finished with the legs, he began to bash the crab's head on the hard wood, finally cracking it along the seam and opening it up like a lid. Inside were gill fans, mushy-looking gray organs, and some muscle-meat near the leg-joints. He teased that out first, and then ate most of everything, handing over the really unidentifiable stuff to Gluck.

Finished, he quickly tossed the remains of his meal over the side, as he knew what dead crustacean was like when it was left in the sun for while—it became so pungent it attracted predators from miles away.

Andy licked his fingers and tossed the last shell over the side. His hands were sticky and smelled already. He rose to a crouch.

"Wait there, buddy."

He climbed down, staying within his tree root cage toward the water, and leaning down, dipped his hands in to rub them together. He was about to turn away when he chanced to look deeper and there, sure enough, was a long gray shape that dived below the log.

"*Ah*, not you again."

It seemed his friend from before hadn't quite given up and was following him down the coast. Andy was about five feet up from the water and his tree was quite stable. Barring hitting surf, he should stay high and dry and out of trouble.

He clambered back up to his root nest and stood to crane his neck and look out at what was ahead—there were no more spits or white-water areas that might have indicated a reef, bank, or even shallow water.

His only problem was the coast seemed to be receding, and he was heading straight. Slowly but surely, he had gone from being 50 feet from the shoreline to now about 150, and the water here was impenetrably dark.

For now, I'm okay, he thought as the tide was still on run-out and was taking him with it along the coast. He was moving fast and guessed he must have crossed many dozens of miles. Trying to trek through the jungle would have taken him days to do what he'd done in a matter of hours.

There came a wet hissing sound like a soda bottle being opened and Andy looked down at the water to see the mosasaur surface. It exhaled through its snout, blowing water and air upward, and then sucked in another huge breath. Its nasal flaps closed over the snout holes and back down it went. But not before it turned one enormous and very human-like eye on him for a second or two just to make sure he was still there.

Mosasaurs were marine reptiles, but they breathed air just like sea turtles. Over the millions of years they existed, they had evolved enormous, long lungs and could stay down for an hour. It meant they were excellent ambush predators, waiting down deep and then coming up fast to catch something unaware on the surface.

Andy exhaled and looked back down southward. How long would it track him? Possibly in the next few hours, they'd reach the tide's peak low point, and then there'd be a period of calm before the tide started to run back in. At that point, he was planning to leave his makeshift cruise liner. The danger was he now found himself a good 200 feet from the shore.

He looked down and saw the shadow pass underneath his tree trunk again.

Well, that's just great, he whispered. *I only just made 50 feet, how am I ever going to make 200?* He looked back over his shoulder; did it now mean he was stuck and going to have to ride the tree back up the coast again? Would the massive sequoia finally beach itself, or would it eventually be washed out to sea where he'd slowly starve or die of dehydration?

"*Gluck.*" The small flying reptile found a few extra shreds of drying crab in amongst the bark and pecked them up and ate them. Andy smiled down at it.

"Don't worry, little guy, I'm never going to eat you."

It hopped up on his leg and sat down. The tiny pterosaurs weighed next to nothing; a combination of having a small frame and hollow bones just like a bird.

"Besides, there's no meat on you." Andy stroked its head. It was a warm, leathery feeling, with a few bristles on its hide, perhaps early forms of feathers. It was like touching a warm, plucked chicken.

"I wish you could fly…for your sake." He leaned back into his tree root chair. *But I'm glad you can't*, he thought. *Because if Gluck was ever able to fly away, I'd be left alone.*

Andy started to hum a tune, and then broke into a song. It made him feel good, but homesick. The weird thing was, he needed to hear a voice, any voice, even his own. Deep down, he knew Gluck talking to him was really his mind so craving interaction, it had created one for him.

We humans are weird, he thought. We all want to be left alone, until we really are. Then we all want to be with someone.

He sat in the Cretaceous sunshine and let his mind wander as he sailed ever onward. What would he do when, if, he saw Helen again? His eyes watered.

"I miss you, sis."

He sniffed, still trying to decide his future. There was a place up in North America were there was an explosion of evolution around the time of the Late Cretaceous Period, right about now, that led to all manner of new forms.

Why did new species come out of there? What was so special about that place? He desperately wanted to see it, and maybe he could talk Helen into staying and coming and seeing it with him. He bet she'd like it.

Andy immediately brightened. *Hey, maybe that was why she was coming. She missed* him*, and she wanted to do what he did—explore.* He grinned. This might turn out to be a really cool idea after all.

Andy looked down and saw the long, shiny, but clearly reptilian body come to the surface, roll, stare, and then sink back down. He suddenly knew what it reminded him of—a massive Komodo dragon lizard, with a smooth body, and flippers where its legs should be.

"I wish you'd just fuck off." He sat back and tried to ignore his nemesis. It was still hours until the tide turned. *I still got time.* He hoped.

*****

Andy had been right about the different hues of seawater representing different currents. The massive continents of Appalachia and Laramidia were in the middle of a massive ocean-wide northern hemisphere current that came up along its external coasts, and was drawn in the northern opening to then return to the southern hemisphere via the inland sea, exiting down where Florida would be one day.

While the tides moved in and out along the coastal areas, the current further out was a constant southward drift. And that was where the mosasaur had bumped his tree trunk.

Andy didn't yet know it, but for him, there would be no tide change. His trip was one-way and would take him all the way out into the depths of the prehistoric ocean.

*****

Another hour sailed by, and Andy's tree trunk ride was veering even further away from the coastline. He was hungry but didn't want to eat his last crab just yet.

From time to time, he had been lowering his bag into the water to keep the crustacean fresh. And so far, every time he'd done it, there had been nothing down there but deep blue ocean.

He dared to hope that the water hunter had finally given up. He eased back in amongst his nest of wild roots. Without the constant presence of the mosasaur, he thankfully only had one problem to worry about now— getting to dry land.

Gluck busied himself further down the log, finding something interesting in among the rotting scales of bark. It cheered him a little to think that at least he seemed to be finding something to eat.

He turned to watch the land pass by. He was now a good 500 feet from the shoreline now, and he bet he had traveled hundreds of miles. As there was no coastline on the other side, he couldn't be sure if he was now heading out into the open ocean or was still traveling down along the edge of Appalachia. But the key thing was, he was still heading down the coast.

He sat forward. Why? Why was he still heading down the coast? Then it hit him—the tide never changed. He got to his knees, making the small pterosaur raise its head in alarm.

"Hey, we should have been going the other way by now. Or at least becalmed as we hit mid-tide."

He put a hand over his eyes and squinted in at the shoreline. There they were, those stripes of different colored water, the lanes, and as he watched, they passed by mounds of floating debris, fast. No, that wasn't right. They were going one way, and the debris in closer was going the other.

"Oh, shit no, we must be in some sort of sea current."

Andy continued to watch for a while, and then he guessed it didn't matter. The basic fact was, they were still going the way he wanted, but his priority was he needed to be closer to the shore or he would eventually starve, or in the next storm be tipped into the water where there was death in a hundred massive forms lurking below.

Andy squinted at his tree trunk. He needed something—maybe a makeshift paddle, or rudder, so he could at least steer his log, even if it was just a little. He carefully got to his feet, making sure to hold onto a lengthy root. Further down the tree were long branches, some still with the remnants of dried leaves. Perhaps if he could break one off, he could use it.

He walked carefully along the log and came to the first—it was about 15 feet high before it broke off, and as thick around as his waist. He'd need an axe to chop through it. Further down, there were smaller ones, but that was where the end of the mighty tree got thinner, and therefore its buoyancy was reduced—and that meant the entire log was lower in the water.

"Oh boy," he whispered.

The sea around him was deep blue, and shafts of light vanished into it for perhaps a few dozen feet. Below that, it turned to ink. But he knew from below, up here in the sunshine he stood out clearly even from the depths. That meant anything down there could see him long before he got to see it.

Andy braced his feet and stared at the spray of branches. There were a couple of longer ones that were thinner half way up, and maybe he could at least snap them off.

The log bobbed in the dark blue water and seemed to be stationary even though he knew they were drifting fast now in some sort of sea current. He looked from the water to the branches again and mentally calculated how much time it would take to get there, snap one off, and then scurry back.

"Seconds," he whispered.

"*Gluck.*"

The small flying reptile was watching him keenly, and it didn't look happy. Andy took a few steps.

"*Please don't do it.*"

There was no doubt that the pterosaur was calling him back.

"Yeah, I hear you." He blew air through his lips. "But I'll be greased lightning, I promise."

He widened his stance, getting ready to run toward his target branch. In his mind, he saw it all in slow motion—him darting forward, snapping the limb off, and being back before anything was the wiser.

"*You'll never make it. Ple-eeease don't, Andy!*"

"Shush." He turned and put a finger to his lips. "Just keep a lookout for me okay, little buddy?" He drew in a breath and felt the knot of nervousness in his empty belly.

"Ready, set… *go.*" He sprinted forward.

The log surface was sun-dried and traction was good. He only had to travel about 15 feet to the first large branch, dodge around it, and then run another 10 feet or so to his destination branch.

At the first massive limb, he slowed, turned his back to it, and edged around it. He slipped a little as the curve of the log was closer to the waterline, meaning it had become a little more waterlogged and greasy.

But just as he came back up to the top, the creature exploded from the water. Andy screamed and stumbled back to the top, but way too fast. He went over the other side.

In seconds, he was spluttering on the surface and looking up at the top of the branch some four feet above him and too high and steep to climb. Up there, the mosasaur hung, having come right up out of the water to get at him. Its massive seal-like body writhed and thrashed as it looked to either roll back into the water or keep going to get to Andy over the top.

Andy gave up the idea of trying to climb back up here and swam to the root ball at the rear. The predator curled its body and with a thunderous splash, flipped back into the water on the other side, making the massive log bob up and down half a dozen feet in the water

Now, it and Andy were both in the monster's domain. But fear gave him energy and he was in among the roots in seconds. He didn't stop as he then clambered back up into his root cockpit, cutting and grazing himself in his haste.

"Fuck." He lay back, breathing hard. The small pterosaur hopped up onto his leg and actually pecked his thigh.

"Ouch."

He looked down at the tiny creature as it turned one tiny red eye on him. Andy continued to suck in deep breaths as his heart raced in his chest.

"Yeah, yeah, I know, you told me so."

Andy pushed the wet hair back off his face and looked about. The land seemed even further away. "This might not have been a good idea after all."

Andy turned toward the branches, knowing now that getting one was an option that was never going to materialize. He needed another plan, he needed something, anything, and even a little luck would do.

He continued to stare at the branches. "You know what they say? Necessity is the mother of invention." He looked down at the small flying reptile. "So, all I need is a chainsaw, 50 feet of soft rope, and an outboard motor, and we'd be outta here, little buddy."

He smiled, sighed, and then rested his forearms on his knees. In the distance, there was a smudge on the horizon, and the hint of a cool breeze kicked up to gently ruffle the surface of the sea.

He groaned, knowing exactly what that could mean. "Not good. Very not good." He rubbed both hands up through his long hair and leant back. "I need to think about this while I've still got a little bit of time." His adrenaline had now leaked from his body, leaving him bone tired and feeling a little sick.

Andy tilted his head back and closed gritty eyes; the sun was warm and dappled on his face as it worked its way through the root canopy and into his skin.

After another moment, he dozed.

CHAPTER 29

HALIFAX RIVER MOUTH, DAYTON BEACH—PRESENT TIME

RE-EVOLUTION: 025

Gil stood at the river mouth where the warm water was shallow and there was about another dozen feet to go before the deeper water of the channel drop off. It was just coming on dawn, and he was first out, pegging out the best fishing spot.

Even though there was still a slight chill in the dawn air, he was in his new trout fishing pants and warm as toast. He hummed softly as thoughts of his struggling hardware business were far, far away.

Where he fished, the river emptied out into the ocean, and the tidal flats were just flooding as the tide came in again. The sprats shot across the surface, and soon, the bigger species like sheepshead, snook, and sea trout would follow them in as the water deepened. He might even snag a lemon shark, which always made for a good tale back home.

He had his net at his waist, and even though the water came to just above his knees, he felt now that the sun was coming up he could probably work his way a little closer to the channel.

Gil knew he could stick to fishing shallow and was sure to pick up a flounder or two, but he thought they were a bastard to eat—every time he flipped one over on his plate, he ended up with a shirt front covered in lemon and butter. Tasty though.

Gil blinked as the lights went out and he looked over his shoulder but there was nothing at all around him as if he had been dropped into the depths of space. Just as he turned his face to the sky, everything came back to normal.

"Well." He snorted softly. "Don't tell my doctor."

He reeled his line in, walked further out toward the deep channel, and recast. He had a good-sized bit of fish bait on a razor hook, and he kept his fingers lightly on the line, sensitive to every tap, bump, and tiniest of vibrations—after many years of fishing, by feel alone, Gil could tell the difference between the sea bottom, weed, and a fish nibble—and most times, he could even tell what sort of fish was doing the nibbling.

The line suddenly got heavy. "Whoa there."

Gil reeled in, but the line stopped dead. "What the hell?" He clicked his tongue in his cheek at the thought of maybe getting himself hooked up on a snag—sunken log probably. There'd been some rain a few weeks back, and maybe something washed down the river and was stuck on the bottom.

He tugged again and took a few steps closer to the channel drop off. He continued to reel, and thankfully, the line started to slowly come up. But there was still weight on it. He knew what a shark or big ray felt like, and it was similar to this—dead weight.

But at least it was still coming, so that was a good thing. He reeled in more line and tried to calculate how much he'd reeled back in verse how much line was still down in the depths. As Gil reeled in, he stared into the water, looking for 'color' as they called it, the first glimpse of a catch, to get an idea of what exactly he had on his line.

He squinted. Gradually, something was taking shape from the darker water. "Big ray, maybe." He kept reeling, drawing it toward him. When it was about a dozen feet out and coming up the side of the channel into shallow water, he suddenly realized, and then remembered with a dawning horror, what it could be.

"*Shit.*" He dropped his expensive Shimano rod and turned to run.

The pool-table-sized creature came up from the depths and into the shallows. It was sandy pale, and two fist-sized bulb-eyes popped up from the water to regard the fleeing man.

The emperor crab was one of the biggest crab species to have ever existed, and it had been known to attack dogs, livestock, and even people who were stupid enough to wander close to river mouths at dawn or dusk.

Gil splashed hard, throwing up waves, his bulky trout fishing pants catching some of the surge and beginning to fill with seawater. Unfortunately, he was 55, out of condition, and tiring fast.

The crab never slowed for a second, and as the water shallowed, it lifted up on pointed, stilt-like legs and accelerated. In the next instant, one of its four-foot-long claws reached out to take him by the neck. Gil screamed, but no one heard, and in another flash of returning memory, he knew why.

Don't fish at dawn or dusk.

Why didn't he remember that before and why didn't he remember about the emperor crabs?

The crab was now holding its prize in close to itself, like a footballer holds the ball, and it immediately set about returning to the deep water.

Gil didn't even bother fighting the grip, as it would have been like trying to combat an industrial press. As the crab went over the lip of the sandbank and back into the channel, Gil had one final wish: I hope I drown first.

CHAPTER 30

The water splashing his face brought him to abrupt wakefulness.

"*Gluck, gluck: Andy, wake up, wake up!*"

"*Huh.*" Andy blinked a pleasant dream away where he was in warm, dry clothing, and sitting down to dinner as a Thanksgiving turkey the size of a small car was placed on the table.

It vanished, and he wasn't dry, or in nice clothes, but instead was starving, near naked, and cold.

"What?"

"*Bad things, bad things coming.*" He felt the sharp talons of his little friend on his thigh.

"*Uh*, was dreaming." Depressingly, he was back on his floating log. He put a reassuring hand down on Gluck's shivering back. "It's okay, buddy, just dozed off for a minute, or…"

But as Andy sat up, he knew why the small creature was agitated. The wind was up and dark clouds raced across the sky. Added to that, the temperature had dropped 10 degrees. Waves now lapped the side of his log, and from time to time, the huge tree lurched in the water.

There was no doubt that a storm was bearing down on them—that was the bad news. The good news was the wind came from the west and it was blowing him toward the shoreline.

"Jesus, how long was I asleep?"

Andy looked up at the clouds billowing up from that direction. They were dark, ominous, and held flecks of lightning within them. He then turned to the distant shoreline. *Would he be beached, or swamped by the storm before then?*

Who will win? he wondered aloud.

Another wave and more spray whipped across them. Gluck raised its bony wings, one opening wide and the other deformed one, just only lifting from its body. It held its balance, but it skidded.

"Whoops. Hang in there, little buddy." He reached down and scooped him up. "Better you go back in here where I can keep an eye on you."

Andy popped him in the near empty bag. There was no food or water left now. So something had to change one way or the other.

The tree lurched as a larger wave rocked it. Andy knew that when the storm was fully upon them, he could expect them to be rolled over and he'd be going in.

Slowly but surely, the tree was being washed and wind-pushed toward the shoreline, and Andy squinted into the salt spray. He was way too far out to leave his tree now, but on the coastline, he began to make out landmarks—in the distance was what could have been a single tall tree at the waterline, and all of its branches looked to have been wind-blasted off from one side.

"You're kidding me; that's where our boat is." He grinned. "We made it."

Andy looked about and then toward the shore—he was still about 300 feet from the land.

"Damn, might as well be on another planet," he cursed and wished he had something to throw. He also wished he could look below the water and see if his deadly shadow was still there.

The weather was growing darker, but between him and the shore, a few of the medium-sized pterosaurs still dive-bombed the water's surface and snatched up 20-pound silver torpedoes in their beak. It made his empty stomach rumble.

In another 10 minutes, he guessed they'd pass through the school of fish. Maybe the baitfish might leave some debris on the surface—a fresh fish scrap was better than nothing.

He waited and shivered slightly. With little clothing and no shelter, it wouldn't take long for him to suffer from exposure. Finding shelter had always been his number one priority, and now he was caught out in the open.

As they approached the school of fish that had now moved closer to be only about a few dozen feet to his side, he saw he was still about 200 feet from the shore. But waves now rocked the trunk so much; it bobbed and some even crashed over its surface. However, he was still moving, and for the first time, he felt a glimmer of hope that his tree might wash up before it was tipped by the storm.

And then he felt the first sensation of grinding.

Andy frowned, not understanding what was happening until he caught a glimpse of weed about 20 to 30 feet down.

"Ah, shit no; the bottom."

The grinding continued and then the tree slowed and stopped, its lower branches catching fast on the sea bottom. He looked up—still about 150 feet of open water.

"Well, I'm screwed."

Silver torpedoes shot past his perch on the trunk, and only about 30 feet away, a pterosaur dived to snatch one of the fish from the surface. Up close, he could see these pterosaurs were a fair size and probably stood about four feet in height.

Another came in, grabbed a huge fish, and went to wheel away. However, this time, it never made it. From below the surface, a massive grey beast shot upward, its three-foot-wide head catching the body of the flying reptile and with the sound of crunching bones, dragged it back below the surface.

That could have been me, he thought.

Andy's dark shadow was there; it had always been there, waiting for him, or for anything else.

But for now, it was busy.

To the beach or die trying, he thought madly and dived in.

The water was still bath-warm, but he felt the chill of death all around him. Andy was no great swimmer, but he powered on, one arm over the other. He kept his eyes tightly shut. He didn't want to see any visions of hell rising up to snatch him from the surface and crunch his bones like sticks, like what happened to the flying reptile.

A wave washed over him, causing him to scream and gulp seawater. He spluttered, and then there came a surge of water from underneath him. He shut his eyes tighter, his lungs burning and his testicles shriveling from fear, but he kept thrashing onward.

I've done this before, I can do it again, I can do it again, I can do it again. He tried to think of nothing else but this mantra.

The bag at his side was wallowing open like a parachute as he'd forgotten to tie it closed this time, and it was slowing him down. But he fought on.

Then something touched his hand. He screamed bubbles and yanked it away and stopped to lift his head, but when he changed angles, his feet touched the bottom.

Andy didn't stop for a second and started to run faster as the water became shallower. His feet sunk in the silt, but he powered on with the last remaining atoms of energy and adrenaline he had left in his body.

When he thought he was far enough up the beach, he spun back—save for his massive tree stuck further out, there was nothing.

He cupped his hands to his mouth. "You lose, asshole." He laughed a little madly. "Brains over brawn."

But then he suddenly remembered that if he found his little boat he had hidden, he'd need to sail right back out of this very estuary mouth.

"Hey, sorry about that asshole bit, okay?" He grinned as he sunk down to sit. "Let's just call it even and we all go home happy."

He sucked in deep breaths, feeling like he was 100 years old. Over his shoulder, his bag still leaked water.

He panicked. "Oh no. *Oh, please no.*" He snatched it up and ripped it open.

"*Gluck*." The tiny reptile shook off some water and stared up at him. Andy started to cry.

CHAPTER 31

"EVOLUTION TOOK THEM BACK."

Emma paced, waiting on the call from Ben. She knew from his timetable that they should have arrived down in the Amazon by now. This was their last chance to speak together as Ben would soon be entering the blackout zone, and then it was up to their skill, experience, Andy, and a truckload of good luck.

She tried not to think about what would happen if Ben didn't return from the Amazon. She stood at the window looking out over their estate, still not believing what she was seeing. She knew for sure now the walls were closing in on them.

A while ago, there had been another blackout, this one longer, and then when it was over, everything had changed. Since the first time that they'd noticed time-alterations, she had been doing some hurried research on theoretical changes that could come about due to variations in an evolutionary timeline.

Many of the theorists subscribed to the idea of flora and fauna changes, but also significant environmental changes that could alter entire landscapes. And the experts had history on their side as proof of their theories.

Right here in America, about 15,000 years ago when the mega fauna started to die out, it resulted in significant terrain changes. The massive creatures such as mammoths, mastodons, camels, horses, ground sloths, and giant beavers terraformed their environments. When their populations crashed, a landscape that was once like Africa's Serengeti plains, with countless herds of great beasts, were suddenly changed forever.

Species of broadleaved trees that had been kept in check by huge numbers of big herbivores suddenly began to grow unchecked and quickly dominated the landscape. Soon after, the accumulation of dropped branches, drying leaf mass, and general plant debris saw a dramatic increase in the number of wildfires, which also recast the landscapes, and the species, plants and animals, living on it.

With some plains turning to forests, erosion was slowed, topsoil retained, river courses altered, and with it the entire land reshaped.

Emma felt a tear run down her cheek as she looked out over the countryside that was once lush American forests of Alder, Blue Ash, and Quaking Aspen. Now there were endless miles of dry plains of brown grass and here and there a few lumps of hills with the occasional scrubby-looking tree.

Dust clouds rose from the hooves of the herds. Creatures that could have been deer but had a single horn in the center of their foreheads and also a rough of fur at their throats like that on a lion.

"Zach," she called.

"*Yeah?*"

She half turned. "Can you come down here, please?"

There was a groan from upstairs and then came the rumble of feet on steps. Zach appeared beside her at the window and jammed his hands in his jeans pockets. He looked out for a moment and then up at her. "What's up?"

Emma pointed. "Those animals, what are they?"

Zach frowned up at her as though she was a simpleton. After a moment, he rolled his eyes. "Unicorns, of course."

"Unicorns?" She looked down at him, as if searching for the joke.

"Yeah, why?" He waited for another few seconds. "Anything else?"

She snorted softly as she looked out over the herds of beasts that numbered in the thousands. The landscape was flatter, beaten down, as the exposed ground was nibbled down and churned up from countless hooves to then be blown away in the next dust storm.

"*Unicorns*; guess they made it on the Ark after all in this version of the world." She sighed.

Zach shrugged and zoomed back up the steps.

Her phone rang and she snatched it up, saw the caller ID, and quickly jammed it to her ear.

"*I miss you already.*"

The line was weak, but just the sound of Ben's voice calmed her. "And I you." She smiled as she spoke. "I wish I was there."

There was a pause for a few seconds. "*No, I'm glad you're not,*" he replied softly, and then: "*How's Zach?*"

"He's fine, bored, and thinking I'm losing my mind." *And I probably am*, she thought.

"*And how are you?*" There was a grin in his voice, and she bet he could read her mind.

"Good," she lied. "But…"

"*Yes?*" He waited.

"Everything is different. The animals, the people, and now even the land is changing." She looked out the window. "We're not in Kansas anymore, Toto." She smiled weakly.

"*I know, but we're nearly to the plateau. Stay in the house, and keep an eye on Zach. I want you both safe and sound and waiting for me when I get home.*" Ben sighed long and slow. "*Hey, want to know something weird: we lost one of our people.*"

"Oh no, how?" she asked. "Was it bad?"

"*No, I mean, we lost-lost one of our people—one minute they were there, and the next—poof—just, gone.*"

"I don't understand. You're not even at the plateau yet." She felt her stomach flip.

"*No, no, they, she, just vanished. Only Drake, Helen, and I noticed. Weird thing was, the other guys said she never existed in the first place.*" He chuckled but there was nervousness in it. "*Helen said it was like evolution just took them back.*"

"*Evolution took them back.*" She felt a little dizzy. "It's finally reached us, us humans, I mean, hasn't it? And it seems to be speeding up," Emma said. "I'm scared. I want to scream, fight back, but against who or what?"

"*We'll fix it,*" Ben said confidently.

"But what if the changes that Andy made were already done and bringing him back won't make any difference at all? We might not be here when you get back."

"*Don't say that. Don't even think like that,*" Ben insisted.

"The world could be destroyed," she said. "And only we'll know it."

"*No, it won't be destroyed,*" he said softly. "*But maybe a new version of the world might be made.*" He sounded like he shifted, and the connection began to crackle. "*I've got to go, but stay positive, please. We can't undo what's already been done. But we can certainly stop anything else happening. That's all we got right now.*"

"I know," she said and looked out again at the dry plains of their estate. "Ben..." she began.

"*Yeah, Emm, I'm here,*" he said softly.

"Be careful down there. That jungle you knew before is now probably very different to the one you're entering. Who knows what lives in there now."

"*I know, and I will, I promise. Stay positive; I'll be back in a week...all of us will.*"

He already sounded far away as he signed off.

CHAPTER 32

VENEZUELA, THE AMAZON JUNGLE

Nicolás Manduro paused as the light flicked on and off, like something had been thrown over the sun for a second or two. It passed as quickly as it came and he adjusted his backpack, grabbing a tree trunk to momentarily steady himself.

He had trekked now for many days, and although he had ventured into the jungle before, he had never ever been into the dark region he was now at.

Being a native Venezuelan, his father and grandfather had taught him to hunt, fish, and survive off the land, and it served him well now, mainly by being able to reduce the amount of supplies he needed to bring. Still, his pack sagged with the weight of the meteorological equipment he had brought with him.

He was determined to be at the plateau when the strange weather effects took place. He wanted to see for himself what the meteorological department's electronics' eyes and ears could not. He desperately wanted to know what actually caused their 'eyes in the sky' to become whited-out when trying to see down into that hidden tepui. And what the strange images were that looked like giant bat-like birds in the clouds he had seen exactly 10 years ago.

He had heard the legends of the monsters from the Amazon jungle that came down to claim the souls of the people once every half generation. He didn't believe any of them, but he did believe something strange was going on in there. His suspicion was that somehow the phenomena of the wettest season and the comet Primordia approaching were linked. He didn't know how, but right now, he believed in that more than it being something supernatural rising from the jungle.

He was only a day out now, and the ground was becoming mushy beneath his feet. There would be a waterway close by. He also knew that water and jungles meant insects, parasites, and in most cases, predators who came to drink or lie in ambush, waiting for prey animals to drink.

The only weapons he had brought with him were his hunting knives and his wits. He suddenly regretted not taking his father's old rifle.

Nicolás plodded on, and though the raucous sounds of the jungle masked his movements, he doubted they were hidden from any predators because his sounds were unnatural—two-legged creatures like him just didn't belong here.

After a moment, the buzzing, clicking, and humming of bugs, the scream of birds, plus the rustling of leaf litter all fell away. He stood in near silence in an open space about 10 feet square. It was only noon, but the heavy jungle canopy overhead made it seem like twilight.

Sweat streamed down his face, and the salty residue was attractive to all manner of flying things even though he had lathered repellent on himself and continued to do so every few hours. He knew it usually worked to keep the insects at bay, but it also advertised him blundering through the jungle inside a chemical cloud, probably 100 feet wide.

Nicolás stood quietly, turning his head slowly. He even made his breathing shallow and strained to hear anything approaching. He sensed danger, and the other creatures of the jungle did too. It could be anything—a jaguar, anaconda, or something else entirely. He eased in close to a tree trunk, keeping it at his back, that way he only had to worry about three sides, and if something did attack, he might have a chance of repelling it.

He had the urge to run but stood his ground. One thing was for sure: predators in a jungle were much better at chasing something down than he would be at fleeing.

Come on, he breathed. *Show yourself.*

The hairs on his body lifted and his scalp tingled from tension. He was being watched, he knew it, and he could feel his heart beating in his chest.

He was first grabbed around the neck. Whatever it was, it was fast and very quickly also wrapped around his forehead, and then he felt it sliding around his waist. The pressure was enormous, and with it came a stink that enveloped him and made his eyes water.

Nicolás yelled in surprise and fear and grabbed at the thing, feeling what seemed to be a thick snake, but instead of the dry scale feeling he expected, it was slick, slimy, and his hands slid away and were coated in a jelly-like mucus.

His eyes streamed from the chemicals, and then the pressure increased on his head and waist, and he felt himself begin to be lifted off his feet. He panicked then, punching at it, tearing and scrabbling, but he couldn't get a grip on the revolting thing.

"Help."

He thrashed some more, kicking his legs as he began to be lifted higher into the tree canopy.

"*Help!*"

He tried to grip the tree trunk with his legs to stop being lifted, but the thing that held him was far more powerful than he was.

Nicolás began to panic, becoming scared out of his wits at the thought of what would happen when the thing or things finally had him up and into the dense tree.

His eyes streamed and his breath was beginning to be cut off. He had seconds left.

"*He-eeelp!*"

*****

"Did you hear that?" Drake frowned and turned to Ben, but kept his head tilted, listening.

"Yeah, yeah, I did." Ben held up a hand, stopping the group.

"What is it?" Helen asked.

Chess and Francis hefted their guns; Shawna and Buster turned their backs on them, covering their rear.

"That was a voice," Chess said. "Up ahead; sounds like trouble."

"Yup." Ben nodded. "Let's go; low and quiet."

He and Drake led them out, Chess and Francis right behind, and then Helen, Shawna, and Buster.

Ben burrowed through the wall-thick jungle, making too much noise but not being able to help it. He'd been in far too many jungles now to know the signs of a predator—all around them the rest of the jungle held its breath and just watched.

He also knew from experience there was the pause during the stalking, and then the attack, and just like now, the sounds of the final death struggle. Often it attracted other predators and scavengers. If it was someone in trouble, Ben needed to be quick.

Ben was first into the small clearing and the group piled in fast, spreading left and right. Ben saw the pack on the ground and breathed in the stink.

"What the…?"

"Holy shit." Drake pointed the muzzle of his gun. "*Look!*"

About 10 feet up from the ground, someone struggled furiously. They were held aloft by something wrapped around his neck and waist, but it was what the things were attached to that made the hair on Ben's neck stand on end.

"Oh my God."

"*Monktopus*; bad news." Chess lifted his gun but couldn't fire. "No shot, no shot."

The thing was holding the man in front of it, but Ben could sort of make it out. It was a huge greenish-gray bag, five feet across and sprouting short, muscular tentacles. At the end of each limb, they formed a type of fork, like a two-fingered hand or two-toed foot. The worst thing was the large lidless eyes that were way too intelligent.

"A what?" Drake said, trying to angle his gun.

The snared man's face was turning purple and his tongue began to protrude. Even though the eyes bulged, they were panicked, and he was well on his way to being suffocated.

Ben lifted his gun and aimed—the thing seemed to know to use the guy's body as a shield, and it waved the choking man back and forth in front of it.

And then it moved him a few inches too far one way and Ben fired. The shot took a fist-sized chunk of meat from the bag-like head, and blue blood splashed the surrounding foliage.

It screamed.

"Shit." Drake took a step back.

It was an unnatural hellish sound like nails on a blackboard that made Ben grit his teeth. It threw the man at them and raised its tentacles, opening them like a flower and revealing a parrot-like beak underneath that was as long as his forearm. It snapped at him, angrily, and Ben fired three more times, hitting it again but only once.

Bizarrely, it swung away, as nimbly as an arboreal creature, and in seconds, it was gone. *Monktopus*, Chess had called it—a monkey-octopus.

"*Jesus H. Christ*," Drake said, and his mouth stayed hung open. "What the hell was that?"

Ben turned. "Helen, could that have come from…?"

"The plateau?" She shook her head. "No way. Besides, the doorway isn't even open yet. Nothing like that ever existed in the fossil record, or on any branch of evolution." She snorted. "It was an octopus, for God's sake."

"Like I said, a Monktopus," Chess said casually. "I thought you said you'd been in the Amazon before."

"Many times," said Ben.

"Me too," Drake added. "And never seen anything like that."

"They're rare, but inhabit the darker areas of the jungle, and usually close to a water source. That's where they lay their eggs," Francis said and shrugged huge shoulders. "That looked to be an 8 to10-footer, but they can get even bigger."

Ben turned to Helen. "They left the water."

She nodded slowly, but her eyes were now scanning the treetops. "Theorists always speculated they would. They're intelligent, strong, and adaptive." She turned. "The theorists also speculated that if mankind didn't exist, then cephalopods might one day rule the world."

"All hail our new multi-armed overlords." Chess turned and guffawed at Shawna.

A cough from the brush brought their heads around, and Shawna crossed to the Monktopus victim and stood over him. "Hey, whatta you know, he's still alive."

He coughed again and sat up rubbing his neck, but with his eyes screwed shut. He grimaced. "My eyes."

"Yep, that'd be the ammonia; stings like a bitch, dunnit?" Chess said. "The damn monks are covered in it. Stops them drying out when they're on land." Chess clicked his fingers at Shawna. "Flush it out or he'll be blind for days."

Shawna tilted his head back and lifted her canteen over his face. "Shut your eyes, honey." She first used her sweat rag to wipe his face off. "Now open them." She then let water trickle over his eyes. She wiped them again. "Better?"

He continued to blink as he nodded. "Yeah, thanks."

Ben went and stood in front of him. "Who are you, and what are you doing here?"

"Nicolás Manduro…" He coughed again and held out a hand. Shawna tugged him up. "Thank you again." He turned to Ben. "I work for the Venezuelan National Institute of Meteorological Services."

"You're a meteorologist? What the hell are you doing all the way out here?" Drake craned his neck forward. "Are you insane?"

"Probably." The young man grinned apologetically. "I forgot about the Monktopus. I don't know why I forgot." He sighed. "I came to investigate the source of the wettest season anomaly."

"Great," Ben said and exhaled. "Just great." He immediately knew he was going to get stuck with the guy.

"The wettest what?" Shawna guffawed. "That sounds like one of your porn tapes, Chess."

Chess brayed. "Private viewings only these days, babe." They both continued to laugh.

"That's enough," Ben said. He faced Nicolás. "What are, *were*, you planning to do?"

Nicolás began to grin. "You're going there too, aren't you?"

"I asked you a question." Ben gave him the 'glare' and the young man's smile dropped.

"I plan to scale as high as I can on the plateau and plant some measuring equipment." He frowned. "We can't see it from a distance; it shuts out all our sensors. Need to be closer, I guess." He frowned. "I think there's something strange going on up there."

"Yeah, din-o-sewers, according to these jokers." Chess' grin widened.

"You shouldn't climb the plateau," Drake said and glanced at Helen and then back at the meteorologist. "It's too dangerous."

"How do you know?" Nicolás' eyes narrowed. "You've been there before, haven't you?" He stepped forward. "I've seen something. Last time, 10 years ago, I saw a balloon entering, and then, I think—" He shook his head and then grabbed Ben's arm, "—no, *I know*, it was attacked by something big. Like a giant bat, but as large as an airplane."

"*Ah*, fuck." Ben looked heavenward.

"You *do* know something," Nicolás pressed.

"Yeah, we do. That was us in that balloon," Drake said.

Chess, Francis, and Shawna became silent.

Ben turned to the man. "We lost a lot of people. Only a few of us made it out alive. And three of those four are right here. Believe me when I tell you it's dangerous up there—deadly dangerous. You don't want to go there. There's more than just weird weather up there."

Helen nodded. "He's right, Nicolás. Maybe you can take your measurements from the base."

"That is not possible." Nicolás' expression hardened. "If you're going up there, then I'm going up there."

"Nicolás," Ben said. "The weather is not the anomaly. The weather is only a secondary effect from a magnetic comet that's passing overhead."

"I knew it." He clapped his hands together. "A magnetic astral anomaly; it makes perfect sense." Nicolás straightened to his full height of about five feet eight inches.

"It does?" Shawna frowned.

"Yes," Nicolás replied enthusiastically. "Correlation between changes in amplitude of geomagnetic variations of external origin could account for the significant but temporary, weather fluctuations."

"That was English, right?" Shawna looked impressed.

Nicolás nodded. "But I need to be up there for verification."

Chess snorted. "Buddy, you nearly got killed down here. If only half of what these guys say is true, your life expectancy will be about five minutes from setting foot up there. Here's some advice: fuck off home."

"I'm going," Nicolás said. "With you or without you." He paused. "But, preferably with you." He grinned sheepishly.

Shawna shrugged. "Aw, let the kid come with us. It's his life."

"Gets my vote." Buster's mouth twisted. "Shit goes down, my money is on him buying it first, rather than one of us."

Ben went and picked up Nicolás' pack. It was heavy. He tossed it to him. "How were you going to climb up a cliff face about 1,500 feet with that on your back?"

Nicolás pulled the backpack on. "I've got a power winch."

Drake chuckled. "Of course he has."

"He's not coming." Chess' eyes were half-lidded as he cradled his gun. "He'll slow us down, ghost us, and get us all killed."

Nicolás shrugged. "With or without you."

Drake exhaled. "He's more likely to get killed by himself, that's for sure. At least with us we can keep him under control."

"No," Chess said and lifted his chin to Ben. "Unless you throw in another hundred grand…each."

All eyes swung to Ben. Frankly, Ben couldn't give a shit whether the kid came with them or not. But now that Chess had made it a chest-bumping issue, he decided to play.

Ben's gaze was deadpan. "He comes, and if anyone tries to screw the deal we made, you can head home. Now." He grinned like a death's head. "And when you get home, you'll find your sign-on fee has been reversed out of your bank account, for being an asshole."

The group's gaze now swung to Chess. The big mercenary's jaw worked for a moment before he broke into a grin. "Who gives a fuck?"

He turned away, but Ben caught the lethal glare he threw him. He hoped he wasn't going to be trouble.

"Okay?" Nicolás asked.

"All okay," Shawna said.

Ben shook his head. "Well, you've been warned, but like she said…" He thumbed over his shoulder at Shawna. "It's your life." He turned to the female mercenary. "And you own him seeing as it was your idea."

Nicolás nodded. "Thank you."

"Come on." Ben checked his watch and then looked upward. Huge drops of blood-warm rain began to fall. "We've got about eight hours to get to the plateau base and then climb to the top. And our one-night stand is fast approaching."

CHAPTER 33

8 HOURS TO FULL COMET APPARITION

Comet P/2018-YG874, designate name Primordia, hurtled through the solar system on its approach toward the Earth. The magnetic bow wave that preceded it caused collisions between electrically charged particles in the planet's upper atmosphere, creating an aurora borealis effect over the jungles of South America.

In one of the most inaccessible parts of the eastern Venezuelan jungle, clouds began to darken, and in another minute or two, they started to swirl and boil like in a devil's cauldron, throwing down a torrent of warm rain.

Beneath the clouds, a gigantic tabletop mountain became cloaked in the dense fog, and brutal winds began to smash at its sides and surface. Thunder roared and lightning seemed to come from the sky, air, and even up from the ground itself.

The echoes of roars from throats not heard for many millions of years began to ring out that even drowned out the crash of thunder. Soon, those few roars would become a cacophony of hissing, howls, bellows, and screams, rising to be like those from the dark pits of Hell.

It had been 10 years since the last wettest season and it had arrived again, and with it came the primordial sounds of a world not seen for 100 million years.

CHAPTER 34

Andy rubbed his eyes. He and Gluck had been on the sea for many days now, and he was taking advantage of a breeze at his back and making good time. But a few times, he had ventured so far out that he had begun to lose sight of the land.

His navigation skills were good, and he could get his bearings from the sun, moon, and stars, but if he lost touch with the shoreline and clouds moved in, he could be lost.

His supplies were running low, and he blinked crusty eyes and licked flaking lips. The sea was misty, blurring his vision even more, and only after many minutes did it become clear that it really was an island in the distance.

He had been becalmed for the last few hours and his sail hung limply so he had to rely on the tide and currents to move him along. He guessed he was getting closer to his destination, as the heat was once again tropical. So far, he had been conserving his energy, but now with a goal in sight, he began to gently paddle toward the land.

He knew that the water he passed over here was deep and a bottomless dark blue, so he needed to make as little noise as he could manage. He dipped the makeshift oar in and dragged it all the way back along his boat. Carefully, he lifted it and did the same on the other side.

In another hour, he was closing in on the landmass, and the sea bottom suddenly began to shallow quickly, telling him that the island might have been the tip of an extinct volcano, or even the last in line of a sunken mountain range.

He gently pulled the boat forward and in another hour, he was close enough to see that the island was covered in vegetation, but he hoped small and far enough from the mainland to not support a population of large carnivores. Or better yet, any carnivores at all.

He soon made it to the outer reef, and then waited in his boat and just watched. He could see plenty of small sea pterosaurs just like Gluck, and his small friend seemed to become excited and answered their strange clucking and clicking with his own songs of the sky and sea.

Andy guessed the island was only about a mile around and had breakwaters circling it, creating small pools in close rather than sandy beaches, some small and some larger than swimming pools. The flora to the center of the island were mainly upright trees with few branches on the trunks that had initially looked like palm trees from a distance but were more likely a form of spiky cycad on a large fibrous stem that grew 40 feet in the air. Fast-growing palms and ferns made up the rest of the ground cover.

The more he watched, the more he became convinced there was nothing living on the island but the flying reptiles.

"Just like New Zealand," he whispered.

Andy had visited the island nation off the east coast of Australia once on holiday, and he found it an amazing Petri dish for scientists due to it being an entire biosphere built around one animal form—birds. When it had broken away from Gondwanaland some 400 million years ago, much of it sank, but then several hundred million years later, it was finally pushed back to the surface. But following the mass extinction that ended the age of the dinosaurs, the new rulers came from the sky.

There were the predators and prey, from the herbivores such as giant Moa that stood 12 feet tall, plus a dozen other species of giant parrot, ground dwellers such as the kiwi with fur-like feathers, long-legged wading birds, and also fearsome raptors, such as the Haast, the largest eagle to have ever existed on the planet and weighed in at well over 500 pounds. They could have easily carried off a full-grown man if they had survived.

But thankfully, the tiny island Andy watched seemed home to little more than nesting pterosaurs no larger than seagulls.

"I think it's safe," he whispered and pushed a still-excited Gluck down into the bottom of the boat.

Andy carefully guided his vessel in through rocky corridors of the outer reef, and soon entered calm water that was warm, crystal clear, and only a few feet deep. The first thing he noticed was that the inner pools were teeming with fish, probably trapped by the tides, and he grinned, knowing that food wasn't going to be the problem here.

He pulled his boat up on the rocks. In one hand, he held his spear, while he pulled out his empty water bottles for refilling with the other. He also drew his bag onto his shoulder to carry Gluck to the shore.

"Let's explore."

He put Gluck down and his little friend waddled after him as he crossed the tide-line. Andy noted where the surf had come to, and he surmised that it was close to high tide right now, so his boat drifting away wasn't going to be a problem. Also, the reef barrier should keep out anything larger than a salmon-sized fish, so the large marine predators shouldn't bother him. Though he knew that the sea crocodiles could cross the reef if they wanted to, it was far too shallow for them to conceal themselves.

He entered the thicket and immediately encountered the pterosaur nesting sites. In among the squabbling and furiously scolding flying reptiles, he managed to steal several eggs without losing too much skin from his hands. He did have to rescue Gluck who obviously seemed to think of himself as part of Andy's gang or flock now and went to attack several of the creatures that tried to peck at his big friend.

The one thing that Andy noticed was that the nesting sites weren't built upon one another as he expected from a species coming to the same area over and over. He started to have an inkling of why there were no other terrestrial animals living here.

His next discovery confirmed his suspicions.

Toward the center of the island, piled up against two stout-looking tree trunks, were the remains of a huge animal. Great curving ribs rose high above his head, each as thick as his thigh. A massive skull, 10 feet long, lay on the sandy soil, and on its surface were patches of sun-dried leathery skin.

He saw that it had no arms and legs, but the remains of flippers. Andy went and ran a hand along the skull, and then exhaled.

"You didn't crawl in here, did you?"

He looked around, seeing everything with a clearer eye—this was why the pterosaur nests only looked to be a dozen or so years old, and not hundreds: a huge wave had deposited the massive sea beast's carcass here. More than likely, the area was subjected to huge storms and might be totally submerged from time to time. If Andy were caught here during one, then not being able to fly away like the pterosaurs meant he'd be drowned.

"Short visit only then, I guess."

Andy crossed back to the rocky beach. It was already late when he arrived, and he decided he had time to wade out and grab some fish, shells, or anything else he could catch for dinner. Accommodation was easy, as he had learned that sometimes simply turning his boat over and sleeping underneath was the safest option and cut off his sounds and smells from interested predators.

He waded out into the bath-warm water and as he went, he grabbed one of the pterosaur eggs from his bag, put it to his mouth, and used his teeth to bite through the leathery covering. He ripped it away and sucked most of the fluid out. It was fishy tasting, rich, and oily. If he was back in his own time, his stomach might have rebelled at the strong flavors, but he had trained himself to eat all manner of things to survive, and hunger meant any food was good food.

The contents also contained the beginning of a small pterosaur, and rather than eat this, he lowered it into the bag for Gluck to greedily gobble down.

"You know that's cannibalism, right?" He grinned and then tossed the shell fragments into the water before him where they created a milky cloud as their remaining fluid leaked out.

Fish almost immediately began to dart through it. On the bottom were numerous almost perfectly circular rocks or growths that looked like flat plates about a foot around or perhaps were some sort of scallop, and as Andy lifted his spear over the silver torpedoes, one of the discs opened and something that looked like a stubby, sandy-colored eel shot out.

"Holy shit." He backed up, but then swung his arms, not wanting to set foot on any of the discs behind him.

The thing had been all mouth and teeth, and had grabbed one of the fish and drew back into its lair with an amazing speed. It seemed to be some sort of stonefish species, but obviously something that never made it into the fossil record.

As Andy watched, more and more of the jack-in-a-box ambushes took place due to the feeding frenzy he had created. The ambush-eels didn't seem that large, more double-football sized, but looked more frightening than they were due to their front half being all mouth that was full of needle teeth.

Thankfully, big two-legged land creatures weren't that interesting to them, and as he backed up to the shore, he still managed to spear a few fish on the way. It looked like there was going to be plenty for everyone.

That evening after he and Gluck had eaten their fill, he sat close to the shoreline with his back against a tree and looked up at the night sky. The stars were enormously bright, and the moon so close he felt he could almost reach out and touch it. In fact, it really *was* closer, and the constellations of stars were very different at this time.

Andy inhaled, drawing in the warm scents of the ocean, dry beach, plants, and even the fishy odor of the pterosaur nests. The flying reptiles had quietened down for the night and there was just the soft shushing of the surf out against the far reef. The evening's warmth, combined with the isolation of his little island, made him feel safer than he had in years.

"I love everything about this place." He smiled contentedly as Gluck climbed up onto his lap and nestled down. "Helen will too."

He stroked the pterosaur, and it made a small noise like cooing. Andy sighed and felt a little down knowing he had to set off again next morning. But they weren't far from home now, and the thought of seeing his sister again rallied his spirits.

"Yeah, she'll love this place as much as I do. I *know* she will." Andy leaned his head back against the tree and began to doze.

CHAPTER 35

"A DOORWAY TO HELL BEGINNING TO OPEN."

"There it is." Ben held up a hand and stopped the group.

The rain fell in large drops that felt like warm oil but its curtains still couldn't hide the sight that met their eyes.

Through the mad tangle of green vines and creepers, there was the outline of the monolithic plateau's cliff wall, rising to vanish into the dark clouds over 1,000 feet above it.

"We made it." Nicolás tried to push past him but Ben grabbed his shoulder and yanked him back.

Nicolás shrugged him free. "The abnormal effects—the clouds, wind, and rain, all just over the plateau, exactly as we thought." He turned. "Technically, I know how this happens. But physically seeing it, I still can't believe it."

"You haven't seen anything yet," Helen said from Drake's shoulder.

An eerie bellow rang out, followed by an unearthly shriek that was suddenly cut off. The group looked from one to the other and finally Nicolás swallowed hard and spoke.

"What…was that?"

"A doorway to Hell beginning to open." Ben continued to stare up at the plateau.

"We told you." Drake turned to Nicolás. "It's not just the weather that gets all screwy."

"Whoa." Nicolás blew air between his lips.

Ben checked his watch. The rubberized analog-casing watch still worked as he hoped. "Okay, we've got four hours until Primordia is right over us and the doorway opens. An hour's trek, give or take, until we're at its base where we'll make camp and grab a last coffee. Then I estimate another hour to make it to the summit using the winches. That should put us right on the money."

Ben had pulled free a small pair of binoculars and scanned the jungle ahead. "We can't be there too soon, and need to time it so we are right there when the anomaly is underway—from then, we'll have about 20 hours to find Andy."

He glanced at Helen. "And bring him back."

Another scream boomed out from overhead but was lost amid a rolling peal of thunder.

"Shit, a doorway to Hell, you said?" Shawna looked up toward the top of the plateau where the purple-black clouds were spinning like the center of a small hurricane.

"Consider it an echo," Ben said. "From a long, long time ago." He turned to her. "What, you thought I was making it all up?"

Shawna hiked her shoulders and then turned back to the plateau.

"Okay, let's go." Ben led them on.

The ground now sloped upward, and the jungle opened out a little. The trees began to look more alien, exactly as Ben remembered—possibly hybridized from the seed drift from above, or for all he knew now, entire new species that had evolved through their messing around in the past.

Several more times, the light had blinked out, and each time it stayed dark for a little longer. After one of the times, Chess had yanked him harshly back, and Ben spun to find the lead mercenary putting a finger to his lips and then pointing to a place just up ahead of them.

"*Cryptis*," he whispered. "Bad news."

What? Ben mouthed as Drake and Helen bunched up behind him. He spotted movement and squinted to see through the falling rain. Some sort of creature fossicked on the ground, sinuous and many-legged. It was covered in chitinous scales, and looked like a three-foot centipede, but had long back legs like a grasshopper. But it was out front that the nightmare really began—pincers longer than his fingers and blood red.

"Poisonous," Chess said softly. "And very fucking aggressive." He tugged on Ben again. "And there's usually more in the nest. We go around."

Ben nodded and backed up, thankful the falling rain was masking their retreat.

After another half hour, they reached the base of the plateau and Ben finally pointed to a small open space.

"We do an equipment check. Anything we don't need we leave here. From now on, we travel fast and light."

The group set to dropping packs and arming up—weapons were slung on bodies and placed in sheaths, holsters, and pouches. Food was only a single canteen and a few protein bars.

Drake, Ben, and the mercenaries were like drilled machines as they went over their gear. Helen carefully added and removed items, and Nicolás frowned as he checked much of his equipment pile.

"It's dead." Nicolás held out a small black box. "This ionization meter; it was fully charged when I left, but it's telling me that the battery is now fully drained."

"You heard that bit about magnetic interference, right?" Drake kept reloading his now lighter pack. "Like an EMP wave—knocks everything out and will stay out for the next 24 hours."

"He's right," Ben said. "So leave it here, as it won't miraculously start working if you lug it all the way to the top."

"But…" Nicolás shook his head. "I need it."

Ben stopped what he was doing. "No, you need working equipment. You don't need dead weight. I cannot impress on you the need to be able to travel fast, silently, and lightly as can be." He stared. "Doing otherwise will get you dead."

"Or worse, maybe get *us* dead," Drake added.

Ben sat with his back to a tree and pushed his hat forward to give him some cover from the warm rain. "And now, smoke 'em if you got em." He pulled out one of his protein bars and ripped open the foil cover.

High above them came a long bellow that continued on for several seconds before being abruptly cut off. Ben chewed mechanically, knowing exactly what it was: the world of tooth and claw was waking up—and it was hungry.

CHAPTER 36

Emma froze, coffee cup gripped in one hand, as the lights went out, leaving her in a blackness that was deeper than the void of space. She wasn't even sure if she breathed, but this one seemed to go on and on, and by the time she tried to bring her senses to bear on it, it was over.

When the light came back, the first thing she did was race to the window. The sun was getting ready to go down and evening's dusk was only about an hour away when the blackout had occurred. Nothing had changed about the sunset. But that was about all that was the same.

Her back straightened as she stared. The rolling, dry plains and weird herds of savannah-like beasts that were there only minutes ago were now gone. In their place were colossal trees that each spread over hundreds of feet. They could have been fig trees except for the massive branches hung with basketball-sized fruits like blaring red melons.

Birds swooped from branch to branch; and further in, she could just make out movement at their bases and in their canopies. But the twilight shadows were too deep for her to see clearly what was in there.

The one thing she had learned was that with every change, there came potential new dangers. It was like evolution was trying out different things, showing them all the paths it could have taken with minuscule adjustments along the way. And because she was outside of the changes, she had no idea, no education, nor life experience on how to deal with them.

She picked up the phone. Her neighbors Frank and Allie were good sources of information, so she called them.

The phone rang out, which was strange given the time. They were a few years older than she and Ben and given it was midweek, she doubted they had a dinner date.

She hung up and dialed them again—same result. Emma put the phone down slowly as she continued to stare out the large window toward the massive tree forest. Should she go visit them? She'd been meaning to try and patch things up ever since Ben had been over there demanding their dog back—that she now knew never existed.

She'd spoken to them a few times, but though cordial, there had been strain between their households now. Might be a good idea to get Zach and herself out of the house for an hour or two anyway. She had been going crazy being stuck at home doing nothing but worrying about Ben, and every minute now seemed an eternity. She craved activity, and she knew that Zach needed it as well.

"Zach," she called. "We're going for a drive."

"*Aww*, why?" From somewhere deeper in the house.

She smiled. *Here we go again*, she thought and grabbed her coat and the car keys and headed for the door, pausing at the bottom of the steps.

"Come on, Zachy, we're just going to visit Frank and Allie next door."

The groan managed to contain every atom of indignation a six-year-old boy could muster, and she smiled as she put her coffee cup down on the edge of the table and went to pull open the front door. She was immediately assailed by the new odors of spoiling fruit, plant sap, and rich forest soil.

She exhaled long and slow as she stared—rolling English countryside green hills, to Serengeti plains, and now some sort of giant tree forest. *The evolutionary changes are rolling forward faster and faster*, she thought. It reminded her of those multiple drawings done on the edge of paper, each one slightly different, and when you flicked through them, it made them move faster and faster. It seemed that evolution was in a hurry and speeding to catch up. But to what?

She heard Zach rumble on the steps—but from down in the basement, not from his room upstairs.

"Mum, are you *mad?*" he asked, his features twisted. "Shut the door."

"What?" Emma frowned.

He pointed past her, his eyes wide. "*Shut the door, shut the door.*"

Emma was confused to the point of inaction, and her son ran to her, grabbed her arm, dragging her back inside, and then gently closed the door.

"We shouldn't even be up here now. You know that." He pointed to the window. "*Aw*, Mom, you haven't even closed the shutters."

Emma saw real fear on her boy's face. She suddenly felt rising panic in the pit of her stomach.

"Zach, please, help me understand. I, *um*, had another of my memory blackouts. Tell me what's happening?" She stopped him and stared down into his face that seemed drained of color.

"The time, the *desmos*; remember?" He began to drag her to the basement. But as she approached, she saw it was somehow different. The previous wooden door leading down the stairs was now a fortified sheet of steel set into reinforced concrete.

"The what?" she asked.

"*Shush*, they'll hear us." Zach looked past her, his eyes wide. "The sun's down. They'll be out now."

"The *desmos*? What are they?" She started to raise her voice as panic took hold.

Zach put his finger to his lips, but looked past her, and his eyes widened even further. "Oh no, the bolt."

She turned. Beside the door was now a thick beam and two metal braces where it was supposed to slot on behind the door to hold it. He left her and sprinted toward it. On his way, he knocked her coffee cup from the table, where it hit the tiled floor and exploded into a hundred pieces. He froze from the loud noise, his hands up and teeth bared in a fearful grimace.

Emma had never seen such fear on his face like this, and it broke her heart.

"Zach?" She stepped toward him, just as one of the huge side windows blew inward with a massive spray of glass.

And something came in with it.

It hit the ground and immediately came upright. The thing was roughly man-shaped, but taller and thinner. However, not frail as it was covered in a dark, sinewy muscle, and when it turned to her, Emma felt her blood run cold.

The head was rounded and the face flat with a large mouth and protruding fangs. There was no nose, just a triangular-shaped double slit that operated wetly as it sniffed the room. And above that nasal cavity were two huge black eyes. Though standing taller than a man, it used its long front arms for locomotion as its back legs looked almost comically stunted, and between the arms and legs was a thin membrane.

It clicked, mewled, and squeaked as it sniffed and craned toward them. Emma had frozen in shock, but Zach broke the spell.

"*Run!*" he yelled.

Her muscles unlocked, and she headed to the front sitting room. Zach scurried away in a different direction, and the thing hopped and flapped leathery wings trying to get after her, but found the confines of the room hard to navigate. Still, it was fast and strong. Furniture was pushed aside as it skipped over some and bullocked other pieces out of its way.

"*Hey, hey.*" Emma was frantic, trying to stay ahead of it, as well as consciously trying to lead it away from her son.

Desmos, Zach had called them. Now she made the connection after seeing the monstrosity; she'd come across something like them before when she was cave climbing down in Brazil—*Desmodontinae*—the scientific name for a bat. And not just any bat, but the ones that drank blood; *the vampire bat.*

She winced as she wedged herself in beside the broom closet. They were different than other bats in that, while bats mostly lost the ability to maneuver on land, vampire bats could walk, jump, and even run by using a unique, hopping gait, in which the forelimbs instead of the hind-limbs are recruited for locomotion, as the wing arms are much more powerful than the legs.

This was the ability the bat thing was using now. She wracked her brain trying to remember more details—they had good vision, a sense of smell like a bloodhound, and one other thing, saliva that was an anticoagulant, so when they bit, the blood didn't clot and continued to flow for them to drink.

She heard the thing snuffling and smelled the acrid stink of it. Emma wedged herself in deeper and looked about for a weapon. She didn't get it; vampire bats were tiny and usually no bigger than her thumb. But this creature was huge, standing about seven feet tall. The other horrifying fact she recalled as it closed in on where she concealed herself was they could eat nearly their entire weight in blood. She had no doubt that this beast could completely drain both her and Zach if it got the chance.

Oh God—she had another horrifying thought—it probably wouldn't be alone for long.

Now she knew why the basement was fortified, and why there was a huge bolt for the front door and shutters on all the windows. Zach knew about them, but she didn't. Whether she liked it or not, being immune to the changes going on around her was no advantage and would get her and Zach killed.

Where was Zach?

The creature was closing in on her, and she was at least thankful for that. Because if it wasn't searching for her, it meant it was searching for her son.

Emma needed a weapon, and the gun that Ben had left her was in its holster and hanging by the front door. She looked about; close by was the knife block. She carefully reached out and withdrew the largest carving knife she had, the one with the 14-inch stainless steel, laser-sharpened blade. She gripped it, hard.

Emma had stayed in shape, continuing her rock-climbing routine, and the one thing she could count on was a grip-strength well beyond that of a normal person.

She held her breath as the acrid fumes surrounding the thing grew stronger. She heard it sniffing along the floor, obviously tracking her footprints.

She lifted her knife arm higher.

"*Hey!*" Zach appeared in the doorway and threw something that shattered near the creature. He then darted away, and the monstrous bat immediately turned to follow. Emma launched herself from her hiding space and buried the blade between its bony shoulder blades. The knife sunk in a good four inches, but the bat turned and the hardened blade snapped in half, leaving its tip behind.

It swept an arm back, knocking her off her feet, but she was up and sprinting hard while the thing skittered and jumped, trying to dislodge the piece of blade still in its back.

Emma rounded the corner and saw Zach at the basement door, holding it half ajar—his teeth were bared and his eyes were as wide as she'd ever seen them. She could tell by the way his eyes moved from her to just behind her that the thing was bearing down on her.

"*Move!*" she yelled.

He stood aside and she dived. In a single motion, he slammed the door, just as a huge weight crashed against it.

Emma rolled onto her back and placed her feet against the door. She didn't really need to as the solid steel was designed to keep the monsters out—she just didn't know it until then.

She turned to face Zach, still breathing like a steam train. "Desmos, *huh?*"

He nodded slowly. "Did you have one of your forget-about-things times again?"

She nodded and smiled.

He came and hugged her. "I'll remember for you."

"Thank you." She returned the hug, and then held him back so she could talk to him. "How did they get so big?"

"They've always been that big." He seemed to get it then. "Oh, you don't know. Well, Mr. Abernathy, our science teacher, said they used to feed on big animals like the land whales, but…"

"Land whales?" Emma lifted her head for a moment before easing it back down. "Save it for another time."

Zach nodded, "…they used to feed on big animals like the land whales, but when they all died out, they started looking for other things to eat."

"Like us." She snorted softly.

"Yeah." He shrugged. "They can have the night, and we can have the day. Works out okay." He waggled a finger at her, grinning. "As the saying goes: you'll be able to sleep at night, as long as your windows and doors are locked nice and tight."

"That's good advice." She let her head rest on the concrete and knew then that this was not their world anymore. She shut her eyes and breathed deeply. "So what comes next?"

CHAPTER 37

SOUTH AMERICA, 52 MILES FROM THE PLATEAU—100 MILLION YEARS AGO

2 DAYS BEFORE PRIMORDIA

Andy ran, hard, keeping his head down and arms pumping as he used his slim frame to dart, burrow, and dodge through animal tracks that were little more than tunnels bored through the tangled green maze of the jungle.

Behind him, the predators closed in—a pack of them, theropods, *Austroraptor* probably—about 400 pounds each, covered in tiny, shimmering feathers that looked like scales, and with their long hard snouts filled with razor teeth, they seemed like a cross between a bird and an upright alligator.

They had flushed him out before he could find cover, and he prayed that the jungle stayed as closed in as it was because he knew that if he broke into open territory, he was as good as dead.

Unfortunately, they were a large raptor species and big and strong enough to bullock their way after him, and their sense of smell meant there'd be no hiding behind any fallen logs.

Andy had been trying to move as quickly as he could manage back to the plateau in time for the arrival of Primordia, and he stupidly had been breaking all his own rules for survival—travel by night, be quiet, invisible, silent as a ghost, and where possible, coat himself in mud or plant sap.

Instead, he had taken to wearing strings of vines over himself like a homemade ghillie suit that had worked a treat to break up his outline and also cover his odor. Well, it usually worked.

But he forgot that the raptors were smart, and learned quickly, and you could only fool them for so long before they worked out what was really happening. He recalled from his paleontological studies that they were probably as smart as dogs—he knew now that wasn't true at all— they were far smarter than anyone realized, and he guessed he should have been thankful that at least this one species was wiped out during the great Cretaceous–Paleogene extinction event or instead of humans, it would have been them as rulers of Earth if evolution had allowed them to progress.

Andy paused for a split second at a fork in his green tunnel. It was long enough to hear that the lead pursuer could only have been 50 feet at most behind him. He chose, going left, the smaller tunnel, and he crouch-ran as he burrowed onward.

Then to his horror, he broke cover into bright sunlight and had to sprint hard to cross a small clearing unusually devoid of any plants. Behind him, the *Austroraptor* broke through as well. Andy's eyes were wide with panic, as he knew he had never been a sprint champion, and even though he had a head start, he was racing something as fast as a cheetah.

Andy's teeth were bared as he concentrated on the opposing wall of jungle, but he could already hear the hissing breath of the carnivore as it must have been craning forward, mouth open, to sink its row of razor teeth into his shoulder.

And then he was falling.

Beneath him, there was no more ground, and as Andy fell into space, his mind screamed: *sinkhole*, way too late, as he had already fallen through the thin layer of vines hiding the deep cavity in the earth.

He wasn't the only one, as he heard the massive raptor fall as well.

Andy splashed down first into the pool of dark, fetid water, followed by the larger eruption as the creature fell in beside him.

He came to the surface first, tasting brackish, stagnant water, and something sweet like corrupting flesh. He immediately thrashed to the slick rocky shore.

From above, sunlight streamed down, throwing a halo of light onto the sunken pond. The raptor rose up as well, but was more stunned and confused, as its larger body had undoubtedly struck the bottom of the shallow basin of water.

Andy seized the moment to clamber higher in the darkness and squeeze himself in between two boulders, trying to wedge himself in as far as the tiny gap would allow.

The theropod stayed in the middle of the pond, tilting its head to look upward. It began to make a series of short barks, and from high above, it was answered. A number of boxy-looking reptilian heads craned to look down, but its pack could do nothing.

You're trapped like me, sucker, Andy thought as his eyes began to better adjust to the gloom.

Andy quickly looked around to better understand his predicament: they were in some sort of sinkhole pocket. There was a pond of soupy water at its center, and the walls were slick and rising sheer for about 50 feet to then curve in toward a small opening at the top. Depressingly, Andy also saw that there were animal bones lumping the water and around the pond edge—this sinkhole had probably been trapping unwary beasts for thousands of years.

Turning back to the roof, Andy saw what could have been vines hanging down. He might be able to climb out when the time was right—he looked back down at the pond and at the raptor standing at its center—and if he could survive long enough.

Above, the raptor pack pulled back and then vanished. The lone creature stuck in the hole with him let out a long hiss that turned to a scream of frustration. It stomped around in the small pound for a few seconds, swung its head to look along the slick walls, and then stopped to stare into the crevice where Andy was hiding.

Oh shit, he thought and stared back while trying to wedge himself in even tighter. He glanced up at the vines and knew he'd never make it.

The box-like head began to swing slowly away, when a tiny voice floated up from the bag tied over his shoulder.

"Is it gone?"

Andy grimaced and clutched at the bag, squeezing the small pterosaur to silence it as the head swung back to them. The *Austroraptor* began to move out of the water, its head now craned forward and directly at him.

Andy quickly looked up again, calculating, but no matter how many options his mind presented him, he knew the reality was there was no way he'd be able to clamber to and then up a vine quickly enough. Plus, the slick walls were impossible to scale, and from what he could make out in the darkness, the cavity they were in was pretty much the size of a double bedroom so he had nowhere else to go—he was royally screwed.

The raptor took another step toward him, but then suddenly became motionless. It slowly turned its head to the side as if listening. Andy also froze, thinking that the thing was trying to get his bearings again—it had night vision like a cat, hearing far beyond his own, and a sense of smell like a bloodhound. It would eventually ferret him out, no matter how dark it was, or how well he concealed himself.

But then it slowly turned away, and began to hunch over and hiss into the darkness. Behind the column of light streaming into the center of the sinkhole, Andy thought he heard another sound—a soft noise he could just make out that was like a typewriter's keys being struck. He eased out a fraction, concentrating his senses.

The raptor turned again, obviously aware of the sound and probably a smell that was beyond Andy's senses to detect. Whatever it was, the raptor could hear and smell it, but hadn't found the source yet.

Then came the soft *zizzing* of water as if something was being poured into the stagnant pool.

"I think we got company," Andy whispered.

The theropod stayed in the light with its mouth hanging open, small arms outstretched and shoulders hunched in an attack posture. Andy felt a chill run up his spine as he saw that the fearsome raptor had detected a threat that was even creeping *it* out.

Then from the dank water behind the great beast, something began to rise up, higher and higher. It looked like a flattened pipe, and Andy at first thought it was a snake or the long neck of a creature, but that thought was dispelled as sharp legs began to unfurl all along the body, dozens and dozens of them, and then they stretched outward, as if they longed for an embrace.

It continued to rise, nearly 10 feet and above the theropod. He recognized it now, a centipede, and in the sunlight, its head was a glossy, fire engine red and at its front, a formidable pair of pincers opened about two feet wide.

Andy knew that right here in this land, in modern times, lived the *Scolopendra gigantea*, the largest centipede in the world…at that time. It grew to nearly 16 inches long, was venomous, and loved living in caves where it fed off bat colonies.

But in the Cretaceous, there lived its ancestors, evolving from the mighty *arthropleura*, an eight-foot-long segmented insect of the Permian Period. Andy didn't need to be told that this thing was a hunter and they had both fallen right into its killing ground.

The theropod must have become aware of the centipede as it spun, but faster than it could react, the massive arthropod darted forward, fixing its wickedly sharp pincers into the *Austroraptor*'s neck and then its body wrapping around like segmented tape to then allow its sharp legs to hook into the flesh.

The raptor screamed with a noise that made Andy want to cover his ears, and he wasn't sure if the thing was injecting venom, or who would win, as he couldn't look away.

"*Now, Andy, now, now!*" a voice screamed at him from within his bag.

Andy didn't need to be told twice. If he didn't get out, then he'd be the next thing being filled full of prehistoric venom and devoured slowly in this miasmic sinkhole.

He ran along the pond edge and reached the first vine, grabbed it, and tugged.

"Nope."

It broke free and fell down heavily to the cave floor. The sounds of battle continued and he quickly glanced back to the pond. He saw that another long and flattened body had risen up in the dark water.

"*Crap*, there's more."

He tried again.

"*Shit.*"

Same result, and the next as well. Andy started to feel giddy from fear and refused to look back to the water now, even though the sounds of thrashing had ended as the battle had been decided.

He tried again and finally found one that supported his weight and began to clamber upward.

He didn't stop climbing, arm over arm, for once thanking his meager diet for shrinking his body weight. Nearing the surface, he felt the vine begin to stretch and then jiggle. He chanced another look back and to his horror saw the blood-red head of one of the massive centipedes coming up the vine after him.

He whimpered and felt his hands and arms go weak from fear for a split second. In his mind, he could imagine the large pincers closing on his bony ankles and then dragging him back down into the darkness.

Fear then gave him a shot of adrenaline-fueled energy that made him cover the last 15 or so feet in seconds. He poked his head above the surface, didn't even bother looking for the raptor pack, rolled to the ground, got to his feet, and sprinted into the jungle.

At the first huge hairy tree trunk, he stopped to look back and get his bearings. He tried to slow his breathing and the nausea he felt from fatigue.

Andy could see the broken vines over the hole in the ground and for a moment something started to breach, but perhaps the sunlight made it change its mind, and nothing eventually emerged.

He exhaled, and then doubled over and vomited. Nothing came up but yellow bile.

"*Gluck?*"

Andy opened the bag and smiled in at the tiny pterosaur.

"Yeah, you're right, we were nearly bug food. But we're okay now."

He wiped his mouth on his forearm and turned toward the east, the direction of the plateau.

"I damn well hope this is worth it."

Andy got to his feet and continued on.

CHAPTER 38

FULL COMET APPARITION

"This is *fucking* madness." Chess' eyes were slits as he hung onto his rope as the wind exploded around them, making him twist and bounce.

Ben checked his watch—the time distortion should happen any minute now, according to his calculations. They had started their climb half an hour ago and were all suspended at different levels of between 500 and 600 feet up from the jungle floor.

Above them, the sky on top of the plateau was purple-black and boiling like a witch's cauldron. Heavy rain fell, but the wind was so erratic that the drops lifted and seemed to be coming from everywhere at once and then heading upward as though being sucked up into a vacuum.

Ben knew that the comet Primordia was reaching what was termed its *perigee* or maximum observable focus, as it had reached its closest point to Earth. They *must* continue on, and must do it now.

"Hang on!" Ben yelled back. "It'll soon…"

The magnetic distortion reached its peak, and with it was generated a form of stability. The hurricane-like winds that had been roaring above the top of the plateau ceased, and the boiling clouds dropped to become a mist that moved through a primordial forest.

"…stop," Ben finished.

Torrential rain still fell around them, but high above, Ben could now see an oasis of light forming. He knew that on the plateau the sunlight would be breaking through.

But the anomaly was that it wasn't breaking through on their world, or in their time. Where they were going was somewhere far older and far away. But only in time.

"Climb, now!" he yelled and engaged his winch that began to drag him higher.

Now was the time, now the season of Primordia had begun.

PART 3—Pellucidar is but a realm of your imagination.

"A man who dares to waste one hour of time has not discovered the value of life" — Charles Darwin

CHAPTER 39

SOUTH AMERICA, AMAZON, 100 MILLION YEARS AGO

Andy had scaled to the top of a tree and lifted his head above the hair-like fronds to stare up at the plateau.

Even though he had lived, or rather, survived, for 10 years in this time, and seen creatures living that were long just fossilized bones in a museum, it still amazed him when he saw evidence of time passing—the monolithic flat-topped mountain, or tepui, was only just beginning to have the surrounding jungle weathered down around it. Over the millions and millions of years to come, the jungle would sink, while the harder granite 'plug' would erode more slowly, making it seem to rise like an island into the sky. But now, it was just a slightly raised area in a vast primordial world.

Rain had started to fall an hour or so back, but that was nothing compared to what was happening over the plateau—surrounding it was a curtain of rain, almost like a shield. It reminded him of some sort of titan's shower stall with the splash curtain pulled around it. Overhead, the clouds were boiling and turning slowly like they were being stirred, and the constant sheets of rain made it indistinct.

Andy grinned. "Behold the return of the great God, Primordia," he whispered.

Andy looked up, but there was nothing to see above, as the clouds were too thick. But he knew they wouldn't be for much longer. Soon, when the vortex stabilized, the maelstrom would dissolve and sunshine would rule on the plateau once again.

He smiled, wondering if someone was already on their way coming to look for him. He wondered when they arrived, what would it look like? Would they beam down and materialize from the future like they did in a Star Trek teleporter?

His grin widened, remembering that it wasn't that special, and in fact, it had been as simple as walking through a gossamer sheet, that had made him feel slightly flippy in the stomach for a second or two, and then he was there.

As he watched, the cloud started to drop, creating a misted atmosphere on the plateau. It would still be dripping with humidity but he knew now that at its center, the cloudbank would break and rise.

The oily curtain remained, but beams of light began to shine down like beacons. Andy eased back down in his treetop perch and watched for another few moments. His hand was half-mutilated, his skin was covered in scars, and his body that was once slightly pudgy was now whip thin and nothing but stringy, sunburned muscle. Hell, even his teeth hurt, not from any sort of sugary diet, but from having to, at times, eat food that was bordering on being tougher than boot leather.

He opened his bag to let the small flying reptile out. Gluck immediately set to hopping around and chasing down bugs for a quick meal.

"Save some for me." He grinned and then turned about, looking back along the valley. Things hooted, squealed, and screamed out of a green world. Things that looked like thick tree trunks rose from the green ocean and at their top were explosions of spiky leaves. Medium-sized pterosaurs glided from tree to tree, some chasing insects as long as his arm that glittered on membrane wings.

There were other massive trees that climbed into the clouds, some primitive pines, gingkoes, and redwoods, with smoke-like mist curling in and around the canopies, and he knew below them the forest highways created by eons-old animal tracks would also be shrouded in mist—perfect for an ambush, he knew from experience.

Andy cupped his fingers into a box and brought them to his lips. He filled his lungs with the humid scent-rich air of the Late Cretaceous and blew long and carefully into his hands. It produced a long mournful bellow that traveled along the valley floor.

He finished and waited. Sure enough, heads the size of small cars lifted on tree-trunk-thick necks from the endless green, and as he hoped, responded. They called back to him, the sauropods, the largest creatures to have ever lived on land. 120 feet from nose to tail and around 80 tons, the creatures were walking mountains.

Andy blew into his cupped hands again, and once again, they responded. But this time, they looked toward him. He waved. *What would they make of a tiny creature like me?* he wondered. He was nothing to them, a bug, an anomaly out of place and out of time. And where mankind ruled for a few thousand years, these things ruled for many millions.

He smiled as he watched them, and his chest swelled and eyes watered. This was his land, and his alone. And it was as magnificent as he imagined and hoped it to be.

He turned back toward the plateau. Right now as the comet Primordia was overhead, everything was thrown into chaos—the atmosphere, the weather, the magnetic orientation of the Earth, and even time and space itself, as a portal or doorway to another reality was thrown open.

He had a little over 24 hours. And at the end of that period, when the comet pulled away and the time distortion ended, the two realities went back to being ordered once again, the two worlds separated by a distance so vast it was hard to even comprehend.

He remembered that Ben Cartwright had seen himself as being marooned here in the Late Cretaceous. But Andy never saw it that way. If his sister came to find him and try to take him home, what would he do or say to her?

He smiled; she couldn't take him home, because this *was* his home now, wasn't it?

Andy was torn. He had so much more to do and see in this world. It had taken him a decade, but he learned how to survive in this place. He peeked over the edge of the tree canopy, looking at the growth below him.

He made a plan: she would try and convince him to come with her. But instead, he would convince her to stay here with him. He had so much to show her. She'd love it.

He looked down from his perch—there were broad and fleshy leaves, bulbous hanging fruits, and a mad tangle of vines, some with hooked barbs that tore at the flesh, cycads, and tongue-like ferns. And on the trunks of those titanic trees, there were brilliant red and orange fungi, like flatbread growing out from their bark, and their lower branches had what looked like strings of green pearls hanging from them.

It was a wonderland, except in among that wildness there were the predators—big or small, they all spelled death for a soft-bodied mammal. But he knew how to avoid them. He had something the other creatures didn't: a giant brain.

He looked back once again at the plateau—there was another reason to go no further, turn around, and just head back into the jungle. Up on that plateau were monsters, but not just massive two-legged theropods, or flying reptiles the size of airplanes, or waterways filled with carnivores that made sharks and alligators seem like goldfish.

Andy felt the tremble in his stomach at the memory—the monstrous snakes known as *Titanoboa* were creatures that were like some sort of elemental force. The entire plateau was where they thrived, and it was like a pit of vipers on a monstrous scale.

"*Gluck.*" The tiny reptile hopped up on his leg, obviously now having had his fill of insects and fruit. "*Don't go there, Andy.*"

Andy smiled flatly. "I don't really want to go."

"*Gluck.*" It cocked its pointed head. "*And Helen?*"

He sighed. "I know if there's a chance my sister is going to be there, then I should at least meet her. After all, it'd be rude not to, if she's just come a few thousand miles and 100 million years to see me." He pulled at his lip. "Be also good to get some supplies. Even a new knife would do."

He looked down at his emaciated frame. He was covered in scars, missing a couple of fingers, his skin covered in dirt and a deep tan, and he bet his long hair was filled with twigs, seeds, and all manner of debris. Andy smiled; he was a prehistoric Robinson Crusoe. Yeah, he needed some supplies. But that was all.

"Gluck." The tiny flying reptile turned one suspicious eye on him.

"Don't worry, I won't leave you. I'm not going anywhere."

Gluck climbed up his leg, and then used his sharp beak to open the bag and burrow in. Andy grinned.

"What, so I'm a kangaroo with a pouch now?"

He looked in at the tiny bird-like thing.

"We'll just take a look, a quick one." He went to close the bag but paused. "And no snoring in there—silence is the key up where we're going."

Andy began to ease down the tree and felt more vulnerable every foot of the way.

CHAPTER 40

Still several hundred feet from the top of the plateau, Ben was the first to find and then enter the cave mouth. There had been several caves he had bypassed, but what attracted him to this one was it had dappled light falling at its rear.

As he scrambled in, he stayed pressed in tight to one side, gun up, as the others came in behind him. He motioned to his eyes and then to the cave interior, and Chess and the mercs, plus Drake spread out. Ben waved Helen and Nicolás in behind him.

He sniffed—there was no smell of the acrid ammonia that he remembered from the previous massive snake pits he had encountered up here, so he hoped it was a place they weren't using for nesting.

"Clear," Drake said, and the word was repeated along the line by the mercenaries.

Ben kept his gun at the ready and eased in toward the bars of light being thrown down into the cave. When further in, he took one last glance about then tilted his head to follow the beams up to the cave ceiling. He couldn't see the sky, but at about 100 feet above them, the cave ceiling curved away to a shelf, and he bet that was the start of a chute that led to the surface.

He squinted, and then pulled his small scope which he held to his eye—it looked weird, oily, as though underwater. There was definitely some sort of hanging layer of distortion in front of the cave shelf mouth, like two different liquid densities, one upon the other.

Ben knew what it was—during the comet's apparition, it threw open a doorway, and either grabbed the top of the plateau, sending it back in time, or it allowed the distant past to be brought forward to now. But though the area that the anomaly covered was the entire mountaintop, it only penetrated down 100 feet or so. Anything below that wasn't affected.

They'd need to pass through this veil that indicated the doorway between one time and the next.

Drake appeared at his side and nudged his arm. "Looks like our ride—and we've all got tickets."

"Yep, so up we go," Ben replied as he fixed another rope to the caving dart, aimed, and fired toward the jutting lip of the rock shelf over 100 feet above them. The dart sped away, taking the rope with it, and embedded with an audible *clunk* into the hard stone about six feet from the opening. He tested it once, before attaching it to his power winch.

Ben turned to his friend. "Looks like the fun's about to start."

Drake grinned and saluted. "After you."

Ben nodded, hit the retraction button, and he lifted off. He sailed upward as the group watched from below. He took it a little slow, cautious of every nook and cranny that could be used for an ambush, and then in a couple of minutes, he was at the ceiling.

Ben hung there for a moment, just looking along the rock shelf. There was definitely light streaming in from a good-sized opening. Thankfully, there didn't seem to be any of the football-sized packages that were the monstrous snake droppings.

He looked down at all the upturned faces. "Looks okay. I'm going in." He kicked off the wall and swung the rope to the right, picking up momentum, and then swinging back to the left, and when at full extension, reaching out to grab a horn of rock. There were good hand and foot holds, and he was able to disengage the rope and clamber up onto the lip of rock.

Below him, Drake grabbed Ben's rope and attached it to his winch and started to come up behind him. The others assembled, waiting their turn.

Ben entered the cave, and then passed through the oily distortion layer. He got the familiar weird sensation in his gut, as if he was falling, and he became slightly dizzy for a few seconds. Sand grain-sized particles hung in the air as if there was no gravity, and there was also the absence of sound—he felt like he was between time and space for a moment, and he pushed on, feeling the dense air acting like a liquid, sucking at his body and slowing him down. But then he passed through it into the new cave.

He felt his senses rush back in at him, as though he was waking from a deep sleep and as the light grew stronger, he slowed, becoming more cautious. Ben now crouch-walked holding his gun before him; the cave wasn't huge, but more than big enough for human beings. The problem was, he knew that the massive snakes didn't need much room, just enough to get their heads in and then it was all over for anything in front of them.

The air was moving now, rising up and gently pulling past him. He didn't like it as it meant his scent preceded him, and he didn't get the return favor—anything outside the cave would know he was coming long before he could hear or smell it.

In another few minutes, the cave angled slightly upward, and Ben climbed a narrow chimney all the way to the top, and then the light exploded before him, and with it came all the sights, sounds, and smells of the primordial world.

Ben felt both sick to the stomach and entranced. "Pellucidar is but a realm of your imagination," he whispered, the words of an author long gone. Edgar Rice Burroughs was a writer similar to Arthur Conan Doyle in that they both wrote of fantastic places, people, and animals, and in doing so, displayed magnificent imaginations.

But Burroughs' strange world, *Pellucidar*, was at the center of the Earth, and given he personally had proven that Conan Doyle's Lost World on the plateau was real, would someone one day find that hidden place far beneath the dark ice and snow of the Antarctic? He did wonder.

Ben rested on his forearms. "Nice to see you again. Do you mind if I just visit for a while?" He half smiled. "I don't want any trouble this time."

He then heard Drake talking softly to the mercs as Helen slid in beside him. Nicolás crawled up next to her, and the three of them stared out.

"See anything?" she asked.

"Nothing yet. And that's the way I want it to stay." Ben put the telescopic scope of his gun to his eye and moved it along the foliage. "Nope, nothing."

"We should scan some more," she said.

"Yeah, we should. We should scan a lot. But we need to balance caution with haste. We need to be out there, find your bother, get back, and then all get the hell out of here before the doorway closes. I am not, repeat *not*, staying in this place again." He meant it.

"I get it." She looked out at the jungle. "It's been 10 years; we might not even recognize him."

Ben chuckled. "Here's a tip; if we see another human and it's not one of us, odds are it's going to be your brother."

"Oh yeah." She grinned back.

Drake and the mercs finally belly-slid up to them.

"Holy shit." Shawna's mouth dropped open. "That is one weird-ass jungle."

Drake grunted. "You have no idea."

Through the curtains of mist that swirled through the underbrush, there were huge tree trunks, rod straight, and growing 150 feet into the air. At their top, just becoming visible now that the mist had fully fallen, were pompom type bunches of fronds. At their base were heavy-leafed palms with massive tongue-like leaves, a dozen feet long and five across, and ropey vines tangled everything.

There were flowers, enormous fruits or seed pods, some with dangerous-looking spines, and also fungi as toadstools or in ragged shapes like torn bread.

"It's like the Garden of Eden," Shawna whispered.

"Yeah." Chess snorted. "Complete with the devil snake, according to these jokers."

"I can smell it," Buster said. "Stinks like shit out there."

"Because that's probably what it is," Helen replied. "Dinosaur shit."

"Look." Chess pointed with one fingerless gloved hand.

Something the size of a brush turkey sped past the cave mouth, paused to stand so still that it looked like it had become frozen as it seemed to be listening for a moment, before it unlocked and then sprinted on.

"Did you see that?" Chess continued to point. "That was a…"

"Yeah, yeah, we know," Drake said and turned to Ben. "What do you want to do, boss?"

Ben slid forward so his elbows were on the lip of the cave mouth. He stuck his head out and looked left, right, then craned his neck to look above them.

They were about six feet up from the ground, and vines were hanging across their cave mouth, partially obscuring them. Helen was right, they should do a lot more watching and waiting, but they were on the clock. There didn't seem to be anything close by, so he guessed it was as good as they were going to get.

"We mark our position, and then we head out. Follow me, stay quiet, low, and in tight."

Ben eased out and dropped to the ground. He held a hand up and just crouched for a moment. He turned his head slowly, and then looked up above them. There was a rocky hill behind them, mostly covered in plants, and even from where he was only a few feet in front, it was hard to make out the hole he had just climbed out of.

He waved them out, and one after the other, the men and women jumped lightly to the ground. The mercs and Drake had their guns up and all pointed out at the jungle.

Helen also leapt down followed by Nicolás. The young man just gawped as he turned slowly.

"This is not real," he breathed and fumbled for a camera, but cursed when he saw it was dead. He turned to Helen. "How can this be real?"

"We told you. You just didn't want to believe us," she said. "This world is our world. But it's from about 100 million years ago. Somehow, the comet that is passing overhead distorts time, opens a portal to long ago, and right here, on this tabletop mountain, we get a little slice of the Late Cretaceous period."

Nicolás continued to stare. "This is where those giant bat-birds came from."

"Yes; pterosaurs," Helen said softly.

"Hey." Drake nudged Nicolás back to attentiveness. "And I'm betting there's something else you didn't believe us about this place…it's the most damned dangerous one on Earth."

Nicolás nodded, his eyes blinking. He turned back to the jungle as Shawna looked over her shoulder.

"Buster was right: it stinks."

Helen pulled out a small scope and held it to her eye, shifting it to thermal, and turning slowly. "Rotting vegetation, sap and plant resin, early flowers, and one extra thing—lots and lots of dino-poop."

"Big shits mean big assholes," Chess said. "Stay in tight, people." Keeping his eyes on the wall of jungle, he moved in closer to Ben. "Which way, Cartwright?"

Ben turned to the female paleontologist. "Helen?"

The woman looked up, sighting the sun for a moment. "Even as a kid, he wanted to see what America was like in the past." She held out an arm. "So I'm betting he went up north, and if he came back, it would have been coming from that way."

"Then let's meet him halfway," Ben said. "Francis, take us out."

The big man grunted, kept his gun tucked under his arm, and went to move off into the jungle.

"Wait," Helen hissed.

Francis turned.

"Some of the creatures here, the snakes, *Titanoboa*, also use the trees. Make sure you stay aware of what's above you."

"Those tinyboas; that's them big snakes you mentioned?" Francis' voice was deep but untroubled.

"*Titanoboa*, but yeah." She nodded. "Be careful."

"And the dinosaurs." Shawna grinned. "They can fly as well."

"Francis, also big damn spiders, just like you hate, right, Drake?" Chess chuckled.

"Yeah, that's right," Drake sighed.

"Oh man, this is getting better by the minute." Francis shook his head. "Hope I live to get that big paycheck."

He turned back, scanned the tree canopy for a moment, and then led them in.

CHAPTER 41

HUMBOLDT COUNTY, NEVADA, PRESENT TIME

RE-EVOLUTION: 409

Barry Ryebeck pushed the mower around his large grass backyard for 20 minutes before stopping, grabbing the brow of his cap, and lifting it to wipe his streaming brow with a forearm. It was hot, damned hot, and the Nevada summer was going to be a bitch as always.

His home in Humboldt County was a good 3,000 square feet with a few orange trees, camellias for color, and plenty of flat ground for his magnificent emerald-green grass. It was Kentucky Bluegrass Supreme, and was soft, thick, and a pleasure to walk on in bare feet. Everyone commented on it. It made him feel as proud as a rooster.

He took a moment to inhale the sweet smell of fresh cut grass, and then jammed his cap back on and was about to check his progress when the lights went out.

"*Huh?*"

As soon as he noticed it, it was all over and the sun shone hotly once again on his upturned face. He blinked, turning one way then the other.

Musta been my imagination, he thought and straightened his cap and looked back to his work. He was pretty much done, with just some tidy up to go around the trees, and along the hedge line—he'd tackle that one first.

Barry pushed the mower along the hedge line, coming to a hole in the hedge at ground level that was roughly the size of a hubcap. He pushed the mower on past, and then just as he was beyond it, something that felt like molten daggers stabbed his calf.

Barry screamed and went to the ground while the damn mower continued on without him. He turned over, gripping his leg, and just caught sight of two black stick-like things repositioning themselves just at the hole opening in the hedge.

As he grimaced, confused, he felt the spreading coldness work its way up his leg to his groin. And then begin to rise higher.

"*Help me!*" he shouted but his words were weak as already his chest was succumbing to the spreading numbness.

Then he remembered. "Ah damnit." It was Meso season. He should have known better—those big bastards, the *Mesothelae*, were the world's largest and heaviest spiders. They lived in burrows, and a big one could get to be two feet across and weigh 40 pounds.

Barry began to take short breaths, as it was getting hard to breathe. He turned his stiffening neck and saw it then, the Meso, as it eased further out of the hole in the hedge. Just as he thought, it was a big sucker, and had been in its burrow, lined with silk, just waiting for an ambush.

The spider came out slowly and in the sunlight, its skin looked like polished plastic. The eyes, two big central ones and many smaller ones surrounding them, were glossy black buttons devoid of soul, but Barry knew every damn one of them was focused right on him.

Below those eyes was where the shit got crazy—the two chelicerae, the things that housed the fangs, were an angry red, and those twin curved daggers were as long as his big fingers.

"*Shit, shith, thithhh,*" Barry whispered as the numbness spread to his face. He lay back then on his magnificent grass, and it felt like a soft, sweet-smelling pillow. "I gith thup."

Barry didn't feel the spider's first touch, as he was totally numb now. And thankfully, he didn't feel when it began to drain him of his body fluids. He just felt dumb for not remembering sooner.

CHAPTER 42

THE PLATEAU—100 MILLION YEARS AGO

Drake tried to look everywhere at once. Ten years ago, he escaped this hellish place with his life and little else. He promised then to never return—he groaned for a moment—but now, here he was.

Out front, Ben had taken over the lead, and next was Helen. He never stopped thinking about her, and when things went well for him or he ran into trouble, it was always her he wanted to talk to. *Guess I'm still hooked*, and her coming was probably why he was really here. *I'm dumb like that*, he thought and snorted softly.

Ben paused to look again up at the jungle canopy. Sunlight filtered down, but it was shredded into thin bars by the thick leaf cover. At their feet, mud pulled at their boots, and roots thick as Drake's thighs lifted from the slime to plunge back down like the muscular tentacles of a massive mud-slick octopus.

Drake turned slowly. The jungle in this place was like being on another planet. He was no botanist, so nearly everything was unidentifiable. But here, nothing was even recognizable—large fronds like green dining tables hung over scrambling plants that shot out curling hair-like strings to cling to the stalks of hardier plants to lift themselves higher. Large flowering growths that smelled like old gym socks bloomed open, and fungus of all shapes, sizes, and colors fed on rotting logs, each other, and in one case, the skeleton of some gargantuan fallen beast.

"What's the hold-up?" Chess asked from the rear.

"Stinks like shit in here," Shawna repeated for the 10th time as her mouth turned down. "And worse than that dino-poop."

"It's the swamp methane," Chess replied. "I thought you liked that stuff. That biker boyfriend of yours reeks of it."

She returned a short hoarse laugh. "I dumped that ass-wipe long back. Got my eye on something younger and prettier now." She turned and winked at Nicolás who blushed and looked away quickly.

Ben turned with his teeth bared and waved them to quietness. Shawna continued to guffaw, and Drake knew it'd be impossible to close them down completely. And it would stay like that until they saw something that freaked them out, or one of them got dead—*education the hard way*, he thought grimly.

"Hey." Francis walked a few paces across a small, shallow pond.

"Looky here."

"Whatta you got, big guy?" Chess tried to see around him but Francis' shoulders were like a wall of muscle.

"Got the biggest, ugliest frog I ever seen." He half turned and chuckled. "It's all head."

"Lemme see! I love frogs." Buster began to slosh toward him.

"Slow down," Helen said, also moving toward Francis.

"*Ah*, goddamnit." Ben looked to Drake, and then nodded to the mercs.

Drake knew what he meant—*they were his buddies, so do something about them*. He followed.

Francis pulled a long blade from a scabbard on his belt and crouched. "This thing is massive." He began to hold it out.

As Drake approached, he could make out what was capturing Francis' attention. There was some sort of frog or toad that looked like an upturned brown and green bucket. On each side of its head over its eyes were horn-like protrusions, and a pair of large glassy eyes was fixed on Francis...and the guy was right, it seemed to be all freaking head.

"Is it alive?" Shawna asked.

"Let's see." Francis reached forward with the blade.

Helen moved quickly. "Don't..."

She went to grab at Francis' shoulder. But just as she lunged, the toad opened its mouth and sprayed Francis' hand and arm with something that immediately pitted his clothing and the acrid smell of it stung the eyes.

Francis dropped his knife and recoiled. "What the hell?"

"Fuck you." Buster kicked out, landing a boot into the center of the amphibian that sent it flying into the bushes with a soft thud.

"It's burning." Francis' normal baritone had gone up a few octaves.

"Put it in the water, quickly," Helen said.

The man did as he was told and grimaced. He lifted it, and Helen came in closer. Her hands hovered just over his arm. The glove he wore and his tough jungle-proof sleeve was all abraded, and the dark flesh on his arm underneath was red raw.

"Interesting," Helen said as she craned forward.

"You think?" Francis shot back. "That damn thing just spat acid at me."

"That looked like a *Beelzebufo ampinga*... otherwise known as the devil frog. And it's interesting because their fossils have only ever been found in Madagascar from the Cretaceous Period. But we always thought they might have existed here." She looked up. "And now I know they do."

"So damn happy for you," Francis grimaced.

She opened her canteen and let more fresh water run over his wounds. "You'll need to dress that."

Francis nodded. "It still burns."

Helen looked to where the giant frog had been. "Yeah, hydrochloric acid—because it has such a large mouth, it eats big prey whole. I guess it needs a strong acid in its gut to break them down quickly. Never knew they could spit it."

"Lemme guess, and now you know that too." Francis' brow furrowed.

She smiled up at him and nodded. "Their closest living relative lives right here in South America. This is proof that these things crossed over land bridges."

"Fuck it." Francis half turned to look over his shoulder. "Buster, shoot that damn thing."

"It's already gone, buddy." He lifted his gun. "But I'll shoot the next one."

"Is it bleeding?" Ben asked from their rear.

"Not now," Helen said.

"Does it smell like raw flesh?" Ben pressed.

Helen sniffed, and then Francis. Francis shook his head, but Helen just looked at him.

Ben grunted. "Like the lady said, bathe it, and then bind it, thickly. Many of the things in here hunt by scent." He turned to look at the man. "And you just made yourself very interesting to them."

Francis stood. "Hey, listen, man…"

"Shut up." Ben shot back and looked along each of their faces. "You touch nothing in here. This is no jungle you've ever been in. You wise up right now, 'cause I don't give a shit if you get yourself killed. But if you put me and mine at risk, I'll kill you all myself." He glared. "Clear?"

Chess held up his hand. "Be cool, asshole, we get it."

Drake doubted it.

*****

Ben worried about Emma and Zach with every step he took. The world was changing, animals were changing, and people were changing and even disappearing. New animals were emerging like some sort of conjuring trick, and everyone just seemed to remember them as though they'd always been there and suddenly recalled the oddities.

The landscape was altering, and he wondered what would happen if they failed to find Andy. What would they be heading back to? It was telling that when they'd last flown into Caracas 10 years ago, the city had a population of two million people. Now it was little more than a town with no airport, no buildings over two stories, and a few thousand people living behind a high wall.

Ben didn't know whether the jungle consumed them, or if the town just never got a chance to exist as they knew it.

Please don't let that happen to Ohio, he silently prayed. *Or anywhere back home.*

His thoughts stayed with home. Emma was the smartest and toughest woman he had ever known, and he had confidence she could deal with anything. But knowing that just didn't make him feel any better about being here while she was back there.

His lips flattened as he thought about it—back there? Did he mean back there in America? Or back there, 100 million years in the future. It didn't matter; it was just a long, long way away.

They'd been trekking for three hours now, and he'd stop soon for a break. He'd already laid down the rules: you have something to eat, you bury the wrappers. You take a piss or shit, you dig a hole first, and cover it over—the deeper the better—and you better be damned quick. The smell of fresh feces was something he had learned the hard way that brought the predators running.

If anyone ever wondered why dogs look at you real strange when they're taking a dump, it's because they know for that few seconds they're hunched over, they're vulnerable. And they're looking to you, their pack leader, to check you have their back.

As Ben marched, he tried to recall any landmarks from his previous time here, but couldn't. Though he knew the lake and caves were at the interior, the fact was he left this plateau as soon as he was stranded in this time. It was the only place he found that the *Titanoboa* lived.

He looked up—the sun was just past its zenith. The snakes were more active at night, and they still had a few more daylight hours yet.

His one hope was that they saw the creatures before the creatures saw them—it at least would give them a fighting chance. That was the reason the mercs were with them—more sets of eyes to watch out and bodies trained to react quickly. He looked over his shoulder at the group coming up behind him. Drake nodded to him, and he returned the gesture. Thank God for having a few people here he could trust with his life.

Ben's objectives were simple: first prize, they found Andy and everyone went home. He doubted they'd win that medal, but there were levels of achievement underneath that. So, second prize was Andy must be brought back or stopped. With rifle or sidearm, Ben was a crack shot, and Drake was even better; one way or the other, Andy must not be allowed to have any more effect on this time zone.

Ben led them through the damp and claustrophobic jungle. The mists that were still curling around the hairy tree trunks and through the broad palm fronds were now beginning to settle and drip like rain, soaking them all in a warm and oily moisture.

Ben was first to break out into the small and unusual clearing, and as the team filed out, Helen came and grabbed at his elbow.

"This isn't natural," she whispered.

Ben nodded slowly. "You're right; been scratched out of the jungle." He half turned. "Eyes out, everyone."

The clearing was roughly 50 feet across, and around its edge, plant debris was piled there that had long rotted down. Something had scraped everything away from the center. There were mounds every few feet that were about a foot high and a yard around.

"Snakes?" Ben asked.

"I don't think so," Helen still whispered.

"Eggs," Chess said as he used the toe of his boot to dig into one of the mounds. He succeeded in crushing some of the oval spheres, and the fluid made the spill glisten in the muted light.

Nicolás leaned forward. "I once saw an ostrich egg; they look like this."

"Yeah, maybe." Chess crushed another of the eggs with his boot.

"Stop doing that," Helen hissed.

Something moved within the glutinous fluid, and she moved closer.

"Are they edible?" Buster said, and also began to uncover another mound.

"Gross." Shawna blew air through her lips and held her gun up. "Looks like an ugly baby bird."

Helen crouched beside the egg clutch and used her knife to peel open more of the shell fragments. She stared.

"What is it?" Ben asked.

"A bird," Shawna insisted.

"Bird? I wish it were. This is something far more dangerous." Helen got to her feet and turned slowly, scanning the surrounding brush. "I think they're *Troodon*, otherwise known as *wounding tooth* theropods. Yeah, Shawna, they're like birds, but only in that they're covered in hair-like proto-feathers. But they have jagged teeth, stand about three-to-four feet tall when fully grown and probably weigh in at about 100 pounds apiece. They were one of the few dinosaur species that developed an angled digit like opposable thumbs—only other species to do that were apes and humans."

"So they're big turkeys with sharp teeth that can also thumb a ride if they need to," Shawna sneered, and Buster laughed and bumped fists with her.

"Real funny," Helen said. "These *turkeys* eat meat and hunt in packs. They also had the largest brain size per-ratio of any dinosaur. They were damned smart. If they didn't go extinct, who knows where they might have ended up in the evolutionary pecking order." She turned to Ben. "We need to get out of here."

"Let's go. This way." Ben began to lead them out.

"Are you brain dead?" Drake seethed.

Ben turned at the sound of Drake's voice. He saw his friend was glaring at Shawna who was crouching over the nest with one of the eggs in her hand.

"What? Just wanted a souvenir."

"Well, it isn't going to be a freaking dinosaur egg, so put it down." Drake jabbed a finger at her. "*Now.*"

"Lighten up." Buster shook his head. "Look around, there's tons of them here."

Drake's jaw jutted. Shawna grinned back at him, but slowly her face began to drop. "Oops, sorry, mama."

Ben saw that the female merc wasn't actually looking at Drake, but just over the man's shoulder. He eased his head around, and then squinted in at the jungle. It was almost invisible in among the foliage, but there was a head sticking from between two fronds. The eyes were large and front facing, and though the face looked heavily boned, he could see black and white down-like feathers covering the crest and neck.

"We got company."

Ben gripped his weapon, and though the thing was totally motionless, the unblinking gaze was unsettling. Worse was the way the mouth curved at the back and made it look like it was wearing a cruel smile.

Helen spoke with barely any movement of her lips. "It. Won't. Be. Alone."

Nicolás nodded to the wall of jungle. "It isn't; there's another one in there."

Ben looked to where he had planned to exit the small clearing and noticed in the dark, green tunnel another set of ruby red eyes peering out. "They're all around us."

Chess lifted his gun, racking in standard shells. "Say the word and I'll make a hole."

"Let's try and back out first." Ben cradled his gun in his hands now, the muzzle pointed at the foliage.

"Like I thought: *Troodon.* Try and keep facing them," Helen whispered. "They'll prefer to attack their prey from behind."

The group eased backward, one step, two, and then came the wet crunch from behind them.

"*Ah*, shit." Buster had planted one of his size 13 boots on an egg mound.

That must have been the last straw, as the herd, pack, or flock of *Troodon* burst from the foliage with a hiss like airbrakes being engaged. They were fast, and though the gunfire of multiple weapons in the hands of experienced shooters struck home, for every creature they took down, more were disgorged from the jungle.

Ben marveled at their strategy; they usually came in pairs, darting and jinking, and some moved back and forth in front of them, while their pack-mates came at them from the sides. It was a co-ordinated attack, and Ben could see their intelligence at work.

Francis cursed as his shots went wild, and Ben turned to see one of the *Troodon* hanging onto his already wounded arm. It was bicycling its legs against him, and red stripes appeared on his thigh as long claws on its center toes ripped through his tough jungle clothing.

The huge man then grabbed it by the neck and swung it like a club to the ground twice before flinging its broken body into the jungle.

Shawna changed up her rounds to jam powerful Raufoss into her M82 rifle and the explosive booms were near deafening in the enclosed clearing as she punched big tunnels out into the jungle with each discharge. But for every *Troodon* she hit, she missed twice.

"Standard rounds," Ben yelled.

Shawna's teeth were bared and she aimed again, just as one of the bird-like creatures flew from behind to land on her shoulders. Its backward-curving teeth went for her neck, and its talons stuck like twin daggers into the meat of her back. She screamed her agony, one arm going for the thing and the other waving her gun.

Francis held his damaged arm in close to his body, and simply swung his other arm, massive fist clenched at the beasts' heads, knocking them over like ten-pins.

Then the big man looked up, meeting Ben's eyes, and they widened as Ben could see what was coming a mile away. Just as the thing on Shawna's back flexed again, digging its talons in even deeper, her muscles automatically spasmed and then contracted—including her hand that was still wrapped around the M82's trigger.

"*No…*" Ben sprinted and dived, taking the huge Francis around the waist, knocking him down.

Shawna's gun discharged, wildly, but unfortunately for the large form of Buster who was next in line and busy clubbing one of the beasts, it was aimed directly at him. Worse, Shawna still had her explosive rounds packed in.

One minute, the 6-foot 3-inch man was upright, and then next, the Raufoss round took him between the shoulder blades.

Buster's top half disappeared in a flash of blood, bone, and gore as his head, neck, and most of his chest was sprayed all over the jungle. Weirdly, he stayed standing for a second or two, and even took a staggering step, before the headless body crumpled to the ground.

"*Fuck!*" Chess yelled, and then turned to rack and pump shots into the jungle. But as fast as it started, it was over, and the small clearing was filled with smoke, misted blood, and leaf debris that rained down like confetti.

Shawna groaned and rolled over. There were long stripes of blood on her neck and back.

"What happened?" She shook her head and groaned.

"You just fucking killed—"

"*Shut it!*" Ben yelled and helped Francis up.

"Oh fuck, man; that coulda been me." Francis stared at the shredded remains of his colleague, then to Ben. "You saved my life."

"Don't worry about it." He slapped his upper arm. "In this place, I'm sure you'll get a chance to return the favor."

"We must hurry." Helen kept her eyes on the wall of jungle. "The big hunters will be here soon."

"Right; we get the hell out of here, patch ourselves up, and keep going. *Now move it.*"

Drake dragged Shawna to her feet. She moaned loudly and tried to see over her shoulder.

"Where's Buster?" She winced as Drake grabbed her arm.

"Gone," he replied, dragging her after Ben.

"Spread all over the jungle," Chess spat.

"*Aww*, those goddamn lizard turkeys," she replied.

"Yeah, them." Drake carried her out of the clearing, with the group all hurrying to follow Ben.

CHAPTER 43

The home of gods and monsters, Andy whispered as he stared, both horrified and transfixed—the monstrous snake had wrapped itself completely around the body of a juvenile *Ankylosaurus*. The powerful herbivore dinosaur was only about 12 feet long, and as an adult would grow to twice that, but it was still larger and more powerful than a full-grown rhino.

The snake began to compress as the dinosaur bleated like a lamb. It struggled, but it wasn't going anywhere. Andy shook his head and blew air softly from between his lips in awe as he heard the first crack of its heavily armored body.

Unbelievable, he mouthed.

The *Ankylosaurus* was almost completely covered in massive knobs and oval plates of bone, known as osteoderms or scutes, which were also common on crocodiles. And on these beasts they were so thick and dense they would have been like iron plating.

To add to their defensive kit were two rows of spikes along its body. Additionally, its head was long and low, with prominent horns projecting back and to the sides and shelf-like plates protecting its eyes.

Finally, there was the club on the end of the bony tail that whipped back and forth now, but only managed to kick up dirt.

The snake's titanic coils compressed some more, and there came popping and cracking all along the body. The *Titanoboa* kept its head clear, its gaze dispassionate, as its body squeezed the life from its prey.

The pulverizing served two purposes; the first was to suffocate the creature and the second was to compress the thing down to near pulp. Most of the bony plates would be indigestible, but they'd be excreted along with the skull and bone fragments later.

There came more tightening of the coils, and the bleating became hoarse gasps. And then the mouth hung open, and Andy gaped as what looked like some of the *Ankylosaurus'* stomach was pressed up and out of its windpipe. At last, an eye popped free, before it finally stopped moving.

The snake would continue to compress, and sure enough, it sensed the battle was over and moved its mouth around to the front of the plant-eater. The maw opened, showing rows of tusk-like backward-curving teeth, as it began to push the head and shoulders into its mouth.

It would take almost an hour to swallow, but it had time, and up here, there were few predators who would take on a fully-grown *Titanoboa*.

Andy exhaled, feeling scared shitless but exulted. He was a paleontologist, like his sister, and also like her, he specialized in this very creature. But where they had studied bone fragments, he had now seen several specimens alive, and they were more formidable, frightening, and admirable than he ever expected.

He smiled almost dreamily; he knew more about the creature than any person living, now, or in the far distant future. He knew they kept their nests underground, and also weren't solitary, as they preferred to live in communal habitats. They had all the sensory skills of the large modern snakes like anacondas and boas, plus they were a size that made them the most feared creature on the plateau.

There were still answers to some questions that evaded him—why did they congregate up here? It might just be that there was an abundance of prey, or the micro-climate was ideal, or even that the ancient tepui being riddled with caves was perfect for their nesting sites.

But the biggest and most perplexing question of all was: why did they go extinct? He'd heard all the theories, and even postulated some himself, and they ranged from climate change, to competitive tension from other species for food, to disease, and even a theory that something evolved that preyed just on them and wiped them out.

But he didn't buy any of it—other large snake species survived, and this monster had all their advantages and many more of its own.

Why aren't you with us today? he breathed. *What happened?* Andy backed away slowly, glad that the monstrous thing was feeding and not hunting. Otherwise, it'd be him being pushed into that giant mouth right now.

He gave it one last look. *I need to know, and I'll find out,* he thought as he vanished into the jungle.

CHAPTER 44

THE HOME OF GODS AND MONSTERS

Ben held up a fist and his team froze. He then carefully waved everyone down, and the group eased into the dripping ferns, or any places of concealment they could find. No one said a word; they just waited, all eyes on Ben.

His soldier's intuition made the hair on his neck prickle. He didn't need to know that they were being watched; he had felt that for hours now.

After several minutes, Drake crept up beside him. "What have you got?"

Ben looked along the jungle, and then above, and spoke while keeping his eyes on the jungle. "Nothing…and that's what worries me." He turned slowly again. "Listen."

The raucous noise of the jungle had ceased—there were no chirrups, buzzes, or clicks of insects. Nor any squeals and squeaks of tiny animals, or even the thud as clumsy, leathery-winged pterosaurs slammed into tree canopies overhead.

It wasn't quite total silence as there was the constant drip of moisture in the humidity-laden jungle. But there should have been more.

"Yeah, nothing. You think we got company?" Drake asked, now also scanning the foliage.

"I think something's out there, watching us," Ben said and turned to wave Helen up. He then signaled to Chess, pointed at his eyes, and then to the jungle on either side.

Chess nodded and motioned to Francis and Shawna to spread a little into the jungle, where they'd do a quick reconnoiter. Nicolás simply stayed hunkered down with wide eyes.

"That doesn't look right." The path or animal tracks they had been following ended at a wall of vines and Ben squinted toward it. "Eyes out while I take a look."

He eased to his feet and walked carefully toward the end of the track. Oddly, it seemed firm like packed earth or stone beneath his boots, and he pulled his gun in tight to his shoulder.

He used his peripheral vision to track the foliage beside and above him, as he closed in on the unnatural looking wall of green. When he was a few feet from it, he paused and eased his gun barrel forward to part the hanging green drapes. He half smiled.

"Hello again."

He waved Drake and Helen up to his position. As they approached, he half turned.

"Found an old friend."

Behind the wall of vines was a stone idol, roughly human-shaped but with the head of a snake. Its lower half was covered in gnarled roots, and the pitted nature of the stone hinted at eons of weathering.

"Look." Ben pointed with his barrel to the idol's feet. There were smaller carvings of people, many dismembered or without heads. "Still feeding the snake Gods, I see."

"This looks far older than the previous ruins we encountered," Drake said. "What do you think, Helen?"

"Well, humans have lived here ever since they crossed the Bering land bridge around 15,000 years ago." She scoffed softly. "I mean, from modern times that is. This looks definitely pre-Columbian, and the weathering on this hard stone could make it easily 5,000 to 7,000 years old."

Drake snorted. "Gotta give these guys full marks for persistence. They kept coming, kept trying to establish outposts or temples, and they kept getting massacred."

Helen reached out to rub a hand over the degraded snout and fangs. "Well, they regarded this place as the home of Gods and monsters, so they believed that ascending here every 10 years meant they were bringing themselves closer to their Heaven…and their Gods."

She looked down and wiped aside some of the greenery they stood on. "There is, *was*, a pathway here." She scraped some more, and then looked up. "How long did it last this time before their hungry Gods turned into the monsters they feared?"

"Hey, check this out." Drake had moved to the side and pulled away some monstrous-sized palm fronds. There were steps leading down to a dark passageway that was about six feet around. He sniffed and held his gun up. "Bad news."

Ben and Helen did the same.

"Yeah, I think we've found a nest," Helen said.

"The natives built it, and the snakes took it over. Just like last time." Ben turned to see the mercenaries appear out of the jungle. He lifted a finger to his lips and then motioned toward the foliage. "Let's get out of here."

The group silently vanished into the dark wetness of the primordial jungle.

*****

From deep inside the lower chambers of the dark cavern, a leviathan *Titanoboa*'s tongue flicked out to taste the air. Its glass-like eyes were unblinking in the near total darkness, but it saw well with nocturnal, motion sensitive, and also thermal vision.

The fallen magnificence of the room it nested in was lost on its reptilian brain, and the magnificent columns, carvings, and glyphs telling stories of mighty empires that once lived were no more than the rock they were once carved from.

From outside, it detected the tiny exhalations of the creatures at the tunnel entrance, and though it had never sensed them before, an inherited memory was triggered and it became excited by the sweetness of their warm breaths.

It began to slide forward and from beneath it came the sound of crunching as bone fragments, some age-browned and some still with traces of marrow, were pulverized beneath its 5,000-pound body.

At the tunnel entrance, it paused for a moment to taste the air again. It was able to determine the small herd's number, their size, and the direction they had taken.

The monstrous snake poured forth from the cavern like a green and brown-scaled river, only just fitting through the opening.

It knew its hunting territory and knew what was up ahead. It took to the trees to follow the small herd of biped animals.

CHAPTER 45

GREENBERRY, OHIO—THE CARTWRIGHT ESTATE

RE-EVOLUTION: 1089

The night passed slowly. Emma got very little sleep and when morning finally came, her eyes were dry and crusted and she was still exhausted. She had kept her arms wrapped around her son, who thankfully slept easy.

And why wouldn't he? she asked of herself. To him, nothing that was going on was abnormal, or even some sort of new normal. To him, it was just the facts of life of everyday living, and always had been.

The thing about the future was it always became the present. But now, the past was also becoming the present. For her and Ben, they were cursed with the sensation of actually registering the changes. They knew that tomorrow would be vastly different to today. But as the re-evolutions occurred, it was as if people's consciousness, memories, and experiences were the last thing to be altered—like a computer program updating but only in batches and saving the most complex until last.

She carefully eased her arm out from under her son. The light was still on in the basement and she saw that the space that had once been for storage, with a few bottles of Ben's father's and grandfather's wine, old furniture, packed books, and broken toys, was now something so completely different. It was as if it belonged to someone else—there were kitted-out rooms, a kitchen, and well-stocked pantry, and it was spotless, as well as fortified.

It was an entire other house down here, and obviously where they were supposed to sleep now that above ground was too dangerous because of the freaking giant vampire bats that had evolved.

"They can have the night, and we can have the day," Zach had said about them. *We've surrendered half our world already, and never even got a chance to fight,* she thought.

She stood and walked from one table to the next, looking at maps, a radio, computer equipment, and even a gun and ammunition rack. It was exactly how she imagined some of the doomsday preppers probably lived—except doomsday was real and it was like an approaching storm that was creeping up on them faster every day.

She opened up the computer and also flicked on a bank of external cameras from their upstairs. She saw that inside the house was a mess; that's what happens, she guessed, when you "forget" to lock doors and pull down the external window shutters; the monsters got in, *real* monsters. She then flicked to external view and saw the morning light shining down on a mist that snaked through the massive banyan-type forest outside. It looked almost mystical.

A few antlered animals browsed on the dew-covered lawn and seemed more interested in the grass than potential predators—*must be safe now*, she thought.

Yesterday evening, she had planned to visit her neighbors, Frank and Allie. Now she wanted to speak to them more than ever. She'd have to play dumb, but at least she thought she might learn something that could keep them safe.

Right at this moment, as a parent, she felt she was well out of the loop when it came to defending her family. How could she protect Zach from this world's dangers, if she didn't even know what to look out for herself?

"Morning, Mom." Zach sat up and rubbed his face and eyes. "What time is it?"

"Breakfast time." She smiled. "Eggs over easy?"

He nodded. "And do the thick toast."

"You got it." She headed to the pantry. "I'm going over to Frank and Allie's later. Do you want to come or do you just want to hang out here?"

"Hang out here if that's okay," he replied.

"Will you…be alright by yourself?" She turned to him.

"Sure, why not?" He stood and headed to their bathroom.

"Yeah, *why not?*" she repeated. She wanted to keep Zach with her, but right now, here was safe, and out there she had no idea what was or wasn't.

On the way out, she grabbed a holster off a rack with a 9mm handgun already in it and threw it around her waist.

*****

After breakfast and a few hours later, Emma was driving toward her neighbor's property, but now along a rutted dirt track that she knew was once a fully paved road only a week ago.

Looking out from her windows, she saw what had once been open fields, gently rolling hills, and a few stands of emerald green trees were now like iridescent mountains of gargantuan trees that were punctuated by dark arboreal caves tunneling through them, just like the one she was traveling along now.

Luckily for her, the sky was clear and the sun shone brightly, otherwise, it'd be like night-time underneath the heavy canopies.

She grunted as she hit another pothole—the dirt surface was uneven, pocked and rutted, and in some cases so overgrown; it looked more like a horse trail than a road. It took her nearly two hours to traverse the winding track where it used to only take her a third of that.

At last, Emma came out of the trees and saw Frank and Allie's friendly little cottage on the hill, and in seconds more, pulled up out front. She stepped out of her car and saw that overhead there looked to be crows or some sort of large birds circling the property.

Oddly, Frank and Allie's front door was ajar, something she would never think to do now, and given these guys should be more aware of risk than she, it seemed jarring. Perhaps the daytime was safer than she expected and more normal than she gave it credit for.

They can have the night, and we get the day, she remembered.

"Frank? Allie?" She called and walked up the last few dozen feet to the house.

She knocked on the doorframe, and then called again. But there was nothing but silence from inside. She tugged on the partially open screen door that squealed on rusted springs. The heavy wooden door was already pushed right back against the wall, so she stepped inside.

She tried again. "Hey, Frank?" She waited with her head tilted, but after several seconds of empty silence, she decided to head on in.

Wait, she thought. There were sounds—the babble of people talking.

"Frank?" She moved lightly but quickly along the hallway, checked the living room, and found her voices—the television set was on, playing softly.

Emma then checked a small library-sitting room at the front of the house—empty as well. She continued toward the back where she knew the kitchen was.

Entering, she saw that the table was set for dinner, and there were bowls of stone-cold potatoes, carrots, and something green that had dried out and curled. There was also a frying pan with two cooked steaks sitting in it that had been pushed aside, and thankfully, the element had been turned off. Something happened to distract them while they were cooking—enough to stop what they were doing, but perhaps not urgent enough to forget about the heating.

That might be good, she hoped, but warning alarms were still going off in her head.

There was one last place to look, and she saw that the door was cracked open—their pantry. She and Ben had been to Frank and Allie's for dinner many times, and she had seen the inside of their fair-sized pantry room before. But entering now, she saw that it had changed and was now exactly like their own fortified room—except it was swung wide, and more worrying, there were shotgun shells scattered on the floor.

"Please God, no." Her hands instinctively went to her hip, drawing the gun and holding it in a two-handed grip with the muzzle pointed down.

"Frank?" Her voice was softer now as caution and a little fear sharpened her senses.

She crab-walked to the back door. It was bolted up and down with several heavy-duty locking mechanisms—no one came in or went out of here in a hurry. There was a heavy diamond-shaped glass panel at head height and she looked out through it. The backyard was empty, and the only movement came from a couple more of the black birds shooting overhead and heading out front.

Crows again, she thought. And then, *carrion eaters*.

She quickly checked the upper-level rooms and found they were empty. The beds were still made, and thankfully, there was no sign of any sort of struggle. Looking out from one of the upstairs windows, she could see in the distance that the black birds dotted one of the far fields, and there was a tangled lump of them squabbling at its center...squabbling over some *thing*.

Her stomach sank and she rushed downstairs, shouldering open the screen door, and quickly crossing the field.

She began to run, her stomach knotting as she could see the large glossy birds worrying something at their center. It took her several minutes to close in and even up close the bodies, wings, and thick plumage of the birds made it impossible to yet make out what was in there at the core of the tangle.

"*Heyaa*!" she yelled and waved her arms. "Go-on, *get*."

The birds turned her way, but then continued to squabble and climb over each other to get at their prize. "Oh, *piss off*!" she yelled even louder, and then finally drew her gun and fired it into the air.

Its effect was immediate as the birds exploded up and away, revealing what had attracted them and what they had been fighting over. She slowed and then stopped a dozen feet out.

She didn't need to go any closer to see it had once been two people. The bodies had been obliterated and the bones scattered. Even the skulls were separated from the top of their spines. Shreds of flesh still clung to the bones and tattered gore-stained fabric also hung like wet streamers from the ribs and hips.

"Oh God." She put the back of her arm over her face, as even though the cool of the morning had contained most of the odors of the kill, she didn't want to inhale anything up close.

Emma turned about, looking to the forest line, but there was nothing ominous crouching there. She walked in a large loop around the bodies. There were no tracks—whatever attacked them came from overhead, she bet. She looked back to the massive trees, wondering, were hidden in among those mighty boughs the bat-like creatures, roosting now, perhaps sated after their bloody feast? And did they catch Frank and Allie out in the open?

She often wondered about the "remembering," as Zach put it. When the re-evolution changes flashed through them, it seemed everyone else rapidly had their brains rewired as though it had always been like that.

But she knew it wasn't. It was fine to think that's the way the world now worked, but what happened if they were caught out when one or more of the lethal changes occurred? When *the way the world worked,* safely, one day, suddenly became *another way the world worked* that was deadly?

Emma remembered the scattered shotgun shells in the pantry and her imagination started to fill in the blanks—she saw Frank being far out in his field as the sun was going down. Then the re-evolution wave change washed over them and re-ordered everything, and suddenly the elderly man was a long way from home when the vampire bats attacked.

She saw Allie, hearing Frank's distressed calls, rushing to the pantry and fumbling for the gun, hurriedly packing in a few shells and dropping the rest. She would have charged out into the field, knowing it was probably suicide to do so but going anyway. She'd have done the same for Ben.

Emma looked again at the mutilated remains. What happened if Ben was successful? Would all of these changes be reversed, or would there be no more changes from then on? She knew that because Andy had been there that he would have already affected the timeline in some way. But if he had lived on for another few years or even decades, then the changes would be continuing and getting more significant.

She knew from personal experience that the passage of time could make tiny things, big things. So a small ripple in a pond that continues to occur will eventually erode the shoreline. Perhaps this is what Ben and his team could stop before it gets real bad.

"Bad?" she scoffed, disheartened. "It's already real *bad.*"

Emma looked back at the obliterated bodies. "I'm so sorry, Frank and Allie." Her brows rose slightly. "Will you come back from the dead if Ben is successful? And if you do, will I, or you, even know that you were dead once?" she wondered.

She looked up at the huge trees. "And are the vampires now things that have gone from our dark fairy tales to reality now destined to stay that way forever?"

She dropped her gun hand and sighed, closing her eyes for a moment. *We truly are in a nightmare,* she thought.

Emma started to trudge back to the car. She'd call the sheriff's office, as there was nothing she could do here.

As she walked through the sunlit field, crickets chirruped and cicadas *zummed* all around her. The sunshine was warm on her shoulders, and for a moment, it felt like it was the same sane world she had always known.

Then the sun went out.

She froze as the tingling washed over her from toes to scalp. Seconds passed and then even more seconds, and she knew why—the more complex and significant the changes, the more nature needed time to reset.

When everything blinked back into focus, it seemed the same, but she knew that was just wishful thinking. Something had changed, something big. She suddenly had a terrible thought.

"Zach," she gasped, and then started to run.

CHAPTER 46

Ben pulled a boot from the sucking mud with a wet fart-like blurt. Every step here was the same, and the next footstep the ooze separated around it as he sunk again to the ankle, and then held on tight when he pulled it out.

The same noises were coming from behind him, with the occasional curse from Francis, Chess, and Shawna. Drake eased up beside his left shoulder.

"We sound like a herd of elephants."

"Yep; a herd of elephants with gas." Ben looked around. "I don't remember this bog being here. And I'm sure I traveled through this area before."

"Ten years ago; things change. Maybe last time it was some sort of dry season," Drake said.

"Yeah maybe. But if I had known, I'd have skirted it. Don't like swamps." He looked up at the canopy cover overhead. There was almost no light coming down on them, and at the ground, or rather, water level, there was moss, algae, and slime upon slime. He'd been in jungles that had swamps and bogs as miasmic as this before, and they were places that rotted the flesh inside your boots, had water-borne parasites and diseases, and sucked the energy from your bones as quickly as they did the state of mind. Bottom line: they were shit places to be stuck in.

"We need to be out of here," Helen whispered.

"No kidding," Ben replied.

She squelched up to his right shoulder. "I know, I know. But seeing that frog a while back got me thinking about these swamps."

Ben glanced at her, waiting.

She looked around warily. "The dinosaurs filled every eco-niche on the planet for many tens of millions of years. After them of course came the mammals and birds." Helen seemed to be gathering her thoughts. "And before them, the very early life on the planet was crustacean and bony fish. But there was another biological group that is overlooked because of the dinosaurs, and they flourished in the primordial swamps—the amphibians."

Ben grunted. "I'm guessing you're about to tell me that the hell-frog we encountered isn't the worst thing that could be in here."

"Not by a million miles," she responded.

The bog was becoming deeper by the step. The slime was still on the bottom and algae on the surface, but now it came to just below their knees.

"Okay, give it to me." Ben sighed. "What should we look out for?"

Drake sloshed up next to them as Helen cast a glance around. "In this part of the world?" She bobbed her head. "The last holdouts of the *Eryops*; a six-foot amphibian with a bear trap for a mouth."

"Six feet?" Drake snorted. "A tadpole."

Helen scowled at him. "Or we might run into the last of the *Metoposaurus* species. A 10-foot salamander with interlocking razor teeth."

"We can deal with those too," Drake said and winked at her.

"Only if you see them coming." Helen turned back to Ben. "Also, we might have the misfortune to run into a *Mastodonsaurus*. They grew to about 15 feet. That thing was like a slimy tank with row after row of teeth like a great white shark."

"Okay, we'll avoid that one," Drake scoffed and then faced Ben. "Hey, how did you survive in this hell for 10 years?"

Ben half turned to his friend. "Pro tip number one, stay out of the damn swamps."

"*Ugh.*" Helen sank into a hole to her groin. "Could have been worse. Down in Australia and Antarctica was something called a *Koolasuchus*; that amphibian grew to about 20 feet and was basically all shovel-shaped head and mouth."

"Lucky Aussies," Ben said.

Ben held up a hand and the group halted. Light beams waved out over the reeking water where a heavy green mist curled around moss-covered tree trunks, roots lifting like tentacles from the bog, and interspersed with bubbles of methane popping to the surface.

"Getting too deep," Ben said.

"Gotta be coming to an end soon. Place isn't that big," Drake said.

"We're at a disadvantage and our blind spots are getting bigger every inch that water rises." Ben put a scope to his eye and turned it slowly. "We give it another 10 minutes, and if it doesn't begin to shallow out, we back up and go around. Okay?"

"We'll lose a lot of time," Helen protested, but then: "And I agree with you 100 percent."

A large bubble of gas rose beside them and then popped with a shitty vegetable smell. "Nice," Drake said and waved it away.

"Okay, stay tight. Chess, bring up the rear. Francis and Shawna, take the left and right flank. And everyone keep your eyes open, we may pick up some interested critters along the way." Ben shook his head. "And Shawna, carry your own damn gear."

Nicolás seemed to be now carrying some of Shawna's pack.

"I don't mind." The kid shrugged.

"Whatever." Ben turned away. "Let's go."

*****

Just a hundred feet out to their right side, bubbles of methane came to the surface and popped. Some were Alka-Seltzer size and others were the size of tennis balls.

In an area devoid of trees, two large bubbles came to the surface, close together, and instead of popping, they blinked open. More of the creature surfaced, hanging in the water like a smooth-skinned crocodile, its mud-colored skin almost invisible in the murky, brackish water.

It watched the line of upright animals passing by it. They were just too large to swallow whole, which was its favorite attack method based on a mouth three feet across in a wedge-shaped head. But it also had the strength to attack larger prey and drag them under. It only needed to hold them down for a short while and then the water did the rest.

It would then wedge them in among the twisted stilt-like roots of the swamp trees, and wait for the warmth and bacteria to soften the flesh enough for it to be pulled from the bones.

The *Mastodonsaurus'* short, strong legs and a thick paddle-like tail propelled it forward as it plotted an intercept course to set up an ambush.

*****

Shawna dropped back to walk beside Chess. "This is fucked up." She grimaced as she took a hand off her gun to touch the back of her neck that was still heavily bandaged after the attack.

"You got that right," Chess said, letting his eyes move over the putrid water. Drake had told him to watch the trees as well, but he knew if there was going to be an ambush in here, it'd come from below the surface. He'd been in alligator-infested swamps before and he knew how they operated—get in close then finish their final run at you from under the water.

Nicolás plodded along just in front of them, and Chess was happy for the young Venezuelan to act as their stalking horse.

"Can't see shit in here," Shawna complained.

"Sure can't." She was right; the mist hung over the water's surface like a veil of gauze. Added to that, the water was the color of dirty coffee. And it was further obscured by bubbles and ripples, and other signs of things coming and going below the surface.

That asshole Ben Cartwright was leading them into deeper and deeper water. Bad for them, but real good for any predators lurking about.

Shawna sloshed closer. "I say we back out. Head home. We've got hundred grand each in the bank. Good enough."

Chess kept his eyes on the water as he spoke. "But I want a million. This is my retirement package." He grinned. "Only reason I'm here."

"Yeah, well, ask Buster whether $100,000 would have been enough." She sneered. "A dead millionaire is just dead."

He nodded. "I hear you, babe. But give it a few more hours. We're nearly done here." He turned. "Remember, we find this asshole or not, we get outta here and we're rich. And it's all over in another half day. You can suck it up for that long."

"Yeah, I guess," she agreed. "But we gotta keep these guys alive as well."

He laughed, hoarsely. "Only the money man, Cartwright."

"Ri-*iiight*." She visibly cheered at the thought.

"And anyone else that gets to go bye bye, well that just adds a little more pressure to go home." Chess slowed down and put a hand out, also slowing Shawna. "So let's let these suckers get a little ahead." He winked at her. "Bait."

"*Ahh*, now I get it." She grinned. "And the more I get it, the more I like it."

Chess slowed them down even more as he caught sight of something. "Head's up."

The group was now a few dozen paces ahead of them, with Nicolás just on half that.

Then the attack came.

The surge of water was followed by a scream and then Helen went under.

*****

Ben began to turn just as from the corner of his eye he noticed the V-shaped water movement. Even before he finished turning, the thing was launching itself from the water—all he had time to see was a massive mouth gaping open and snapping closed around Helen's waist. There was a short scream, more like a squeak, as she was quickly taken under.

From behind him, Nicolás also shouted his shock and fear in Spanish. Immediately, Ben saw the water moving again, this time in a lumped wave as the thing tried to get back to whatever den it lived in, but now taking Helen with it.

Drake and Francis dived, and Ben raised his gun, but knew that with Helen in its mouth and Drake now also below the surface somewhere, if he didn't have a clear target, he couldn't dare fire a single round.

He spun, yelling at the other two mercenaries at his rear, who just stood watching. "Get the fuck after them."

Francis came to the surface, shook the mud and grit from his eyes, and looked about. He then dived back under.

Ben surged after the beast himself, but the going was slow as the water was at waist level now. Ben just prayed that the predator was territorial and big enough to keep others away. The amount of noise they were making would have attracted anything else for half a mile.

"No shot!" Ben yelled and tried to run harder just as there came an explosion of water up ahead. The creature breached and Helen was still in its mouth, battering against the slimy, shovel-shaped head. But now Drake had both hands gripped around its paddle-like tail.

The huge form of Francis came back up again gasping for air, but he had swum underwater in the wrong direction.

Nicolás, who was closer, surged forward and dived then, grabbing Drake's ankles, and the combined weight obviously created enough drag to cause the creature to spit the woman out and turn on Drake. Ben didn't need a second invitation, and as soon as Helen came free, he fired.

Before the massive amphibian had a chance to get its jaws around Drake, it had lifted itself out of the water, and then Ben's high-powered shell entered the wide-open mouth, punching the glistening head back and blowing a fist-sized hole out the top of its skull.

The shot echoed out over the brackish water and the massive beast rolled on its back, its stout legs bicycling and large taloned feet clutching at the air like webbed hands.

Drake pushed it aside and raced to where Helen grimaced in the muddy water. He pulled her to him and wiped hair from her pain-wracked face. Ben charged closer and quickly turned to the mercs.

"Keep a look out."

He then helped Drake lift Helen up out of the water and onto some exposed roots.

She held her chest and breathed in and out rapidly through clenched teeth. She threw an arm out around Drake's neck.

"Thank you."

"I just thank God you're safe. I'm going to take a look, okay?" He lifted her rapidly reddening shirt.

Drake turned to Nicolás who was streaked in mud and his brown eyes, blinking probably in surprise at his own bravery. He slapped the young man on the shoulder.

"Thanks, buddy."

Nicolás smiled weakly. "I feel sick."

"Makes two of us." Drake went back to pulling Helen's shirt away.

Helen let him and looked away. "Is it bad?"

Drake looked over the wounds and pressed various places on the ribs. She exhaled loudly when he did.

"I don't think you've got broken ribs. That's good. But there's a lot of lacerated skin in here." He turned to Ben. "We need to get to dry land, clean this up, ASAP."

"I heard that." He turned. "Chess, you and Francis get ahead, double time. Find us some dry land or a place out of this damned hellhole."

"You got it." The pair waded ahead.

Ben then turned to Shawna. "Keep your eyes open. And don't shoot anyone."

*****

In another hour, they finally managed to find the end of the swamp and Drake and Nicolás carried Helen up onto a dry bank.

"Keep watch," Ben ordered the mercenaries.

The female merc's jaws ground together for a second, but the three did as they were asked.

Drake opened her shirt, and Helen sucked in air. The lacerations were mainly in two half-moons on both sides of her body where the thing had grabbed hold of her.

"Take it off," Ben asked.

"*Huh?*" Helen frowned through her pain.

"The shirt; its soaked in blood and I need to try and rinse it out." He held out his hand.

"Oh." She let Drake help her peel out of the red and brown-streaked top, and Drake then tossed it to Ben.

He went to the bank, took one last look out at the water, and then dipped it in, rinsing and wringing it several times to flush it out. It came out covered in fine silt, but at least much of the blood odor would be gone.

Ben dunked it one last time and held it out. He began to brush the slime from it and saw the wriggling creatures dotting it—they looked like tiny crustaceans, like isopods, and he hoped that they weren't some sort of parasite, as there was no doubt they'd be in Helen's wounds.

Give us a break, will you? he whispered. He shook the shirt hard, flicking them away.

When he got back, he saw that Drake was wiping out the wounds and squeezing iodine into them. Helen sucked air in and out quickly, as it must have stung like a bitch and probably felt like she was being seared.

"You do know that you're the only person alive today who was bitten by a prehistoric salamander?" Ben half smiled as he handed her the cleaned shirt.

She started to chuckle, but then pressed a hand to her ribs. "Helen, meet Mr. *Mastodonsaurus*, and vice versa." She reached out a hand to Drake. "Did I thank you for not letting me be the only person in history who was taken away to be eaten by a prehistoric salamander?"

He smiled as he worked on her. "Buy me a drink when we get home."

She squeezed his arm. "You said that last time. Next thing I knew, you had me in bed."

He shrugged. "What can I say, I'm pretty charming like that."

Ben cleared his throat. "Nothing like being attacked by a monster to reignite the flame of love." He looked above them. There was a small break in the tree canopy overhead. "Well, what do you know?" He could just make out the small eyebrow-like streak directly above them. "Primordia," he whispered. "It'll probably be at its closest point now."

"Yep." Drake followed his eyes. "And that means, it'll be heading away soon."

"Yeah." Ben opened his pack and took out a squat pistol. He cracked it open and loaded a stout brass plug into it. He then aimed for the hole in the branches above them and fired. The plug streaked away and then high above them it exploded in a red star that began to settle slowly toward the earth.

"Time to let our prodigal son know we're here." He lowered his arm.

"Come on, Andy," Helen breathed as she sat up. "Come home, little brother."

*****

The red flower bloomed high over his head. It seemed so strange, so incongruous, that something so modern could be appearing over a prehistoric jungle. Over *his* prehistoric jungle.

"Oh wow." Andy smiled as he said the words. "She came."

"*Gluck.*"

He shook his head. "Oh, you told me so, did you?"

Andy tried to plot where the flare had risen. *Not that far*, he guessed.

As the small red star fell back to Earth, the pale blue sky was left unmarked save for a small eyebrow streak just up and to the left. He continued to stare at the streak that was like a single artist's brushstroke that seemed to hang there, locked in place. But he knew that the celestial body would be moving at hundreds of miles per second.

"That's my sister's ride—she just got dropped off." He peeked into his bag. "You'll like her."

"*I know I will; will she like me?*"

"Of course she'll like you." He grinned and shut the bag.

Before he ventured further, he found a small area of mushy ground and took a few moments to lather on some more mud. He carefully coated every inch of his body, paying attention to his groin and under his arms and anywhere else that his scent was strongest. Though humans didn't have scent glands, bacteria combined with sweat gave them a distinctive pungent odor. It was this odor that predators homed in on.

He faced the thick jungle, aiming himself toward where he suspected the flare was fired from, and then began to burrow in. He moved through hanging vines and under huge spiked cycad fronds, and also past rice-bubble-spotted tree trunks.

Up on the plateau, the climate was slightly cooler than in the valleys, but it was still damp and humid. It would have been easier going out in the clearings, but the chance of being spotted and run down was too great for the small benefit of drawing some clean air.

Andy estimated he had about a half mile to cover. Any normal place, it'd take him less than an hour. Here, it'd be more like 3 or 4 times that.

His lips moved silently as he burrowed on: "*Silence is the key, silence is the key.*" And then: "*Because the bad things live up here.*"

He got down on all fours to slither through a tunnel in the brush, and then slowed. *Maybe the bad things are us*, he thought, and felt like he'd been struck by a thunderbolt. *We're the bad things.*

He crawled on for several more minutes before this time freezing as another thunderbolt struck him.

The *Titanoboa* fossils were only ever found deep in caves and mines of South America. And he had never encountered them once in his travels anywhere except here.

What if they were more rare than anyone really knew? What if these were the total breeding population that ever existed? What if these were the last?

And then: *How many have we killed?*

CHAPTER 47

SOMETHING IS OUT THERE.

The pair of three-fingered hands slowly pulled the foliage aside to watch the line of bipeds pass by. The pack leader knew they were clumsy, loud, and soft. But they had stingers that sounded like thunder and killed in a blink.

The *Troodon* pack leader made clicking sounds, and guttural coughs and squeaks, telegraphing the information to its pack. More heads poked through the green wall to watch.

Their hunting party was 20-strong, and they needed meat. They were always successful on their hunts and had many animals to choose from on the plateau. But this day, they had chosen to target the bipeds for another reason—revenge.

Their brood nests had been decimated just as the hatchlings were due to commence. Blood would be had, as well as meat.

The pack leader saw how the line of bipeds was strung out, and how they seemed to tend to the injured member of their group. It decided on a strategy and then pulled back to organize their attack.

*****

Drake, Ben, and Helen led them out. Ben tried to watch everywhere at once as the jungle was thickening and turning into pathways that were more like green tunnels that bored through a near impenetrable green tangle.

Drake helped Helen who was full of painkillers and wrapped in bandages but was so far managing okay. Ben hated that there were blood spots on her shirt and it told him that her wounds were still leaking—open wounds meant blood and that meant the smell of a wounded animal wafting through the jungle to any hungry predators.

Chess and Francis were just behind a few paces back, and then came Shawna and Nicolás, who was once again carrying much of the blonde merc's pack. He didn't care anymore, and frankly, right now he'd prefer one of the mercs to be hands-free rather than the kid.

Ben held up a hand and the team halted. A few moments back, the jungle had fallen silent and Ben half turned, pointed to his eyes, and then to the foliage. Every single one of them looked from one side to the other and then also overhead.

Ben looked for odd shapes, eyes, or anything unusual, but he knew that the things that hunted in this primordial place had evolved millions of years of natural camouflaging abilities that rendered them near invisible.

"You think we got company?" Drake whispered.

"Yep, and the jungle thinks so too," Ben replied.

"Can't see a damn thing," Chess hissed. "You've stopped us in a freaking kill-box, Cartwright—walls all around. Keep moving until we find some open space."

Ben turned to the pathway ahead. They'd been moving along some sort of animal track, but it was impossible to know if it opened out further along, and in fact, to him it looked to close in even more just up ahead of them.

"Captain Cartwright?" Francis' deep voice sounded apprehensive and the big man was looking above them. "You think it might be those tinyboa monsters?"

"Don't know," Ben said. "But something is out there."

"There's nothing." Chess eased forward, held the muzzle of his gun out, and used it to part the curtain of hanging vines in front of them. At about waist level, hanging just inside the dark green hole he had just opened, he exposed a boxy head with ruby red eyes and a weird grin full of needle teeth.

"*Jesus.*" He dropped the vines and went to aim his weapon as the jungle exploded around them.

"*Troodon!*" Helen yelled.

One of the small dinosaurs flew from the jungle to land on Chess' front. Even though the big man was more than twice as heavy as the 100-pound creature, it knocked him backward. Other *Troodon* swarmed from the jungle walls, and a small group broke away and headed straight for Helen.

Perhaps it was the smell of blood, or due to her being a smaller target, but in the blink of an eye, they'd knocked her down and began to drag her away.

Drake lifted his gun and blew a hole in one of them, as the remaining few dragged the woman down the path. Drake sprinted after them, firing as he went.

Ben and Francis set off after them as well, as their world became filled with clicks, squeaks, and hissing, as well as yells of furious human beings and the blasts of shotguns.

Strangely, no *Troodon* followed them, and as Ben, Drake, and Francis closed in on Helen, and just as Ben raised his gun to fire, the creatures dragging the woman dropped her, peeled off left and right, and immediately vanished.

Drake was first to Helen who lay flat for a moment, her clothing shredded where they hung onto her. From well back now, they still heard

Chess yelling, the booms of shotgun blasts and the hellish squeals of the *Troodon* making for a madhouse cacophony.

"Keep watch," Ben said to the towering Francis, who immediately swung to scan the jungle while keeping his gun in tight at his shoulder. Ben knelt beside Drake and Helen. "How is she?"

"She's okay." Helen groaned and sat up. "I hate this damned place." She grimaced as she pulled her tattered shirt closed and then checked a wound on her upper arm.

Drake quickly set to patching her up as the sounds from behind them gradually began to fade away.

"Let's get back," Ben said, trying to see back down the track.

He and Drake helped Helen along as Francis gave them cover. In just a few minutes, they rejoined a very bloody and battered Chess, plus Shawna breathing hard, bleeding from multiple wounds and looking like she just fell out of a moving car. Dead *Troodon* littered the ground everywhere. Ben counted about 10.

Shawna stared. "Hey." Her brows knitted. "Where the fuck is Nicky?"

"What?" Ben spun to her. "He was here."

"*Ah*, bullshit, man. I thought he went with you," the brawny woman said.

"For fuck's sake." Ben ran a hand up through his hair. "Spread out."

"They took him?" Shawna said softly. "They took my little Nicky?" She turned slowly and it told Ben they had no idea even which way they'd taken him.

*****

Nicolás skidded and slid as he was dragged through the jungle. He felt like he had nails driven into his flesh as talons dug into his skin and leathery hands gripped him by the arms, clothing, hair, and legs.

He looked up, and one of them turned to stare down at him—large front-facing red eyes that belonged on the devil itself, set in an intelligent pebbled face that had black and white downy feathers starting at the neck. It grinned at him with blood covering its lips, and he couldn't tell whether it looked more like a large bird or a lizard.

The two creatures continued to stare at each other, and Nicolás could see that between its eyes was a distinctive v-pattern of scales or horns that gave it a heavy-browed look and also made it seem like it was scowling at him.

But there was clear intelligence there, and he wondered if he might be able to communicate. He bounced as he was dragged over a rock, and it caused a talon to dig painfully deep in his arm.

"*Stop!*"

He tried to pull away and writhed hard, trying to at least slow them down a little.

"*Stop, please.*"

They were traveling so fast, he knew his friends would never be able to keep up, and soon, they'd never even be able to find him. *What would happen then?* he wondered.

As if in response, a set of jaws like a bear trap lunged at the side of his face and ripped his left ear completely away. The pain was excruciating and he didn't need to look to know that his ear was greedily gobbled down.

He knew then what would happen to him.

"Please, no," he begged insanely.

The things, the *Troodon*, Helen had called them, clicked and squealed excitedly to each other, and he was aware they were communicating.

They then burst through into a clearing, and Nicolás immediately recognized where he was—there were obliterated egg nests, fragments of shell, and glistening yolk everywhere.

"I didn't do this," he pleaded.

The *Troodon* pack started to nip at him, but a sound like a barking cough from one of them caused them to stop. He was then held as the largest creature leaned in close to sniff at him, especially where the blood ran down from the side of his mutilated face.

"It wasn't me."

He began to cry, as what he assumed was their pack leader brought its face even closer to his. It sniffed him, and the red eyes never blinked as they looked deep into his own eyes and began to examine him. It lifted one scaly, demonic-looking hand that had three fingers and another that acted like a thumb and hooked it into his shirtfront. It peeled downward, ripping it open and exposing his chest and stomach.

"I have food bars." Nicolás began to urinate from fear and the smell seemed to excite the pack even more. He threw his head back. "Help." He gulped air, feeling he was going to be sick. "*He-eeelp!*"

It was hopeless, he knew it, and he finally lowered his head. "I'm sorry."

The pack leader darted in, its jaws snapping, and it took the tip of his nose. The other creatures took it as a sign and also began to nip and pick at him, taking fingers, small chunks of meat from his shoulders, chest, and other parts of his body.

They worked on him for many minutes, killing him slowly as they ate him alive. Their revenge was as sweet as his flesh.

*****

Ben and his team moved as fast as they dared. Though the *Troodon* were formidable adversaries when hunting in packs, there were other huge predators that would obliterate them if they caught the tiny band of humans off guard.

All Ben could hope was that seeing the jungle was so dense and tightly tangled here, it would have made it difficult for larger predators to enter or at least chase them down.

At first, the signs of Nicolás being dragged were clear, but they became fainter and fainter, and then they vanished altogether. After another 20 minutes, Ben held up his hand.

"Stop."

They piled up around him, guns pointed out at the mad, green tangle. It wasn't silent anymore, as the living, breathing sounds of the jungle had restarted all around them. He knew then they'd lost the trail.

"He's gone," Chess said.

"*Aw*, shit." Shawna's mouth turned down hard.

"Quiet." Ben tilted his head, listening. He thought he heard a scream, but he couldn't be sure. He waited, but it wasn't repeated. Then he heard nothing. Chess was right: the kid was gone.

"They knew what they were doing," Drake said. "Going after Helen was only meant to draw us away; to distract us. They'd probably targeted Nicolás all along."

"He was the only one that didn't carry a weapon," Shawna said.

They turned to look at her. *Shit, she's right*, Ben thought. He turned to Helen. "Could they be that smart?"

Helen was still bent over, flushed and breathing hard. But after a moment, she looked up at him from under her brows. "An hour ago, I would have said no. But now…" she shrugged.

Ben nodded and exhaled, feeling his anger build. He bared his teeth and kicked at a clod, sending it into the underbrush. "This fucking place." He looked up. "We should never have let him come with us."

"Yeah, well, that's on you, Cartwright." Chess' lip curled. "The kid was as good as dead the moment you let him tag along."

"No, he was always going to come with or without us," Helen said. "It's not his fault."

"Bullshit. There's a hundred ways you coulda stopped him from coming." He pointed one large blunt finger at Ben's chest. "Ask the kid's corpse if he would have rather had a busted jaw or be eaten alive."

Ben's jaw jutted and he went to move in on Chess, but the mercenary just angled the barrel of his gun a little. "Uh uh, let's not get dumb now, big fella."

"Leave it." Drake grabbed Ben's shoulder. "Now's not the time." He turned his head slowly. "C'mon, we should move."

Ben knew Drake was right. Much as he wanted to stomp Chess flat, right now he needed the asshole. "Yeah." He looked out at the walls of the steaming jungle. "Sorry, Nicolás. I just hope… I just hope it was quick."

Shawna stayed for a moment longer, one side of her mouth pulled up a little. "The nice ones always disappear." She sighed. "Goodbye, Nicky." She then followed them into the green.

*****

Ben and the group trekked slowly, wary now of every shadow, broken twig, or swaying branch in the jungle. It was wearing them down and fatigue was turning the group on each other, and instead of remaining on high alert, they spent more time bitching at one another.

They needed a break, and soon. So it was with relief that they finally found a more open space in the jungle that was between two boulders on one side, tree trunks the size of redwoods on the other, and a thick green canopy overhead, with some good-sized holes in the branches above to let in a few columns of light.

In the absence of a cave, it was dry, defensible, and there was no sign of any predators. Chess had climbed to the top of one of the boulders and had his scope to his eye and moved it along the foliage.

Ben waited at the bottom and was heartened to see the mercenary taking his time, checking even the overhead canopy. "What've you got?"

Chess grinned as he stared. "You won't fucking believe it." He pulled the scope from his eyes. "A space ship."

"A what?" Drake turned.

"Yeah, yeah, *there*, look." He pointed up into the huge Banyan tree.

Ben spun and sure enough, looking like some sort of massive overgrown hanging fruit, was a space capsule.

It was about 15 feet up from the ground and still hooked up by parachute cables. Vines had snaked all over and around it.

Ben walked toward it and stood below looking up at it. "I'm pretty sure it's popped open. Looks old, 50 years at least." He tilted his head and walked a little further to one side. "I think it's one of ours."

Searching the ground underneath the capsule, he found the helmet and shook mud and plant matter from it. He wiped a sleeve over the forehead plate.

"Gordon," he said, reading the stenciled name.

"*Red Gordon*?" Drake crossed to him and took the helmet. He shook his head. "I'll be damned." He looked up at the hanging module. "He was a fearless test pilot in the late 50s. But he vanished while attempting to be the first man to orbit the Earth."

Drake held the helmet up and wiped more debris from it. "According to official records, they believed his rocket exploded on re-entry

184

somewhere over South America. His loss set us back several years in the space race."

Helen grimaced from the pain of her wounds and hobbled a little closer. "Do you…do you think he survived the crash?"

Ben looked up at the open capsule. "Yeah, I think he survived the crash and got out." He looked around. "But how long after that, who knows."

"The Bermuda Triangle." Drake snorted softly. "I remember you telling me about that World War II Corsair fighter that had crashed here. Anything that's unlucky enough to be caught in the magnetic distortion effects as Primordia is passing over ends up coming down here. And then vanishes from our modern world, just like in the Bermuda Triangle."

"Yeah, I think this place solves a lot of mysteries," Ben said. "Because no one is ever going to find these lost souls, no matter how long and hard they look."

Drake crouched to place the helmet on the ground and laid one hand on top of it. "Rest in peace, Red."

Ben turned to Chess, still perched up high. "Anything else?"

Chess quickly took a last look with his scope. "Nope. All clear." He lowered his hand. "Smoke 'em if you got 'em."

"Okay, let's take 20," Ben said. The team exhaled with relief and started to drop packs, finding places to kick back.

Ben watched as their small group spread out a little. Drake smiled and spoke softly to Helen as he re-checked her wounds. Shawna seemed a little lost and sat with her head bowed and elbows resting on her knees, and big Francis patrolled the perimeter. Chess stayed atop the rock sprawled out and watching over all of them.

Ben paced, looking from the wall of the jungle to the canopy overhead. Experience, and his gut, told him there was no safe place at all in this world. There were some places that afforded shelter or security, but only for a while. And that "while" only lasted until you were found.

He looked up again and through one of the holes in the tree canopy: from this angle, he couldn't see the streak of Primordia and only spotted a few of the bat-like creatures that flapped awkwardly from branch to branch. But they weren't bats at all, as the mammals wouldn't evolve for millions of years yet.

Beside him, there was a small shrub with simple bell-like flowers, and within them a few insects that looked like flies moved from flower bell to flower bell. He'd seen them before, and after his time in the primordial jungle, he had researched them when he got home—he had learned they were primitive bees, and he remembered Helen telling him that insects had been around longer than most other creatures on earth, but bees evolved around the Cretaceous in response to the flowering plants.

If you build it, they will come. He smiled as he continued to watch the tiny bees. *Who came first?* he wondered. *You for the flowers, or the flowers for you?*

Ben sighed. Evolution was crafty. It watched and then acted—if something was beneficial to the survival of a species then it was grabbed, amplified, and replicated. And if it wasn't, well, nature was also brutally fast in her rejection.

Unless something intervened to accelerate or hinder that rejection, he thought, and continued to watch the bees. These tiny creatures had proved to be enormously important to the modern world, and for all he knew, this very hive was one of the keystone species. If it was wiped out when it was supposed to survive, then potentially everything changes.

He continued to stare. *A small change today can change our tomorrow. A small change 100 million years ago can change everything,* he thought.

Can't let that happen, he resolved and slowly stood. "Because that's why we're here," he said to the small bees.

*****

Chess watched the group from upon high. Time was moving on, and frankly, he couldn't give a shit whether they found this Andy guy or not. Either way, he got paid.

Shitty luck about Buster and the kid, but he was damned sure it wasn't going to happen to him.

His lips turned up in a cruel smile. If he had to take bets on who would be next, he'd give short odds to it being the wounded woman, Helen. He bet by now she must smell like fresh meat with all those cuts all over her body. It was the reason he never walked too close to her.

Chess rubbed his chin, watching them. Or maybe it'd be Francis, or even Drake or Ben, as all three of them seemed willing to jump into the fire if they felt it was needed. *Heroes die first, ladies and gentlemen.* He grinned down at them.

His eyes settled on Ben. He'd love to see that asshole buy it. And if he didn't think it would cause him a problem getting his money, he'd gut him when no one was looking and leave him to bleed out in this godforsaken shit hole.

Just a little longer, he thought. *You can hold it in until then, Chessy Boy.*

Chess then carefully reached into a pocket and pulled out a small string bag of tobacco. Papers and a few striking matches were also tucked inside. He kept an eye on Drake and Ben Cartwright as he bet they'd blow a gasket if they saw him lighting up.

He snorted. He did say light 'em if you got 'em, and no one complained, so…

He rolled the small cigarette, twisted the edges, and stuck it in his mouth. By the time they smelled it, *if* they smelled it, he'd have stubbed it out—just a couple of red-hot draws, and he'd be all good.

He lit the match between his thumb and fingernail and held it to the end. It glowed orange, and he sucked in the sweet smoke. He let it drift out from between his lips.

"Ah-*hhh*."

He dragged on the slim cigarette again, hard, taking the smoke in deep and feeling the burn all the way down to the bottom of his lungs. He hissed the smoke out, trying to spread it, and then pinched off the glowing tip and flicked it away—no mess, no trouble, and no one was the wiser.

That was better, he thought, and drew the string tight on the tobacco bag, then began swinging it around his finger. Chess sniffed—the smoke had already dissipated, but… he lifted his chin to sniff again. There was something new, something that smelled a little like cat's piss.

His brows came together and he first sniffed under one of his arms. Then he turned. The small bag of tobacco stopped spinning in his finger as he stared into the face of the devil himself. Right behind him hung a four-foot-wide diamond-shaped head, with two large glassy eyes on each side. The scales were a mix of brown and green and looked like heavy armor plating, but it was impossible to tell exactly how big it was, as the snake trailed away into the trees well beyond his vision.

"*Gah*." His brain tried to initiate a call for help, but his tongue and lips refused to translate it into anything coherent as cold fear short-circuited his lower face.

Those eyes; they hypnotized him, held him frozen as the monster stared deep inside him to the bottom of his soul. The tiny bag fell from his hand.

Then it struck.

✶✶✶✶✶

Ben sniffed, smelling the cigarette smoke. *That asshole*, he thought as his anger began to rise. He turned to where Chess had been perched, about to tear the guy a new one for smoking, but saw that the rock he had been on was now empty.

"Hey." He turned about. "Shawna, where'd Chess go?"

The female merc lifted her head from her reverie and looked quickly up at the rock perch and then shrugged. "Probably takin' a leak."

"Jesus wept." Ben seethed. Nobody, but *nobody*, was supposed to be going anywhere by themselves without telling anyone.

"*Ben*."

He turned. Helen was now back on her feet and standing with Drake. She waved him closer.

"That smell," she said, and her face was bleached of color.

"Yeah, that asshole Chess was probably smoking. Might be okay, as the smell of burning shouldn't…"

"No, no, not that," Helen said. She sniffed again. "Like the smell of the reptile room."

Just the woman saying it made Ben's heart rate kick up a notch. "Oh shit." He spun, gun up. "Heads up, people, I think we got company." Ben backed up.

"*Wazzup*?" Shawna, sensing the alert, leapt to her feet and also pulled her rifle from over her shoulder.

Francis planted trunk-like legs and swept his gun barrel over the foliage. "I got nothin' here."

"Holy fuck, in the trees." Shawna's eyes were so wide they threatened to pop the eyeballs from her head.

Ben looked to where she was pointing, and at first saw nothing but thick leaves, branches, and the wider tree canopy, so effectively had the monster concealed itself.

It was the jungle boots that he found first. Just up and to the left, a massive snake hung in the boughs of the tree. Sticking from its maw were two legs, and horrifyingly, they watched the legs kick, showing their owner was still alive. Then, the peristaltic motions of its throat drew them down into the gullet. Ben didn't need to be a genius to know whose legs they were.

"There's another one," Drake said from behind him.

Sure enough, staying still as a statue, another snake hung in the trees. Its weight even caused the titanic boughs to bend downward. *If they could spot two, how many more were there*? Ben wondered.

It was too late for Chess, but he'd be damned if they'd lose anyone else. Fight or die, it was all they had. He racked his gun.

"Take 'em down."

Gunfire erupted from rifles, shotguns, and even Helen's handgun. Then came the thunderous booms as Drake and Ben had now racked in the explosive Raufoss rounds. Helen had her teeth gritted, held her handgun in a two-handed grip, and fired continually up into the trees.

The explosive rounds blew out bucket-sized chunks of scales and flesh, and the snakes went wild. The one that had just devoured Chess vomited, and the man's body was ejected to the ground before them.

"Aw, fuck me." Shawna's face twisted in horror as she glanced at it.

Chess' body was now about eight feet long, and nothing but a red and brown twisted mess of crushed flesh and pulverized bone. If the boots weren't intact, it might have been hard to even recognize it as once being a human being.

Drake fired, racked, and fired again, and the crack shot scored only once on the now thrashing monster. Leaves rained down on them like a ticker-tape parade.

"*Yeah!*" Shawna yelled. "Come git some!" She also pumped and fired over and over.

"*Stop.*"

The voice was unfamiliar.

"Please, just, *stop.*" The bedraggled skeleton ran into the center of their camp and pushed Drake's gun up and away from its target.

"Andy?" Helen's mouth dropped open. "*Andy?*"

Helen immediately dropped her gun hand, and Ben and Drake ceased firing, but Francis and Shawna kept punching out rounds at anything that moved in the upper canopy.

"Just please stop, *now.*" He held his hands together as if he was begging.

"Andy." Helen smiled through her pain. "We came…"

She went to cross to him, but Ben held out an arm. "Why?" Ben scowled and kept his gun pointed at the thrashing monsters. "Why not kill them?"

"Why the fuck? They killed Chess." Shawna blasted again.

"Stop!" Helen shouted. "Hear him out."

"Hold fire!" Ben yelled. "For now."

Francis ceased firing, and then Shawna did, but took the time to reload.

"Andy's going to tell us why. Right, Andy?" Ben said and stared hard at the giant snakes one last time.

One of them hung in the trees with huge holes in its body, and both of them leaked fluid that rained to the ground. The other *Titanoboa* withdrew, but wasn't in a much better state.

Andy watched it withdraw back into the massive trees, and then exhaled and shook his head. Ben dragged his gaze away to face Andy.

"Welcome back, son."

"Ben." Andy turned. "Drake." He then faced his sister and smiled weakly. "Helen, I knew you'd come. I missed you so much." He went to her.

She hobbled to meet him and hugged his skin-and-bones frame. He returned the hug and she grimaced.

"*Oof.*" She held him at arm's length. "You look like hell."

"No worse than he did." Andy nodded at Ben.

"Bullshit." Drake grinned.

"This toothless old bag of bones is Andy Martin?" Shawna blew air through pressed lips. "You can keep that diet."

"You don't seem that surprised to see me," Andy said.

"We knew you'd be alive. We've felt it," Drake said. "You must have got lucky."

"*Pfft.*" Andy waved it away. "Ben survived by using his Special Forces survival skills and a lot of luck. But I survived because I know dinosaurs and their environment. No luck involved for me, just scientific deductive reasoning."

"Modest as always." Helen smiled. She then looked into his straggly bearded face. "So why not kill the snakes?"

Andy turned to look at the single bleeding corpse of the snake hanging limp now in the tree. "That was a full-grown male. The other one was a female of breeding age; it'll probably die of its wounds as well." He sighed. "I think it's already too late."

"Too late for what?" Ben asked.

"We could never work out why they went extinct. After all, other large snakes survived, their prey survived, and they could even tolerate cooler climates." Andy gave Helen a crooked smile. "We did it, we small group of arrogant humans. We killed them off. Us, right here...and maybe 10 years ago as well."

Andy looked up at the mutilated corpse in the tree again that now seemed deflated. "This plateau was where they lived and survived, and for all we know, those two were the last breeding pair."

Drake grunted. "I'm not sorry to see those things canceled out of history."

"Yeah, who gives a fuck?" Shawna snorted. "Nature boy just wants to let them eat us." She pointed at the disgusting mass of pulp that used to be Chess. "Tell that to my buddy there."

Andy shook his head. "It's too late anyway. What's done is done."

"We're not too sure about that. We've just got to make sure that no more things are changed." Ben nodded toward the female merc first. "That's Shawna, over there, and the big guy is Francis. The rest you know."

Francis nodded and Shawna just stared.

"You came back to see me." Andy grinned. "And I came to see you. I really missed you, sis. I've got so much to tell you, and if you let me, so much more to show you."

"Yeah, we came to see you. But here's the thing, Andy." Ben cradled his gun. "Every time we came back, we changed something. You said that we killed off the snakes, but we think there's a lot more than that. Somehow you being here, and something you've done, are doing, or will do, are making catastrophic changes to the future."

"What? I don't believe that." Andy shook his head, but his forehead creased, as he seemed to think on it.

"True, son," Drake said evenly. "We need to bring you home. Stop the re-evolution effects. Stop what's happening."

Andy frowned. "What's happening? What are you talking about?"

"Things are changing, Andy," Helen said. "Creatures that shouldn't be in our timeline are appearing. And others are vanishing."

"It's bad, real bad," Drake said.

Andy shook his head. "I only came to see Helen. But that's all. Anyway, time is set in stone; it's all too late. Don't you see? What has happened has already happened... 100 million years ago."

"Not from now it's not," Ben said. "You need to come home."

"*This* is my home now." Andy raised his voice and pointed at the ground.

"*Gluck.*"

"And his home too." Andy opened his bag, and then grinned into it. "He thinks I'm his dad." He lifted free the tiny pterosaur, and let it perch on his shoulder. "It's *our* home."

"Oh, for fuck's sake." Shawna shook her head. "He's even got a dino-parrot."

"No, Andy, nothing is yet set in stone," Ben said. "We don't know if you live for another week, a year, 10 years, or how many. But you do something or some *things* that alter our future world. It's going insane back there. We've all seen it."

"Me?" Andy narrowed his eyes, and then pointed to the dead snake in the tree. "Are you blind? Look at that; it's already way too late."

"Please, Andy, you have to come." Helen's voice was small. "You have to."

Andy rubbed both hands up through long straggly hair. "Then maybe I was wrong. Time is changeable." His eyes shimmered with tears, but his vision seemed turned inward. "Maybe time is like a road with a million invisible intersections, and our travels along it are influenced by events, choice, and luck." He took a few steps toward the snake and stared at the carcass as he spoke. "Some of the roads run parallel and others diverge greatly. If we were to go back and choose another, then our lives, and perhaps millions of others, would be vastly different." He turned back. "I don't care; what's done is done. I'm not going with you."

Ben sighed and looked up at the break in the canopy over their heads. The eyebrow streak was moving away to the west now, and the rain had started to fall again. A wind was whipping up all around them. Time was running out, and they needed to be gone in a few hours.

"I disagree." He looked back to Andy, and let his eyes flick to Drake. Ben had no doubt his friend knew exactly what was at stake. "But that all doesn't matter anymore." Ben shook his head slowly. "I came back here, left my wife and kid, dragged these poor souls with me, put these lives at risk, even damned *lost* lives, just to be here and bring you home." His gaze was level. "Or to stop you."

Shawna raised her gun. "Fuck him. Take him back or take him down."

"Don't you dare." Helen looked about to run at her, but instead her eyes went wide.

"Shut up, Shawna." Ben turned to her. "Let me deal…"

"*Huh?*" Ben spun one way then the other, but she was gone. Her gun lay on the ground, but the female mercenary was nowhere to be seen.

"Fuck, no, no, no." Drake pointed. "Did you see…?"

"Where'd she go?" Andy frowned.

Helen held her hands out to her brother. She still held her gun. "Please, please, Andy, do you see now? The changes are accelerating, and moving up the species to the more complex and sophisticated organisms. It's reached us now—human beings. We're disappearing, changing; we must hurry."

Helen stepped toward him, but Andy just stepped back. "You know more than anyone else what happens when you weaken or remove the top animals in the species dynamic—something else rises to take its place."

"Shawna doesn't exist anymore, Andy," Ben said evenly, as he gently drew his handgun. "Because in this new timeline, she never existed in the first place."

"This is a trick." Andy folded his arms. "And it won't work."

"Who's Shawna?" Francis tilted his head. "What's a trick?"

"Only we can see it; those who originally came back into the distortion zone. No one else." Helen held her head. "It's still happening; so we didn't change anything."

"Then stay here with me." Andy took a few steps toward her. "Don't go back. If the world is crap back there, then stay here with me in paradise."

"Paradise? Are you insane?" Drake's jaw jutted as he glared at the bedraggled young man. "We might all cease to exist; the entire human race. And *you-fucking-too*."

"And that's a bad thing?" Andy's eyes narrowed. "Maybe not."

"You idiot; that means Helen too. Eventually, it'll get to all of us." Drake glared.

Helen sighed and looked down at the ground. "You *have* to come. Have to." She looked up. "We don't have a choice; *you* don't have a choice."

"What?" Andy's brows knitted together. "What does that mean?"

"It means we didn't come all this way to take no for an answer," Drake said flatly. "You're coming with us, son. One way or the other, you're not staying."

"You can't make me." Andy began to back up.

Ben brought his gun around. "There's too much at stake, Andy. I don't want to kill you, but I'll sure as hell cripple you if you try and run."

Andy turned. "Helen?"

She remained stony-faced.

"*Gluck, gluck, gluck.*" The small pterosaur was becoming agitated on his shoulder.

Andy reached up to pat it. "It's okay, they won't hurt me." He then grabbed it and it let him tuck it into his bag. He brought his hands together. "Please stay, Helen." Andy was right in front of her now.

Ben and Drake closed in behind him, and Francis also edged in tighter.

Andy glanced over his shoulder at the three men, and then turned back to his sister. "Please, Helen; I have so much to show you. So much left to do and see—the birth of continents, inland seas populated by wondrous creatures, and valleys that sprout dinosaur necks rising three stories into the sky. You'll love it here; it truly is a paradise."

"No, it's not, Andy," she said softly. "And you having so much left to do is what we're worried about."

Andy shot out a hand and ripped the gun from her fingers.

"No." Helen lunged at him, but he pushed her away. He turned and aimed at Ben's chest.

"Please don't make me do this, Ben." He continued to back up.

Drake lifted his gun, but Ben waved it down. "I know, kid, everything seems mixed up. But we can make this right." Ben held out his hand. "Come home. With your sister."

Andy glanced up. Above them, the clouds swirled and began to boil. Wind whipped the branches all around them.

"I could make you all stay, you know. It'd be easy; just keep you from climbing down for another few hours." He grinned, showing a few missing teeth.

The huge form of Francis loomed in from the side, and Ben continued to walk forward, hand out. "Won't work; I know you won't shoot anyone."

Andy still had the gun up, and the barrel wobbled. He backed up another step. "Will if I have to. Just wound you."

He took another step back, his heel jammed against a log, and Andy fell backward.

Ben and Drake lunged.

The gun discharged, and Francis dived.

The bullet took the big mercenary square in the chest, and when he hit the ground, he stayed down. Andy's face was one of alarm and horror, and Helen screamed.

Ben rushed to the big mercenary and lifted his head. "Stay calm, I got you." He looked down at the wound. It bubbled and popped—into the lungs, a sucking wound as they called it. *Survivable, but not when you're in the heart of the Amazon jungle*, Ben thought depressingly.

"You'll be fine," Ben said.

Francis chuckled wetly. "You're a good guy, Ben Cartwright. But a crap liar." He grimaced and there was blood on his teeth. "I know a bad hit when I feel one." He looked up. "And I'm a long way from home."

Francis' eyes became unfocused. "A long way from home…"

As Ben held him, he became blurry and indistinct, like he was in an old photograph, and then he simply wasn't there. Ben was left cradling thin air.

Ben looked to Drake, whose shoulders slumped. He slowly got to his feet and turned to Andy. The young man stared back, his mouth hanging open as he looked from Ben to Helen, and then to Drake.

"I didn't do that." He shook his head. "I didn't do that." He turned and began to run.

CHAPTER 48

8 HOURS PAST COMET APPARITION

Comet P/2018-YG874, designate name Primordia, was pulling away from the third planet to the sun to continue on its eternal elliptical voyage around our solar system.

The magnetic presence that had dragged at the planet's surface, caused chaotic weather conditions, and created a distortion in time and space, was lessening in intensity by the seconds, and in just a few more hours would vanish completely.

The clock was ticking down, and soon there would be another 10 years of calm over the mountaintops of the Venezuelan Amazon jungle.

CHAPTER 49

EAGLE EYE OBSERVATORY, BURNET, TEXAS—END OF COMET APPARITION

"Predictive position plotting now gives us a 99.9999% chance of collision." Jim Henson stared into the viewing piece of the 12.5-inch Newtonian reflector. The massive steel tube was pitted with rust spots on the outside but inside the highly polished glass lenses and mirrors, plus large view aperture, still gave the man crisp images of the solar system, and the astral events as they were unfolding.

Andy Gallagher's hands were a blur over his keyboard. "All cameras online, and NASA, Alma, Arecibo, and just about every other observatory in a prime observational sphere are watching." He looked up at his friend. "This is big."

"Landfall impact?" Henson turned.

"Possible, but unlikely." Gallagher watched his screen, but his hands fidgeted like a schoolboy before an exam.

Henson shook his head. "What happens when a baseball hits a bowling ball—when both are basically chunks of iron moving at hundreds of feet per second?"

"Sparks—celestial sparks." Gallagher giggled. "But seriously, two outcomes are suggested: one, we have a pinball effect. Both are deflected and follow alternate paths. Two: one or both are destroyed."

"And right in our solar system." Henson grabbed his oversized cup of coke and sucked on the straw. He burped and went back to his computer. "Hang onto your hats, boys and girls, this is going to be the biggest show in town."

CHAPTER 50

"THE SHITTY THING ABOUT LUCK IS, IT EVENTUALLY RUNS OUT."

Ben and Drake threw caution to the wind and went hard after Andy. They leapt across fungi-laden logs, skirted weird, hairy tree trunks, and dodged a herd of small, grazing herbivore dinosaurs with barrel-like bodies and squashed beaks that made them look like flat-faced parrots.

"The guy's a fucking gazelle," Drake puffed as they pursued Andy deeper into the jungle.

Rain pelted down and Ben held up a hand, slowed, and then stopped. Drake came in beside him, and while Ben looked down at the mud, he kept his back to his friend so he could keep watch on the undergrowth.

Ben looked up and squinted into the downpour. "Still going fast; that way. Can't let him get away now." He took off again.

In another second, the pair broke out into a clearing.

"*Ah*, shit." The first thing Drake saw was what looked like a bunch of kangaroos crossing the open space 100 yards further down from them. But then the pack swung toward them and immediately became excited by the pair of bipeds running across the clearing. Frills opened at their necks, tiny arms opened wide, showing rudimentary feathers hanging underneath, and then the six-foot-tall theropods opened jaws lined with needle teeth and hissed loudly enough to carry over the downpour. They charged.

"No fucking time for this." Drake shouldered his Barrett M82 rifle. He'd already switched chambers to the high-explosive Raufoss rounds. They were well beyond worrying about noise now, and he pointed the barrel at the approaching pack and fired again and again.

Bodies literally exploded in orange and red bursts that were a mix of blood, bone, and incendiary pyrotechnics.

Some of the creatures were packed in so tight to each other, that as one was hit, the ones beside it were also mutilated and blown over from the blasts. In seconds, panic consumed the pack of predators and they scattered in the foliage.

"Fuck you too!" Drake yelled after them.

The pair entered the thick jungle, and once again, Ben paused to check the tracks. He shook his head.

"This guy must have the luck of the Irish. When I was stuck in this damn hellhole, I used to crawl around on my belly covered in mud." He looked up. "But Andy just barrels along like he owns the place."

Drake grunted. "The shitty thing about luck is, it eventually runs out."

Ben nodded and hunkered down as the wind started to howl with hurricane intensity. He looked up briefly and grimaced.

"Time's running out. He can't be too far ahead now." Ben got to his feet and sucked in a deep breath. "I'm getting too old for this."

Drake looked over his shoulder for a moment. "Well, one way or the other, we're on the last lap. So let's make it count."

"I heard that," Ben said and began to run again.

*****

Helen stayed standing under the foliage for many minutes as the rain pelted down, throwing up mud to her knees. She was alone; there were no people, and no bodies, as they had been consumed by a re-evolution timeline that was taking them all back one at a time.

Evolution seemed free now to try different things with its creations— take some back, replace others, and insert entire new lines of work. It might mean that old models got updated, upgraded, or in some cases, downgraded.

Just thinking about it scared the shit out of her because she knew it would take them too soon. Perhaps it would pause, stop, or maybe reverse if Andy was brought back with them. Or maybe it was all too late.

Helen walked carefully forward to look up at the huge body of the snake hanging in the tree. Even standing so close and looking directly at it, her mind found it hard to believe the thing had been real and alive.

She'd spent her career studying its fossil evidence, but seeing it animated was both as magnificent as it was horrible. *Was Andy right?* she wondered. Were they, Ben, Drake, Helen, and Emma, somehow responsible for taking a creature out of the evolutionary stream before its time?

Each year, in modern times, dozens of species went extinct, so this was just another. Just another taken out when it shouldn't have been taken out; so maybe it was true. *But we killed a legend*, she thought.

She grabbed at her stomach. "Oh no," she whispered as she felt the weird sensation wash through her as another distortion wave passed over her.

Everything went black and stayed black. She screamed but no sound came and when it was finally over, she held her hands out like a tightrope walker for a few moments to get her balance.

Helen moaned and then rubbed her face—it felt strange.

She pulled her hands away to look at them, and saw they were tiny, pudgy, and small, like a fat baby's hands. She felt her face again, and noticed her chin felt smaller and weaker, and was now slightly receding.

What's happening? she wondered and sank down in the drizzle, praying that Ben and Drake came back with Andy, or just that they came back at all.

"Don't leave me here. Not like this," she murmured as she sat, tiny and lonely, in the oily warm torrential rain.

CHAPTER 51

GREENBERRY, OHIO—THE FINAL RE-EVOLUTION

Emma sprinted back to where she had left her car, but then detoured up to Frank and Allie's house—they had a spare shotgun and she knew where it was. If she got attacked, she wanted all the firepower she could get her hands on.

Bursting inside, she saw that the television set was still playing softly and as she went to pass by the living room, the first distortion wave washed over her. Emma went to her knees and tried to focus on the screen, and just before everything went dark, she saw images of a city, buildings, traffic, pedestrians, and other displays of normalcy that she tried to hang onto.

The blackout came and went, and when she blinked it away, she opened her eyes to see the images on the television had changed—it was the same cityscape, but it looked to be consumed by tangled vines, huge trees, with things like monstrous bats flying overhead.

"Oh God, no," she panted. "It's caught up to us...*all of us.*"

The next blackout forced her down onto all fours, and it seemed to last for an eternity. This time when she opened her eyes, she was ill, and finally when her vision cleared, she felt grass under her hands and knees. She wasn't in Frank and Allie's house anymore—because it wasn't there.

"*What the...?*"

She stared at the empty hilltop for a few seconds more and then got unsteadily to her feet. She looked around—perhaps she had somehow wandered around in a daze, like a sleepwalker, and was now on another hill.

No, that was impossible—the track was still there, and the shape of the hill looked right, but there was nothing else, not even a sign that a house had ever been there in the past. She looked along the dirt track—it was a good two miles to her property. Emma knew she had no choice. She began to run.

She checked her watch; it was still only midday—*good*—the goddamn freak bats weren't due to be out and about for ages yet. But it had been hours since the last blackout, and every time one occurred, something changed. And the changes were getting bigger, more extreme. At first, it was as if little edits were being done to their world's story. But the latest changes weren't just edits, big or small; instead, they were full rewrites.

She powered on, her athletic frame easily eating up the miles. She began to speak to herself as she ran, moving it into a chant: *Zach will be fine, Zach will be fine*, she whispered over and over.

She managed to calm herself with the positive thoughts. And then everything dropped into an empty void of blackness.

And stayed black. And empty. And silent.

Emma felt like she was falling, or floating, as there was no sensation of ground, no up or down, cold or warmth, or even if she was even breathing or not. Her stomach flipped and just as she was about to scream her panic, the light returned. And with it came her senses.

That's when the smell hit her—human waste, blood, body odor, and something else she found familiar but couldn't quite place.

Emma got slowly to her feet and found she was dressed in some sort of rag. People milled around, but they were like no people she had ever seen in her life. They were short, overweight, and had small heads and receding chins. Some turned to look at her with vacant, cow-like eyes.

"What's happening?"

Emma backed up as one of them bumped into her, and it felt soft and flabby. She turned about. The green field she had been in, the one she was just running across, was now covered in muck, surrounded with a wire fence, and she was trapped inside with all these strange people.

In front of her, one of the men or women, she couldn't really tell them apart, started to urinate. She backed up as it just let it splash to the ground and onto its feet to add to the fetid mess. It didn't seem to mind, and none of the others even noticed.

"*What the hell is happening?*" She turned about, and then from the far side was the sound of an engine, and she pushed the dumb brutes out of her way and headed toward the sound. "Move it."

But there were hundreds of them in here with her, and when she finally got to the fence where the sound of machinery was coming from, she wrapped her fingers around the links and stared. Some of the people were being herded up a ramp and into a large building, and now that she was closer, she could make out the distinct sounds of metallic thumps, saws working, and grinders.

Emma moved along the fence, pulling and pushing the soft, chubby people out of the way so she could see around the other side.

She wished she didn't.

There was another ramp out the back, and this one was a conveyor belt-type thing, and coming down it to be loaded, were sides of meat.

"No, no, no." Her fingers unhooked from the wire mesh as she backed away. Now she recognized the odor—blood, meat, offal, and the hot smell of a bone saw—an abattoir.

Loading the meat and helping herd the dumb brutes were groups of people in green coats and helmets.

She squinted for a moment and then raised an arm.

"Hey!"

She licked her dry lips. They'd soon see she was in here by mistake.

"Hey you—where am I?"

They turned to face her.

Emma's mouth closed so hard her teeth clacked together.

They weren't people. They weren't even human. They were lizards, with pebbly skin, red lidless eyes, and snouts. She squinted and saw between their eyes a distinctive v-pattern of larger scales, like a brow, but it made the things look like they were scowling at her.

Emma backed away, putting her hands to her face. "Oh, Zach?"

She felt it then, her face; it was round, the chin weak and receding. Tears ran down her cheeks. She lifted a hand to her face and saw the stubby and soft little fingers.

Then she knew—the last black out, the big one, was a major rewrite—the final re-evolution. They, the human race, had lost it all. Some other creatures had now risen to the top, and they were little more than cattle to be farmed and harvested.

She began to cry, and she knew she was carrying the greatest curse of all—she had retained her mind. She knew what they'd done, and she knew what was coming.

We did this, she thought. *We threw it all away.*

She looked up, her vision swimming.

"Curse you, Primordia."

When she looked back down, she saw the lizard creatures were at the fence now and staring in at her, their faces registering naked interest.

She knew then she needed to keep her mouth shut. After all, cows don't speak. She tried to back into the crowd of brutes, but the lizards followed her with their large, red eyes. There were hurried conversations and then a few broke off to head toward the cage gate.

In a minute, they were unlocking a gate and the crowd around her started to become agitated. The human cattle-people started to grunt and harrumph, snorting and whining rather than talking.

The reptiles coming in had picked up long poles with u-shapes at their end—either cattle prods or capture sticks.

Emma backed further away, bumping into one after the other of the docile remnants of humanity. Their near-naked bodies pressed in around her, with their stink and their oily sweat, and their grunting, snorting, and animal utterances.

I'm in hell, she thought, as the capture stick caught her by the neck. They forced her down into the muck and brought a lead.

It was then she slipped mercifully away into unconsciousness.

CHAPTER 52

"I'VE SEEN THE BIRTH OF CONTINENTS, AND THE RISE OF NEW OCEANS."

Ben wiped his face as the rain beat down on them, heavy, blood-warm, and slick. Wind also bent the palm fronds back and made tracking the kid difficult.

"Can't let him get away," Ben said. "Too much at stake." He pulled his revolver. "First prize, we take him down wounded. Second prize, we just take him down full stop."

Drake pulled his gun. "Spread." He charged out to the left.

Ben nodded and did the same to the right. Both big men chased down the wiry Andy who skipped lightly through, around, and over the jungle debris. But Andy was increasing his lead, as his smaller, slimmer body was able to maneuver through the tangled jungle far faster than the two broad men in their bulky equipment-laden clothing.

Just as Ben was going to prop and fire a few rounds to try and wing the kid, something exploded out of the jungle from Andy's side. Ben already knew from experience that this wasn't a place to run blindly through the jungle—noise, scent, and especially movement attracted predators.

"Down," he hissed to Drake as he dived to the side.

The theropod was about 10 feet tall and had a large, pebbled head that seemed all bone, with a mouth full of finger-length, curving teeth. But what would have caused the most damage to Andy was that it leapt and landed on his skinny body, about 800 pounds, with massive feet extended and displaying scythe-like claws on each center toe.

Drake and Ben both came up from their concealment and fired several rounds with their handguns. But their revolvers were inefficient and were just irritants to the beast whose hide would have been like toughened leather.

Andy screamed and his bag fell to the side. From within it, a small squawking creature came out, flapping wings, one deformed, and immediately tried to peck at one of the large feet that held down its lifelong friend.

Ben quickly changed up his weapon's tech and pulled from over his shoulder the big .50-Cal, Barrett M82. He aimed and fired. Immediately, half the creature's head blew apart in an explosion of blood, bone, and gore, and it fell like a tree trunk.

The men rushed over, with Drake keeping watch as Ben tended to the severely damaged young man.

Andy coughed blood, and the tiny flying reptile hopped onto his chest and tried to nuzzle into the crook of his neck.

Andy gently laid a hand on his small friend. "I fucked up." He coughed more blood.

Ben kept pressure on the largest of the wounds in his upper chest, but it pumped and bubbled blood, and he knew it had to have damaged his lungs and heart. They didn't have the kit to mend him, or the place, or the time.

"You'll be fine," he lied.

Andy grimaced. "I can't die yet." He groaned and reached out for the tiny flying reptile and scooped it into the crook of his arm. "There's so much I want to do and see." He coughed, and his lips became glossy red like he wore garish lipstick.

Drake looked at the sky and then over his shoulder. "Ben, gotta go. Our ride is starting to pull away."

"Leave me; it's okay." Andy tried to lift his head. "I'm sorry. Please tell Helen, I'm sorry. I only wanted her to see what I've seen."

"We will," Ben said softly.

Andy laid his head back and stared up at the boiling sky above him. "I've seen the birth of continents, and the rise of new oceans. I've seen monsters from history walking and swimming. And I've seen things that we never even knew existed." He screwed his eyes shut for a moment, either in pain or regret. "I love this place. It's fitting I die here." He laughed wetly and turned his head to Ben. "Told you I was staying."

"We were never meant to be here in the first place," Ben said.

"I know, and I finally learned the truth," Andy grimaced. "We shouldn't be here because we're the real monsters." He reached out to grab Ben's arm. "Leave me. Go home to your family while you still can. Save yourselves and save Helen; hurry."

"We've got time," Ben said.

Drake shook his head, but Ben ignored him. Andy shuddered, but seemed to gather himself. He lifted himself, groaning as he did.

"Promise me one thing."

Ben nodded and waited.

"The only friend I had in this world." He reached for the tiny pterodon and handed it to Ben. "His name is *Gluck*. Look after him."

"I can't." Ben shook his head.

"*Please*, Ben. Just because I die, doesn't mean he has to as well. At least save him." Andy clung on tight to Ben. "Please, he's my only friend."

"Ah, shit." Ben nodded. "Okay."

"Thank you." Andy kept his eyes on Ben's as he relaxed, and let out a long breath that emptied his lungs. They never refilled.

"Is it over?" Drake asked.

"I hope so." Ben reached out to close Andy's eyes. He then grabbed his mesh bag and tried to push the small reptile into it. But it bit him.

"*Gluck.*"

"Gluck you too." He pushed it in and tied the bag closed.

"Time to go, big guy," Drake said.

Ben checked his watch. They now had mere hours. "Double time; we've got the tail of a comet to catch."

*****

Drake was first to find Helen, sitting out in the rain as though daring, or wanting, an attack. She wouldn't look at him at first, and when he crouched in front of her and grabbed her shoulders, she looked up and he was taken aback by her appearance.

Ben crouched beside him and then lifted her chin.

"It's come for us," she said sadly.

"Oh God." He turned to Drake and shook his head. "We didn't change anything."

Helen looked up and began to laugh, in a small child-like voice. "Maybe we did and maybe we didn't. It's got millions of years to ripple forward to us before we'll really know."

Drake helped her to her feet and hugged her tight. He needed to close his eyes to slits as it was like being in the middle of a maelstrom. Above them, the boiling sky swirled purple and black like an angry bruise on the heavens.

Ben grabbed at his arm and yelled back at him. "We gotta go, *now!*"

Drake grabbed Helen's hand in his and he felt how weirdly soft and tiny it was now. He said a silent prayer that she was right and there was still a chance things would be corrected now that Andy had been stopped. If not, then they'd all either vanish from existence, or he and Ben would soon suffer the same fate as Helen.

Ben, Drake, and Helen moved quickly through the underbrush back to where they believed was their tiny cave that would lead them to their drop lines.

Helen was quiet, not asking, and perhaps not wanting to know what happened to her brother. Drake hated that a small part of her thought that he and Ben had been responsible for his death, even though she knew it was necessary to stop him at all costs.

Drake looked up as he ran; the clouds were still purple-black, but tearing open in the center to permit a halo of sky to be seen. He saw out to their right hemisphere he could just make out the eyebrow streak of the comet departing through the whipping tree canopy. Oddly, there was another streak that was almost touching it.

Were there always two comets? he wondered. He put his head down and sprinted on.

In another hour, they began to recognize some of the outcrops on a rocky hill, and then minutes later located the marked crevice that they had slid from only 22 hours before.

Thunder boomed, coming from all around them, and the purple clouds turned like a witch's cauldron above them now. The tiny circle of clear sky had vanished, and with it the last vision of Primordia.

Ben checked his watch. "Eleven minutes!" he shouted over the maelstrom, and then pointed. "Drake, in first."

Without a second thought, Drake leapt in and scrambled further inside. He switched on his flashlight and attached it to his gun barrel—he knew he wasn't ordered in at front to be the first to escape, but to ensure that nothing inside was waiting to make a meal out of them. He quickly scanned the interior.

"Clear!" he shouted back.

Immediately, Ben and Helen followed him in. The trio belly-crawled to where the chute was that would lead them to the lower cave and then out onto the plateau's cliff wall.

Around them, the air was becoming thick and oily like they had submerged into some sort of liquid. Drake knew what it was—the distortion layer. They needed to be below it before the comet's effects were fully undone, or when they emerged, they'd be stuck in the Late Cretaceous, instead of being back home.

Drake moved fast, and then found their ledge. There were several ropes waiting and he grabbed at them, hauling them in and waiting for Helen and Ben to catch up.

The oily layer was making Drake feel dizzy and nauseous, but he swallowed it down. They had mere minutes now, and he needed to focus. He handed Helen one of the ropes and she reached out to grab it but missed, with her movements slow and confused.

Ben took another of the ropes and reached out for her.

"I got her," Drake said. He quickly used his belt to create a harness, and then wrapped a stout arm around her.

"Okay?" Ben asked.

"Let's get the hell out of here," Drake said and jumped off, belaying down the elasticized rope, but faster than he wanted with the added weight of Helen.

Ben came down, trying to keep up. They had over 100 feet to drop to the cave floor, and at about halfway there came a massive crack of thunder, and it felt like they suffered an electric shock.

Everything went black and Drake felt himself falling in space.

CHAPTER 53

EAGLE EYE OBSERVATORY, BURNET, TEXAS—END OF COMET APPARITION

"*Bingo.*" Henson jumped to his feet. "Outta the park." He held both fists up and grinned through his straggly beard.

The cameras were focused on the southwestern quadrant of the sky and recorded the collision event. The smaller asteroid struck the comet—both were rebounded away, like billiard balls, just as both the astronomers hoped.

However, the celestial impact was like fireworks on an astral scale, and it lit up the night-time Amazon jungle like it was noonday. The locals reported hearing thunder from a cloudless sky, but no one could verify it.

Gallagher damped down his enthusiasm and rubbed his face—something was off. The thing was, it was already well *after* the impact. They had been watching like hawks, but somehow they'd missed the actual intersection event. He remembered watching the impact drawing close, but then everything went black in his mind, as if he was somewhere else for a while. But now they were back.

"That's it," Henson said, folding his arms and turning in his seat with a huge grin plastered across his face. "We'll probably never see them again."

Gallagher nodded. "Like you said, *probably*. Neither was destroyed by the collision. Primordia's path was certainly disrupted, but we won't know what its new cyclical orbit is going to be for many years yet, or at least until it stabilizes. For all we know, it'll come back in 10 years, or every 100 years, or maybe even every single year. And maybe next time it'll come closest to New York, or London, or..." He turned and lowered his glasses, "... Texas."

Henson put his hands together and looked skyward. "If you're up there, Superman, please make it happen over Texas." He laughed and then turned to his friend. "*Nah*, Primordia has been visiting us every 10 years like clockwork for who knows how many millions of years." He shrugged. "Like I said before, everyone's luck eventually runs out."

"Well, not us." Henson sat back. "At least they both spun off away from our planet, so I'm calling it as dodging a bullet. No one is reporting any debris falling to Earth so the impact and ensuing fragment disbursement all occurred well away from us."

"Sad, I guess." Henson sighed and turned to his aged and now very gray fellow astronomer. "It always came closest to the Venezuelan jungle. I wonder if they'll miss it, or even notice."

"No one knows, no one cares." Gallagher turned in his chair, shifting his bulk. "After all, my friend, life is like a box of chocolates."

"Oh, shut up." Henson went back to reading his comic.

EPILOGUE

GREENBERRY, OHIO—3-MONTHS LATER

"I woke up in a field," Emma said softly.

Ben nodded. "The rain shut off like a tap. We all fell, but it was like we fell into a vacuum. Like you, we blacked out, I think, or were in some sort of other place…no, more like between places, for nearly an hour according to our watches."

"It was horrible." She turned, her eyes wet. "We had lost everything. We were cattle, farmed for our meat." She buried her face in her hands. "Zach, you, the world, was all gone, and only I could see it."

He rose from his chair and came and sat next to her, throwing a large arm around her shoulders, and she leaned into him.

"We stopped it." He exhaled. "Andy said he had so much left to do and see. Whatever that was, it must have been the major keystone events that changed everything."

She turned to the large windows that looked out on the green fields of Ohio. The sun shone, and there were far trees whose leaves glittered in the sun as a gentle breeze ruffled their branches.

"Was it real?" she asked. "Did it really happen?"

Ben grinned and thumbed over his shoulder to the staircase. "There's a tiny flying reptile in a cage in Zach's room; you better believe it was real."

She returned his smile. "He wanted you to bring him back something cool, remember?"

"Then mission accomplished." Ben snorted softly. "And he can keep it until it grows big enough to carry off a cow."

There came the skittering of paws, and a golden-haired missile launched itself to land between them on the couch. The wriggling golden lab was all wagging tail and licking tongue. Ben grabbed it and rubbed its head, and then looked into its face.

"Belle, if I told you, you came within an inch of never existing, would you believe me?"

Belle just wriggled her enjoyment from the attention even harder, and Emma stroked the dog's head, calming her. Belle relaxed between them and Emma stared down at the dog for a few more moments.

"You know what? We should tell someone," she said.

Ben bobbed his head. "Well, the story was pretty fantastic."

"So tell it, make your ancestor proud." She leaned across to him. "After all, it was his correspondence with Sir Arthur Conan Doyle that started everything."

"Maybe I *should* tell it. As a story, let everyone think it's fiction, but with a message." He tilted his head. "Just not under my name."

"Then use your middle name—Greig—and change Ben to Beck, after one of my favorite singers." She shrugged. "Let's call it Primordia, and use it as a warning."

"Don't mess with the past, *huh*?" He raised his eyebrows.

"Our world, us, and everything in it, is all just a big series of fluke events. We can't mess it up ever again." Emma nodded to him. "Go on, do it, tell the story."

END

AUTHORS NOTES & THE CUTTING ROOM FLOOR

Many readers ask me about the background of my novels—is the science real or fiction? Where do I get the situations, equipment, characters, or their expertise from, and just how much of any element has a basis in fact?

For the entire PRIMORDIA series, in the case of the hidden plateau deep in the Amazon jungle, the novel, *The Lost World*, was my blueprint. And for the re-evolution phases, I nod to one of the modern great Sci-Fi writers by the name of Ray Bradbury, and his tale called the 'Sound of Thunder' written in 1952.

Many of the creatures I include actually existed. However, some do not—these are the ones where I let my imagination run wild and describe what could evolve, and also, if mankind didn't exist, just who or what would be there in its place.

In this story, I further explore the paradox of time travel; can we really change the future through what we do in the past? Some theoreticians say we can. Others say we can't and that time is immutable. I include theories arguing for both cases.

Finally, Emma's words at the end of the story are in fact my words: "Our world, us, and everything in it, is all just a big series of fluke events."

Enjoy it while we've got it!

The Evolution of the Intelligent Dinosaur—Rise of the Dinosauroid

The *Troodon*, a relatively small, bird-like dinosaur (appox. 100lbs) of the Cretaceous Period was among the first dinosaurs found in America. The genus name is Greek for "wounding tooth," referring to the teeth that were lined with razor-sharp serrations.

The *Troodon* possessed several other features which set them apart from their dinosaur and reptilian cousins of the time—they had large braincases, opposable thumbs, and binocular vision. They are also thought to have been social animals. This has led experts to believe that these dinosaurs were on the way to evolving into true intelligent lifeforms.

In 1982, Dale Russell—then at the Canadian Museum of Nature in Ottawa—ran an extrapolation that indicated that the dinosaur's modern-day descendants would have pretty much the same brain volume as humans do. This evolving "larger" brain would have changed the dinosaurs' appearance, giving them more humanoid characteristics. These "dinosauroids" would have stood upright while still having their basic reptilian features, such as the scaly skin, hairlessness, and lack of external genitals.

Russell then employed the services of a taxidermist and together they created a life-sized model of his "Dinosauroid," which looks like a creature from another world (note: I urge you to Google "Dale Russell, *Troodon*, Dinosauroid," as the model is extremely creepy).

Of course, there is a lot of debate over whether dinosaurs could have evolved into sentient beings. But given that dinosaurs had a massive head start on mammals, there is no reason not to believe if they hadn't been wiped out in the Cretaceous–Paleogene extinction event, then it very well could be them ruling this world and not us.

The Paradoxes of Time Travel

I have been interested in time travel ever since watching some of the episodes of The Twilight Zone or Outer Limits. It has also been done magnificently in the movie adaptation of the Time Machine, and A Sound of Thunder.

Interestingly, there is nothing in Einstein's theories of relativity to rule out the possibility of time travel, even though the basic concept of time travel contravenes one of the foundation principles of physics—that is, one of causality.

So, if we ignore the laws of cause and effect, then there automatically arise a number of inconsistencies with time travel that need to be explored, and however poorly, attempted to be explained.

Below are some of the main timeline inconsistency theories—there are so many more, but they each get more complex and more into lower-level mathematics. The ones I have included also have been given movie treatments in the past.

The Predestination Paradox

A Predestination Paradox occurs when the actions of someone traveling back in time actually become part of those past events, and therefore may be the cause of the events that the person was trying to prevent in the first place.

This paradox suggests that things are always destined to turn out the same way, or are predestined, and therefore whatever has happened will happen.

This concept was explored in the remake of the Time Machine (2002) and was illustrated by Dr. Alexander Hartdegen witnessing his fiancée being killed by a mugger. This leads him to build a time machine to travel back in time to stop the fatal event occurring. However, his attempts to save her fail time and time again and this leads him to conclude, *"I could come back a thousand times…and see her die a thousand ways."*

Hartdegen then travels thousands of years into the future seeking an answer to why he keeps failing to rescue his beloved fiancée, to finally be told by the Morlock leader: *"You built your time machine because of Emma's death. If she had lived, it would never have existed, so how could you use your machine to go back and save her? You are the inescapable result of your tragedy."*

The Bootstrap Paradox

A Bootstrap Paradox is a type of inconsistency in which an object, person, or piece of information sent back in time results in an infinite loop where the object has no identifiable origin and seems to exist without ever have been created.

As an example of the paradox, imagine, a 20-year-old male time traveler goes back 21 years and meets a woman who he has an affair with. He then returns home and three months later without knowing, the woman becomes pregnant. Her child grows up to be that 20-year-old time traveler, who then travels back 21 years through time, meets the woman when she was younger, and so on, and so on. American science fiction writer Robert Heinlein wrote a strange short story involving a sexual paradox similar to this in his 1959 classic "All You Zombies."

Grandfather Paradox

This time paradox gives rise to what's known as a "self-inconsistent solution," because if you traveled to the past and killed your grandfather, you would never have been born and therefore would not have been able to travel to the past—hence a paradox.

The Grandfather paradox is similar to the "Let's kill Hitler" paradox. Killing Hitler would have far-reaching consequences for everyone in the world, and would certainly do, and undo, an enormous amount of significant historical events. The paradox arises from the idea that if you were successful in killing the man prior to him undertaking his monstrous actions, then those monstrous actions would not have occurred and none of them would trickle down through history. So, without those monstrous actions ever taking place, there would be no reason to time travel in the first place to cause you to want to make the attempt.

A great film version of this occurred in an episode of the Twilight Zone called "Cradle of Darkness" that sums up the difficulties involved in trying to change history.

Are Time Paradoxes Inevitable and what is the solution?

The Butterfly Effect grew from the mathematical based Chaos Theory, where it was theorized that even minor changes could have devastating cascading reactions that can become ever more amplified over longer periods of time. This is the theory that I make use of in Primordia III.

Consequently, the timeline corruption hypothesis states that time paradoxes are an unavoidable consequence of time travel, and even insignificant changes may be enough to distort history completely.

The Great Lands of Laramidia and Appalachia

From the Turonian age of the Late Cretaceous to the very beginning of the Paleocene, North America didn't exist as a single continent. Instead, it was divided into two landmasses by an enormous body of water called the Western Interior Seaway. At its largest, this sea was 2,500 feet deep, 600 miles wide, and over 2,000 miles long.

The western landmass was called Laramidia and included what is now the west coast of Canada and the United States. To the east was Appalachia, the mountainous island landmass.

As a result of the land separation, the creatures evolved differently on each landmass over that time. In Laramidia during the Cretaceous, the dominant predators were the massive theropods such as *Tyrannosaurus rex*, etc. In addition, massive herds of hadrosaurs, the duck-billed plant-eaters, were perhaps why there were so many predators. The fossil record shows a staggering variety of hadrosaur forms in Laramidia.

Other differences in genera appear between the island landmasses, such as the prevalence of massive pterosaurs dominating the mountain valleys. Also, there were armored dinosaurs such as the nodosaurs that appeared to have been plentiful in the mountainous Appalachia. Nodosaurs were large, herbivorous, armored dinosaurs resembling tank-sized armadillos.

The seaway eventually shrank, split across the Dakotas, and first created a massive inland sea. This sea would eventually also dry up, trapping the massive sea-going beasts that remained there. When they too died out, they provided a wealth of fossils.

The last of the water finally retreated toward the Gulf of Mexico and the Hudson Bay. Around 60 million years ago, the landmasses joined to unite the North American continent.

Vampire Bats and Vampire Plants

The Rise of the Vampires

Bats are an old mammal species. However, since their small, delicate skeletons do not fossilize very well, there is more we don't know about the evolution of bats than we do know. We do know that they are a mammal species that evolved around 60 million years ago, already in the form they are today, and even before the first dogs, cats, and horses.

Most bats today are tiny, some only as long as your thumb. But others, like the golden-crowned flying fox (Philippines), have a wingspan of six feet. They started out as herbivores, and somewhere along the line, some bats included insects into their diet. But then another species emerged, and just 4 million years ago, about the time the first hominids were standing upright, the vampire bats had evolved all necessary adaptations for blood-feeding, a dietary trait called hematophagy, making it one of the fastest examples of natural selection among mammals.

The vampires also evolved physical changes—vampire bats have short, conical muzzles. They also lack a nose leaf, instead having naked pads with U-shaped grooves at the tip. Some vampires have specialized thermoreceptors on their nose, which aid the animal in locating areas where the blood flows close to the skin of its prey. In addition, a nucleus has been found in the brain of vampire bats that has a similar position and histology to the receptors of infrared-sensing snakes—it means they can almost "see" where the warm blood is flowing.

A vampire bat has front teeth that are needle sharp and also specialized for cutting; plus, the part of the bat's brain that processes sound is adapted to detect the regular breathing sounds of sleeping animals—even in pitch darkness, they can find you.

Lastly, while other bats have almost lost the ability to maneuver on land, vampire bats can walk, jump, and even run by using a unique, bounding gait, in which the forelimbs used as the wings are much more powerful than the legs.

We are lucky that vampire bats are small. Because if they had ever evolved to be larger and more formidable, they would have been a terrifying and deadly creature of the night, and something more akin to their legend.

The Dodder vine: The vampire of the plant world.

A parasitic vine nicknamed the "vampire plant" sounds frightening enough, but new studies have found that the dodder vine is even more cunning and creepy than anyone imagined.

No, the dodder hasn't evolved to drink blood (yet), but it earned its ominous nickname for the way it does suck nutrients from its host. The vine wraps itself tightly around a host plant, and where the vine touches the host, it produces structures called *haustoria*. These invade the "skin" of the host and begin to feed from its vascular system—hence, the vampire analogy.

Scientists have known for years about the vine's ability to steal water, sugar, and minor molecules from host plants. However, at the point of contact between the parasitic vine and the host, the dodder is injecting back its messenger RNA into the host. This could be really sinister because these information blocks could be telling the host what to do, and in fact, the parasitic plant is actually controlling the host. It would be in the vampire dodder's interest for the host to be creating more of the nutrients that the parasitic vine seeks, and also for the host to lower the guard of its defenses.

In an eerie time-lapse video, the dodder tendrils waved in the air, seeming to be searching for a victim to attack. And they certainly were, because the dodder can detect chemical signals given off by a suitable host, and once detecting one, they grow straight toward it. Then they latch on, embrace their victim, and begin to drink!

CHECK OUT OTHER GREAT DINOSAUR BOOKS

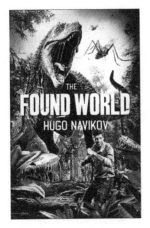

THE FOUND WORLD
by Hugo Navikov

A powerful global cabal wants adventurer Brett Russell to retrieve a superweapon stolen by the scientist who built it. To entice him to travel underneath one of the most dangerous volcanoes on Earth to find the scientist, this shadowy organization will pay him the only thing he cares about: information that will allow him to avenge his family's murder.

But before he can get paid, he and his team must enter an underground hellscape of killer plants, giant insects, terrifying dinosaurs, and an army of other predators never previously seen by man.

At the end of this journey awaits a revelation that could alter the fate of mankind ... if they can make it back from this horrifying found world.

HOUSE OF THE GODS
by Davide Mana

High above the steamy jungle of the Amazon basin, rise the flat plateaus known as the Tepui, the House of the Gods. Lost worlds of unknown beauty, a naturalistic wonder, each an ecology onto itself, shunned by the local tribes for centuries. The House of the Gods was not made for men.

But now, the crew and passengers of a small charter plane are about to find what was hidden for sixty million years.

Lost on an island in the clouds 10.000 feet above the jungle, surrounded by dinosaurs, hunted by mysterious mercenaries, the survivors of Sligo Air flight 001 will quickly learn the only rule of life on Earth: Extinction.

CHECK OUT OTHER GREAT DINOSAUR BOOKS

FLIPSIDE
by JAKE BIBLE

The year is 2046 and dinosaurs are real.

Time bubbles across the world, many as large as one hundred square miles, turn like clockwork, revealing prehistoric landscapes from the Cretaceous Period.

They reveal the Flipside.

Now, thirty years after the first Turn, the clockwork is breaking down as one of the world's powers has decided to exploit the phenomenon for their own gain, possibly destroying everything then and now in the process.

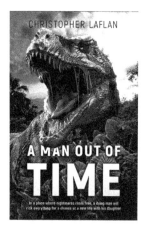

A MAN OUT OF TIME
by Christopher Laflan

Five years after the Chinese Axis detonated an unknown weapon of mass destruction off the southern coast of the United States, Special Ops Sergeant John Crider and the members of Shadow Company have finally captured what they all hope will lead to the end of the war. Unfortunately, the population within the United States is no longer sustainable. In an effort to stabilize the economy, the government enacts the Cryonics Act. One hundred years in suspended animation, all debt forgiven, and a chance at a less crowded future are too good to pass up for John and his young daughter.

Except not everything always goes as planned as Sergeant John Crider finds himself pitted against a land of prehistoric monsters genetically resurrected from the fossil record, murderous inhabitants, and a future he never wanted.

CHECK OUT OTHER GREAT DINOSAUR BOOKS

PRIMORDIA
by **Greig Beck**

Ben Cartwright, former soldier, home to mourn the loss of his father stumbles upon cryptic letters from the past between the author, Arthur Conan Doyle and his great, great grandfather who vanished while exploring the Amazon jungle in 1908.

Amazingly, these letters lead Ben to believe that his ancestor's expedition was the basis for Doyle's fantastical tale of a lost world inhabited by long extinct creatures. As Ben digs some more he finds clues to the whereabouts of a lost notebook that might contain a map to a place that is home to creatures that would rewrite everything known about history, biology and evolution.

But other parties now know about the notebook, and will do anything to obtain it. For Ben and his friends, it becomes a race against time and against ruthless rivals.

In the remotest corners of Venezuela, along winding river trails known only to lost tribes, and through near impenetrable jungle, Ben and his novice team find a forbidden place more terrifying and dangerous than anything they could ever have imagined.

PANGAEA EXILES
by **Jeff Brackett**

Tried and convicted for his crimes, Sean Barrow is sent into temporal exile—banished to a time so far before recorded history that there is no chance that he, or any other criminal sent back, has any chance of altering history.

Now Sean must find a way to survive more than 200 million years in the past, in a world populated by monstrous creatures that would rend him limb from limb if they got the chance. And that's just his fellow prisoners.

The dinosaurs are almost as bad.

CPSIA information can be obtained
at www.ICGtesting.com
Printed in the USA
LVHW111753130819
627498LV00002B/318/P